THE HOUSE THAT BUFF BUILT

Praise for The House That Buff Built

"A Chinese-American woman fears for her life in her first night in the house she's bought in an all-white suburb. The only one who'll help her kung-fu Maoist daughter protect her is a low-rent private dick, Harry Palmer. Dennis Broe's newest meta-noir drops his shamus into the corruption and racism of 1950's L.A. real estate. It's a heady trip among a galaxy of career lowlifes with delirious prose framing this metamorphosis of fact and fiction through a lost and insidious history."

—David James, USC Professor of Film and Television, and author of *Rock 'n' Film: Cinema's Dance With Popular Music*

"Dennis Broe's latest is a farrago of invention not just about Los Angeles in the 'urban removal' era, but about the corporate politics behind that same process in every major American city in the postwar period. Another triumph linking the criminal underworld to villainy in the suites."

—Eric Gordon, *LA Progressive*

Praise for the first Harry Palmer Trilogy, "Calamitous Corruption"

"Broe's trilogy is a compelling read. *Left of Eden* explains the infamous government attacks on liberal Hollywood directors and actors [and] the brutal pressures on these filmmakers' jobs and freedom. *Hello to Arms* explains how the big arms corporations that had profited from the war were lobbying for further war, as without a permanent arms economy they would go bust. *Precinct With the Golden Arm* skillfully combines the cop harassment of Mexicans with a plot concerning the pharmaceutical companies developing opiate painkillers. Readers can enjoy the fast-moving linked plots, and how Broe's explanations of the politics are relevant to our own times. The rise of racism, the pervasiveness of police violence, the drive to war—all these familiar problems were weapons being wielded 75 years ago…"

—Mike Eaude, *Culture Matters*

"An ingeniously plotted look at a side of postwar America we don't often see, and extremely relevant today."

— Ellen Clair Lamb, assistant editor *Books to Die For: The World's Greatest Mystery Writers on the World's Greatest Mystery Novels*

Dedicated to the memory of all the houses and
homes that were built and then demolished
in the name of "modern" Los Angeles

THE HOUSE THAT BUFF BUILT

Copyright © 2023, Dennis Broe

Pathmark Press

A Harry Palmer/Crystal Eckart Mystery

The House That Buff Built

Part 1
of The Dark Ages, an L.A. Trilogy

DENNIS BROE

TABLE OF CONTENTS

"*Dis*possession is 9/10s of the Law"
>
> —Title of an article on
> stripping labor rights from workers

"This is the house that Jack built, y'all,
  remember this house
This was the land that he worked by hand, it was the
  dream of an upright man"
>
> —Bobby Lance and Fran Robbins,
> sung by Aretha Franklin

Cover Photo: Destruction of L.A.'s original Chinatown to make way for Union Station

Act 1

There's No Place Like Home

1

Mid-October 1950

God-damn, it's early, I thought, as I was roused from a pleasant dream in which a buxom hotel clerk with a very suggestive smile hinted that we might retire for the evening to an empty room in a hotel where the paper was peeling off the walls. We were about to enter the room when suddenly a horrific *BOOM* blew my little piece of paradise and the hotel room apart.

The sound was so loud that for a minute I didn't remember where I was. It was then followed by a second and even louder *BOOM.*

This was Bunker Hill, home to all kinds of pensioners, derelicts, transients, and all-around cheap place to live for those who hardly make a buck, and for those, mostly Mexicans, who have just arrived and are looking for work. So, the boom could be gunshots, but the sound was bigger, louder, and more destructive than what mostly amounted to the police—fine fellows that they are—out gunning for innocent hangers-on.

This was really pissing me off. I hadn't had work for weeks and had started a routine of going in late to the office, which of course didn't help matters any. But I treasured my extra time in bed filled, despite the fact that I had a wonderful girl in the Mexican neighborhood of Boyle Heights, with all kinds of pleasant fantasies of women I had encountered in downtown L.A. the day before. Yesterday a very desirable telephone operator with the cutest red, or maybe they were scarlet, nails had given me the eye as I dropped my card at her relay station as a way of hunting up work. I rolled over and tried to picture her using those nails to unbutton—

BOOM! There it was again, and again busting up my now daydream. Will this never stop?

I went to the window. Now, my hotel is not the Waldorf, far from it. There is always a woe-begotten tramp or two hanging around the lobby looking for a free handout or, barring that, possibly able to sidle up to one of the paying customers and see what he or she might be able to lift from their pockets.

But compared to the place next door, this was Buckingham Palace. The building was sinking, and the rooms looked, at least from my window, to be in a state of constant disrepair. Such as they were, those abodes rented sometimes for the day, sometimes for the hour, and sometimes for about 20 minutes, depending on the ability of the paying customer to last, if you catch my drift.

Still, the flophouse also housed a slew of immigrants, mainly Mexican, who spent their days out looking for work and who, from what I could observe from my window next door, spent their nights bunched up three or four to a room as they tried to get a start in a California advertised as "the land of milk and honey."

Was somebody shooting at someone?

I scanned the rooms across from me and, wonder of wonders, they were all empty.

I then pointed my gaze downward and found the source of the disturbance.

Not a gun but a more destructive machine. A bulldozer. At that moment backing up and then charging forward to make another assault on what yesterday had offered if not respectable at least serviceable lodging.

The front end of this huge plow hit the corner of the building at its most vulnerable spot, and a part of the structure ripped off. The bulldozer then backed up and over a vegetable garden that was one of several on the side of the hill, used for the local restaurants, and sometimes poached by those who couldn't afford the local restaurants.

Outside of what used to be the lobby I saw a group of what I guessed were former inhabitants pleading with the owner, asking to be let in to claim luggage, and one of them pointing as if to say, "Where am I to go?"

The owner shrugged and walked away, leaving his former tenants in a bunch, or really a heap, on the sidewalk.

I dressed quickly and went down to my lobby, now at last fully awake.

I walked right past the room clerk and rapped on the door of the front office.

No answer.

I rapped again, this time louder. I wanted to know what was going on and figured it was my right.

At that point, crouched behind the door, a mousy man in a gaberdine suit appeared with bifocals and black hair that was slicked back and oiled to the point where it looked like if you pulled on it too tight the whole mess would come loose from his scalp.

"Ah, Palmer, what is it?" he said, leaning on the door so I couldn't open it.

I wasn't about to take no for answer. I pushed the door open and, seeing he could not keep me out, he retreated behind his desk.

"What goes on here, Johnson?" I asked. "I was roused from a very pleasant sleep and don't like being disturbed."

Mr. Johnson, first name Obadiah, who claimed he was from pure Christian stock and whose moniker came from the Old Testament, fidgeted in his chair, looked displeased, and did not want to give up whatever secret he was hiding.

"They're after us," he finally said. "The whole lot of us."

"Us? What do you mean?"

It seemed like it was hard for him to talk about this, so instead of increasing the pressure I decreased it. I leaned back in the chair he had motioned me to and looked "pensive." That can be either thoughtful or worried, but however he interpreted it, it posed me as less of a threat.

It worked. He came clean.

"They're calling us a 'blight' on the neighborhood," he said. "They claim we're stopping progress and standing in the way of downtown growth."

That I could understand. The business district downtown at the bottom of the slope right below us was always looking to expand westward, up Bunker Hill, and get rid of our little neighborhood of hangers-on and ne'er-do-wells. I'd been living here for three years and there was a nice camaraderie about the place. Nobody bothered you if you didn't want them to, and if you did, once you got to know the locals, they could be quite friendly.

"But who's 'they?'" I asked.

At this Obadiah became more thoughtful—pensive you might say—meaning a look came across his face that was either deeply meditative or fearful.

"I'm talking about the city," he said. "They want to take this whole area. They're telling me they're going to raze the hill, turn it into affordable housing for everyone and get rid of the riff-raff."

"So, what is happening next door is part of a plan to *improve* the neighborhood?"

He nodded.

"Looks more like an assault on the hill, and this morning it sounds like we're in the middle of a war."

The mousy proprietor had gone this far and suddenly he beamed and seemed to want to take me further into his confidence.

"Palmer," he said, "what is it exactly you do for a living?"

Over the past few months that was a hard question to answer but I took a stab at it.

"I find people that don't want to be found, I try to help workers when their bosses take advantage of them, and when the PD comes prowling around making false arrests, I try to clean up the mess."

I didn't come out with it and say I'm a private dick or a shamus because I was starting to smell an opportunity for work and it made me sound more "upright" if I described what my job actually was.

"They say you were on the force yourself until they made you leave."

"Not exactly true," I said. "I left because they don't like the kind of cop I was."

"What kind was that?"

"Honest."

That was stretching a point but it was, in the end, true enough.

Now he was starting to warm to me even more. He leaned across his desk, lowered his voice, and motioned for me to come closer.

"Look," he said, "I don't want to sell. I'm getting pressure from downtown, but I like it here and I want to stay."

"Yeah," I said, "me too."

"I want you to find out who is behind this, what's the real reason they want to clear the area and if there's a chance of fighting back."

"That's going to involve some fussing around City Hall and it may take a while to turn up leads," I said.

"Take all the time you need. Right now, I can withstand the pressure. While you're working, you live here free, and breakfast at the café is on me."

It wasn't an honest to goodness job but since there was little money coming in, and the last case did not have a huge payoff, I wasn't going to look away if Lady Luck smiled on me.

And anyway, who wants to move?

"Where do I start?"

"A couple of fellas came to visit me this morning telling me I should seriously consider the city's offer and sell out."

"Roughnecks?"

"Let's put it this way, I don't think they were from the city planning commission. They didn't leave their calling card, but they did tell me if I wanted to reach them and, if I wised up, I could find them at this bar."

He handed me a card they had left. I didn't know the place but filed it away, nodded in agreement and sidled out of his office and down the hill toward mine, a little older, no wiser, but at least now having free room and board.

***

Anyway, it's work, Crystal told herself. She looked around for a shady spot to sit on a break from a low budget "B" crime film where she had been hired as an extra to sit in a truck stop café with her back to the camera as the star planted himself at the counter. She had started doing this work part-time when she began at Harry's agency. He had gotten her a job at Democritus, the studio that had hired him to babysit their lead actor. She had appeared in two films there, and on the second one she'd even wriggled her way into their giving her a line. "This way, Mr. Ohlrig," she was proud to have said as she led the crass, despicable industrialist to a table in an elegant restaurant.

But Democritus was gone. A victim, Harry had told her, of the blacklist that had unemployed the studio's lead directors, writers and actors. So she looked for work elsewhere—and needed it, as, after last year's big case involving the police which had produced some income from a suit for wrongful arrest, there was precious little work that she or Harry had found.

She had taken to answering casting calls for extras and had been lucky enough on just her second try to be picked for this two-day assignment in what amounted to Hollywood's low-rent district. The shoot paid minimum wage, but luckily the day before had gone into overtime, and there was even talk of having her back the next day as a passerby on a street in Chinatown, which figured for a minute in the plot about a woman who tries to have her husband killed but is found out with the aid of a Chinese maid.

She would make her nut—rent and enough food to survive for this week—to supplement the savings she had hoarded from the two last cases at the agency.

The café location was outside the city in a secluded country spot and, as lunch approached, she had scoped out a felled tree log where she could eat the box lunches the shoot supplied to extras, another perk of the job.

When she collected her box, though, and went to the log, it was occupied by a very fashionable Chinese woman, in an elegantly tailored floral print dress which stretched to her knees. Her dark hair was carefully braided in a tight ponytail. Crystal recognized her as one of the leads but figured she would have her own trailer.

The woman smiled at her as she approached the log and seemed to have assumed Crystal had wanted to sit there. She moved over and made space for her, motioning for her to join.

"I saw you looking at this place earlier and figured we could share it," the woman said, not in halting but rather in perfect English.

They both opened their boxes and found, same as yesterday, tuna sandwiches, chips, and a pear, plus a small bottle of apple juice.

"I'm Anna May Wong," the woman said, offering her hand.

Crystal had heard of her because when she was little, back in Georgia, her mother had once mentioned a "Chink woman" she had seen at the movies, and Crystal had gone and looked her up in the back issues of *Photoplay* her mother kept under her bed.

"I'm, uh, very happy to be employed," Crystal replied, not wanting to give her name since after all this time no one knew it in the industry.

They both laughed.

"I know who you are and that you were very popular twenty years ago, but what are you doing here?"

"You mean in this picture or on this log?" she said.

"Both."

"Work hard to find for poor Chinese girl," she said, lapsing into the Chinese pidgin English spoken in Hollywood films.

"But you were in a lot of pictures in the '20s and '30s. How come you don't have your own trailer?"

"Anna May getting old and old and Chinese in Hollywood not attractive," she said.

"But you speak perfect English and have a formidable reputation."

The woman bowed. "Thank you," she said, "I wish more people recognized that, but for me work is hard to find."

"Don't I know it," Crystal echoed, and they both laughed.

"But there must be some call for Chinese actors."

"I'll tell you a secret," she said, moving closer to Crystal on the log and practically whispering in her ear. "When I was at the height of my career in the '30s, the big Chinese film was *The Good Earth*. I did everything to get ready for the part of a Chinese peasant, but when I went to audition, they told me I was 'too Chinese' and ended up hiring a white girl who played the part in slight yellow face to match the white actor who was her love interest. In this movie I play the Chinese maid, devoted to her master, another in a long line of stereotypes."

"That's disgusting," Crystal said.

"But not unusual in this business or in this town," Anna May countered.

"You got that right," Crystal seconded. "The boss on my day job, who's supposed to be my partner, still isn't convinced we're equals."

At that point, a young Chinese girl caught Anna May's eye, and the actress motioned for her to approach the log.

The two addressed each other in Chinese, and then Anna May introduced the young woman to Crystal. "This is Ester," she said. "She's an extra like you. There is a Chinatown scene shooting later and, when that happens, they pick up people from the street and bring them in a bus out to the set, where they work long hours at the bare minimum to make enough to help their family survive."

Ester bowed but did not speak English.

"Ester's father is a baker who works longer hours than her every day in Chinatown to make ends meet."

At that moment Ester looked up to see someone else approaching the log and, embarrassed, quickly bowed and exited.

A tall Chinese man, in equally carefully braided tight ponytail with an even more richly embroidered pattern of flowers on his buttoned-up shirt, strode over to the log, took Anna May's hand, and kissed it.

"Are you ready for our big afternoon?" he asked.

"Of course, wise sir," she said. "And you?"

"Indubitably, madame," he answered, in a perfect English cadence that matched her own.

"But now I must grab what the Americans call 'chow' and what we might call 'barely edible.'"

He left then in what Crystal noticed was a very elegant stride.

"Is there something going on between you two?" Crystal asked, barely believing that she was gutsy enough, having just met, to ask Miss Wong something this personal.

"Between Philip Ahn and me?" She laughed. "Hardly! We're, as they say, the two hardest working Chinese actors in Hollywood and we frequently show up on the same set. Marrying him would be like marrying my brother."

But then out of one of the trailers, sauntered the female villain, the actress playing the woman who tries to have her husband killed. She was certainly in character, Crystal noticed, with her jet-black hair arrayed in curlicues and in a black dress that clung tightly to her shapely body.

She sauntered past the log and as she did, she oh so subtly brushed her hand against Anna May's. Their eyes did not meet, but there was no denying the electricity in the air in their encounter.

Whatever was going on between them was a subject Crystal did not dare to broach, though she was dying with curiosity and wanting to. At that moment, the assistant director blew his whistle signaling it was time to wrap up lunch and assume places for the café scene.

Anna May patted Crystal's head, said "*Bon courage*" in perfect French, which Crystal took to mean "Good luck." She said she hoped to see her again, and Crystal just sat there for a moment, amazed at the layers she had just uncovered on their log.

That was like Grand Central Station, she thought, not realizing that all of what she had learned would be useful in what, though it started slowly, was about to take off like a fury and involve both her and Harry in a case that would change both of them forever.

2

When I got to the office it was deserted.

I remembered that Crystal was off on a shoot and said she might be back later in the day, but that she was hoping it would take the whole day.

Not a lot I could say, since at the moment we weren't bringing in much money. The only work I'd had for months was a missing persons case, a guy named Quimby who "disappeared" suddenly without a trail but with some traces of his blood on a tire wrench that was found at the scene of the crime along with his car.

The police surmised he was the victim of a robbery that had gone south and that the body was thrown somewhere or burned. They labeled the case an unsolved homicide and stopped the investigation.

His wife was not so sure.

She hired me to, she said, give her some "peace of mind," but I guessed she also thought there might be more to the case.

If you're going to disappear, you're probably going to move as far away from the area you live as possible. He lived in a modest home in the San Fernando Valley, not bad for an insurance salesman.

Crystal started combing the New York City papers for any trace of him, and it wasn't long before she found a needle in a haystack. In a street photo of passersby coping with the summer heat, a man who looked suspiciously like our Mr. Quimby passed by the camera and didn't bother to pull down his hat, probably not having seen the photographer.

I don't know how she does it.

The "widow" who was picking up our tab was willing to spring for a flight, and a few days later I found myself standing at the site the photo was taken in rush hour.

Sure enough, Quimby ambled past, and I tailed him to another insurance company where he was now gainfully employed, the secretary told me, as Mr. Astor.

He had taken the pseudonym of one of the richest men in the world, so I guess he saw himself as moving up in life.

It wasn't too hard to put the finger on him that night as I trailed him after work to a cocktail bar with a lovely little filly on the arm of his two-piece elegantly tailored suit, acting like he owned the place.

I snapped the two of them with my little portable camera, then approached their booth just as he was lunging at her. I told her to scram.

"Who are you?" he demanded.

"I'm the angel of fake death," I replied. "I'm the grinning reaper."

With that I spread the local newspaper clips of his "homicide" on the table in his booth, and he knew the jig was up.

When I told her earlier that day what I'd found, his wife was eager to get rid of him. She wanted a divorce so she too had a chance to start over, but more than that she wanted alimony to help her get started.

It turned out he did have life insurance but had figured out how to divert the payments to his account in New York by setting up at the time he took out the policy that the money would go to a supposed "charity" trust fund he had engineered. He was a good insurance salesman.

But now we had him for insurance fraud.

I laid out the deal I had worked out with his wife.

"Look," I told him, "insurance is just a scam itself so I don't care if you're hoodwinking your old company."

In that sentiment I had help. It turned out in a recent poll that the majority of the country felt the same way, that bilking an industry that was set up to bilk you was not a crime. Actuarial tables were nothing but gambling and, as in a casino, the house usually won.

It turned out also that the payout on the life insurance was bigger than any alimony, so I suggested we keep the scam going.

My own shyster—lawyer to some—had once helped me set up a phony account, and I told Quimby, now self-styled as an Astor in the lineage of old New York wealth, that what his wife wanted was half of what he was making, along with a signed agreement that, if he were caught, she and I knew nothing about her mysterious benefactor.

"What makes you think I won't just disappear again?" he asked, now sitting straight up in the comfortable cushion in his booth.

"If you do, we'll find you like we did last time, only this time, it won't be me, it'll be the police and insurance investigators who will come for you, and, instead of a fancy suit, in your next life you'll be wearing prison stripes."

That took the air out of his tire.

He signed the agreement, I was back to L.A. on the next plane, and Crystal and I got enough money as a one-time payment from his wife to last both of us a few months.

For a while we were coasting. But now, faced with the prospect of possibly having to move from my comfortable and fairly cheap digs on the hill, we needed to find more work.

It was then that I heard a rapping, as the poet says, a gentle tapping, on the door. I have to tell you I do have a hankering for horror and in our down time I was starting to read Poe, whose grim short stories reminded me a lot of my own line of work.

Crystal and I had become avid readers in our forced leisure and we frequently passed books between us. Sometimes we even repeated lines we liked from them. Hey, it beats working for a living.

I got up from my desk, walked through Crystal's outer office, and threw open the door. It was not, as the poet says, "Lenore," but rather a splendidly dressed Chinese woman in a grey suit who had turned her back and was just about to leave.

"Can I help you?" I said, motioning for her to come inside.

She reversed herself on the stairwell, very nervous, as if she was hoping no one would answer her knock, and tiptoed into my office.

She looked to be about 35, slim with a professional presentation, her black hair pulled back in a tight bun, wearing just enough makeup to be presentable but not enough to be gaudily attractive.

She took a seat, and I thought that pulling out of her whatever it was she wanted might be like extracting teeth. Not the case.

"I'm Sandra Chung. I'm a dentist," she said, now sitting straight up in her chair having regained her businesslike demeanor.

"I'm moving out of Chinatown and I might need some muscle."

Talk about not having to pull teeth.

"I'm not generally in the muscle business, but why do you need it?" I asked.

"Because there's some people who are threatening me," she said. "I want you to find out who they are and report them to the police. Meanwhile, I may need some protection."

"Where is it you're trying to move?" I asked.

"The town of Torrance."

All kinds of warning bells went off in my head. Torrance, south of L.A. near the bay and the harbor, was a white enclave known for fiercely resisting outsiders. As for notifying the police, they had a reputation also as making sure that "outsiders," as they called them, moved along and didn't disturb the "peace and tranquility" of their white neighborhoods. They were probably going to be no help at all.

"So, who's trying to stop you?"

"Tomorrow's the signing, and I'm told there will be a crowd outside the owner's place trying to keep me from getting in. That's okay, but the last time we were examining the place my daughter thinks she saw two suspicious men lurking outside on the lawn. When I looked, they had disappeared, but I believe she saw them."

"And why do you want to move from Chinatown?" I asked.

A look of surprise came over her face, that I would even ask the question.

"You mean, why don't I stay in my place?"

"I know it sounds like that, but actually, before taking the case, I just need to get the lay of the land."

She wasn't convinced.

"I read in the ad in the Chinese paper that you could be trusted and would be of help to Chinese people. Is that true?"

I liked her bluntness. She was straightforward as hell. I had just started advertising in one Chinese paper to see what would happen since I had had good luck in drumming up clients with other non-white publications.

I assured her it was, and she took that as a signal to open up and tell me her story. "There aren't many Western doctors and dentists in Chinatown," she began.

"Mostly the people there treat each other with Chinese herbs. My mother owned an herb shop and I was raised with natural medicine. I scraped together just enough money, with help from my mother, to go to dental school and set up a practice about ten years ago. I still use traditional herbal methods from what was my mother's store before she died but, over the years, I've also been able to buy modern equipment, and my practice is now quite popular since in all of Chinatown there's only one other dentist."

But, she explained, buildings in Chinatown were often old and in need of repair. Most were very crowded, a leftover from before the war when the Chinese were still prohibited from coming into the U.S.

"I know about the Supreme Court ruling that says restrictive covenants are illegal and can no longer be enforced by the state. I feel it's my right to live where I want to."

I was familiar with that ruling since my old friend, and former lover, the Negro singer Dinitia, had taken advantage of it to move a few blocks north into a better place after she signed a record deal.

"It's illegal," I said. "But that's easier said than done. After the ruling, what I'm seeing are 'neighborhood associations' springing up everywhere whose intent is to keep white neighborhoods white and the state can do nothing about private matters."

"Don't I know it," she said. "I'm just a little bit stubborn. A few of my friends are starting to move together out into the suburbs, particularly Monterey Park. But that's too far from my work. Mainly, though, I want my daughter in her last year of high school to have the best school possible, and Torrance has some very good ones.

"I also," she said, "want to get my daughter and myself away from the neighborhood associations. Most are harmless but there's still a gangster presence in some of the Tongs."

I had not encountered these groups but I had heard of them, and from what I had heard I was glad to have not made their company.

"So how did you swing this?"

At this her eyes lit up. I saw her beaming with pride.

"The owner of the house, a two-bedroom with lots of space for me and my daughter, didn't know I was Chinese when I went to see the house. I told him my name was Sandra Chase. He believes in doing things himself so he didn't use a realtor.

"When I got there with my daughter, who looks and acts more Chinese than me, he at first tried to shoo us out, but I told him I could pay up front what he was asking and he was eager to sell and get out of the neighborhood and move to the San Fernando Valley. In the end, he didn't care."

"So, happily ever after."

"Not quite, the other homeowners in the neighborhood heard about it. We don't know who told them and if someone is organizing to keep us out, but the next time I went out to the house, I found this tacked to the FOR SALE sign on the lawn."

She passed me a white paper with garish, big, bold black lettering.

KEEP THE MONGOLIAN HORDES OUT OF OUR TOWNS

She rolled her eyes and let out a contemptuous breath.

"My family is from Guangdong," she said. "I have no idea why they call us Mongolian."

"Because they're idiots?" I replied.

That put her at ease and she decided to tell me a bit more about herself.

"My family has always faced housing discrimination and resettlement. When I was growing up, we moved three times. First because the city decided to get us off our land in the original Chinatown which they wanted to build Union Station, then to China City where we luckily moved out before it burned last year, and then to our current location in Chinatown off Broadway, which is fast becoming more a theme park then a center of Chinese culture.

"My mother died young because of this pressure. And my husband died in the war, though at first, when he tried to join the U.S. Marines after the bombing of Pearl Harbor, they told him he couldn't because 'only whites were accepted.' But we knew about the Japanese threat long before the U.S.

did. When I was finishing dental school in the Thirties, I was part of a series of protests against the Japanese invasion of China where we went to the harbor in Long Beach to stop your country from exporting scrap iron to Japan, which we knew was being used for weapons."

"That's a lot of misfortune," I said.

She corrected me.

"Not misfortune, disrespect of one culture for another," she said. "My father was a champion of the Chinese in the U.S. owning, publishing, and editing his own newspaper. But now that's gone, closed because they suspected him of being a friend to the Chinese Communists and destroyed the paper. He's so ashamed that he refuses to live with us. We don't know where he is, but I imagine he sits in his tiny apartment gambling and drinking."

Then she changed her tone and relaxed in the chair.

"But I'm over that now. I just want a good life for my daughter and everything this country has to offer, starting with the signing tomorrow morning. Will you accompany me?"

At that moment, the door to my office burst open and a little fireball entered. She was a teenage whirlwind who immediately pushed her way to the back office to find us.

She was taller than her mother, with the same jet black hair, but not in a ponytail. Instead, her long hair swirled around her and landed on her shoulders which also seemed to be in perpetual motion. She was a teenage whirling dervish.

"What do you need him for?" she said, thumbing her nose at me. "I can protect you."

Sandra looked embarrassed.

"This is my daughter Lyn, who is very forward and impolite," she said.

Lyn, little terror that she was, in black t-shirt and pants, promptly squared off in my direction, assuming a fighting stance with her palms spread flat and her legs ready to kick.

"She's just come from her Martial Arts class and that always stirs up the adrenaline," her mother said, by way of apology.

"And my mother is too polite and passive," Lyn said, moving out of her stance and standing straight up in what was still an imposing pose.

"I don't see why we need to leave Chinatown and go where we're not wanted," she said.

That was aimed at me, who it seemed she thought was forcing them to move.

"It's for your future," her mother said, putting her hand on her daughter's shoulder and gently guiding her out of the office and toward the front door. She had left a card on my desk with the address and time of the signing.

"See you tomorrow, Mr. Palmer," Sandra said.

As they were leaving, Lyn spun off of her and turned to me as I was about to close the door.

She split the air with one of her palms and then raised a fist in a spirit of defiance.

As she was exiting, I saw a black book with red Chinese lettering in her back pocket. I had no idea what it was but Lyn looked back, caught me eyeing it, and smiled.

This girl could be trouble, I thought, for both her mother and me, little knowing that she was to figure prominently in the case in ways I could never have imagined.

3

On the drive out to the neighborhoods in East L.A. where I was supposed to meet Esperanza, I couldn't stop thinking about the difference between homes being destroyed in my little acre of the world on Bunker Hill and homes being guarded and preserved as the residents opposed Sandra Chung's "invasion" of fashionable secluded towns like Torrance.

I had wanted to meet my girlfriend at her home in Boyle Heights where we had some memorable sexcapades and I was hoping for one more.

She said she was too busy, but she might be able to use my help if I wanted to come see her at work. She also said that if I came late enough in the day, she would let me drive her home after work where, as she put it, "You can have dinner and then you can have me."

With that thought in mind, I forgot about losing my home on Bunker Hill and was pumping the accelerator as I drove up Broadway, across to North Figueroa, through Chinatown and east to Palo Verde, one of the three hamlets that made up the area.

I followed her instructions and they led me part way up the Elysian Hills to a small settlement that was more country than city. Goats and cattle were being herded up an incline. I noticed all kinds of vegetable gardens planted on the hill as I drove past a tiny church and toward a small but apparently quite active grammar school.

It was late in the afternoon, still hot in L.A. despite this being October. I parked my car and went inside the school as grade school students were streaming out. I found Esperanza in a classroom with one of the teachers.

She was listening to a tale of woe.

They were speaking Spanish, but when I entered Esperanza explained I had come to help and translated for me.

She was looking cheerful despite the circumstances, dressed in a bright pink shirt with gray pants that, when she got up to let me into the classroom, clung tightly to her curvy body. She saw me looking her up and mainly down and frowned. This was work and she didn't want to mix business with whatever pleasure she had promised for that evening.

When I first met her, she was a card-carrying, active member of the Ladies Garment Workers Union, whose local she represented in her sewing factory downtown.

But, as I soon found out, she was also a fiery activist who had helped elect Edward Roybal, the first Mexican-American member of the L.A. City Council in almost 100 years.

Roybal had recently offered her a job on his staff, which she accepted eagerly, and now she was a housing investigator, pursuing complaints from the L.A. Mexican population.

She was careful to translate all the nuances of the teacher's story and I knew the reason was that she wanted me to get involved.

Rosa Morales, sitting in front of us, middle-aged with graying hair and looking a little frail, nevertheless came to life as she told her story.

She lived on the hill above the village with her father and mother, having never married, since she was instead devoted to her work as a teacher. She was fluent but just not as fluent as Esperanza who could tell her story easier in English.

The family had been there for three generations, but suddenly they were under pressure to sell and leave.

She had been visited by a representative of the city who made an offer for her and her parents' place. She was not the only one. A few members of the village had already sold their property, having been promised that the area was going to be turned into magnificent public housing. All they had to do was find a home to wait for the transformation and they would be let in.

Rosa didn't believe this claim, and her parents didn't want to move, so she said no.

That's when the pressure started. She had received another visit from two city officials saying that if the family stayed, they would lose out and, the next offer would be for far less money.

They still refused, and the last visit was more menacing.

This time one of the same officials returned. She described him as a stone-cold Anglo in a suit and tie, taking photos of the area, who said the family was standing in the way of progress. And he wasn't alone. With him were two men in dark suits who stood together in the Morales' kitchen with arms folded, glaring at them.

The city official threatened that if they did not leave, the city would simply claim the land as something he called "eminent domain," which she did not understand.

How could they do that? This was her family's home, farm, and land for almost a century.

Rosa told the men in her heavily accented English that the family was not interested in selling.

At that point, one of the men in the black suits slammed his fist down on their kitchen table and said, "You better start getting interested."

The city official tried to restrain them, but the man, the bigger and burlier of the two, took a long walk around the kitchen, as if he was figuring the value of everything in it.

He then said, "The city's offer for this shack is more than fair."

The official tried to back him off but the tall man again rolled his hands in a fist and this time slammed it into his other palm right in front of her mother, making a loud crackling noise.

The man from City Hall, who called himself Mr. Beame, then tried to back the big man down, but he didn't seem to want to take orders. It made Rosa wonder who was in charge.

As they were leaving, with the official shooing them out, the smaller of the two stepped back into the kitchen, doffed his black hat, and said, "Miss Morales, as you can see my friend here has a quick temper. I would hate to see anyone get hurt. I think it's best if you just take the offer. It's enough for you to relocate and wait for some beautiful housing to be built."

As he was leaving and adjusting his hat he added, "If me and my friend have to return, it's not gonna go so nice." With that he smiled and exited their home, joining the other two outside.

"¿Qué voy a hacer?" she said upon finishing her story, looking exhausted and turning to Esperanza and me.

I didn't know what she was supposed to do, though I was congratulating myself on being able to understand this last phrase and tiny bits of her story. My Spanish lessons were paying off.

Esperanza patted her hands, which lay folded in her lap in a kind of resignation.

"*Nosotros te ayudaremos,*" she said, motioning to me also. I wasn't so sure I liked the "We will help you," but before I could say anything Esperanza got up to leave, and I followed her out of the classroom.

When we got outside, I started to beg off of this assignment, since I already had two jobs to follow up on. What at dawn was a drought, now was not just raining but pouring.

"Let's take a walk," she said, slipping her two hands around my arm, ambling up the hill and lightly brushing up against me with her thigh.

The hill was filled with modest homes like the one Rosa described. At this hour in the afternoon with school out, it was also filled with kids running and playing along the slope, a few of them herding cows into a makeshift community barn where they'd be milked that evening.

One of the older kids was also driving a herd of goats toward the same structure, where their milk would be turned into cheese.

I wasn't looking and felt a gentle tap on my shoe. I turned to see a turkey prowling the ground and pecking whatever came into its range, including my foot.

I shooed the turkey away, and it ambled into a vegetable garden a few feet from me, filled with lettuce, tomatoes and the staple of the Mexican diet, peppers.

Esperanza then led me to one of the homes. These were made of clay, nothing fancy, but this one featured an altar in front adorned with crucifixes, photos of what looked like the family, their ancestors, and a burning candle.

"It's to ward off the evil that has come their way," Esperanza said.

I then noticed that one of the photos was of Rosa and her class and realized that, while it seemed we were just wandering, my wily mate had actually guided me to Rosa's home.

Esperanza knocked, and Rosa's mother called from inside for us to enter as if she had been expecting us. The door was unlocked, a sign, Esperanza said, of how much the community trusted each other.

Rosa's mother took us inside where her husband was stirring the ashes in a fireplace which they probably used for cooking. Her mother offered us two horchatas, my favorite, with almonds and melon swimming in the sugary concoction. The team—Rosa, her mother, father, and Esperanza—were certainly doing their best to sign me up.

Esperanza translated as we then listened to Rosa's mother tell the story of the visit by the three men. She added something that Rosa may have been too embarrassed to relate. As the better-dressed, smaller man was leaving, her mother followed him out. He had his hand in his pocket but she grabbed his arm, pulled it out of his pocket, pointed to their yard and said, "Please, Meester, don't take our land."

The man snatched his arm away and strode briskly off the grounds not looking back.

We finished our drinks. The old couple thanked us for coming and led us out onto the front lawn past the altar.

When they had gone, Esperanza pointed up the hill and said, "This is happening everywhere here. The city and whoever is behind it want this land they claim for public housing, but in Edward's office we're not so sure that will ever be built. We can't lose homes to these strongarm tactics."

"I know you want me to do this and I'd like to help, but I've got two other cases at the moment and I just don't have the—"

I was looking away from her, not really wanting to face her as I begged off this job.

As my gaze wandered, though, I saw a white piece of paper lodged between the lettuce leaves in the family's small garden. I bent to pick it up, realizing I may have been standing near the spot where Mrs. Morales grabbed the dapper man.

Whatever it was might have fallen out of his pocket. The paper turned out to be a card. I was bowled over. It was the business card of a bar and matched the card I had in my wallet given to me by the hotel owner Johnson this morning.

Esperanza was getting irritated with me and started to walk away.

I caught up with her and showed her the card.

"I'm in," I said, recounting what had happened earlier. "This is two cases for the price of one."

She liked that and put her arm around my waist, holding me tight as we walked to my car.

When we slipped inside, she ran her hand gently over my zipper, making as if to undo it.

She stopped just short of pulling the zipper down, leaned back in the seat, and said, "There's more where that came from as soon as we get back to my place."

This new case, wherever it led, was for a good cause and promised some exceedingly pleasant rewards besides the satisfaction of sticking it to whoever those thugs were and not letting them get away with muscling either me or the Moraleses out of our homes.

4

On the drive out to Torrance the next morning, after a very pleasant evening with Esperanza, I had the radio tuned to my favorite rhythm and blues station, not only because I liked the music, but also because I knew Dinitia had a new album and I wanted to see if they were playing anything from it.

Instead, what I got was the latest news on the Senate campaign. The Republican, Representative Nixon, Richard by name, was running a smear campaign against his female Democratic rival Helen Gahagan Douglas. The newscaster on the Negro station was as suspicious of this guy from the all-white town of Whittier as I was. In his latest salvo, Nixon claimed that Douglas was not only a Commie pinko, but, in a low blow, he said she was "pink right down to her underpants." If she were elected, he claimed, with the country now at war in Korea against what the government said were Communists in the North, she would "establish a beachhead on which to launch an attack on the U.S."

I didn't like the guy because I thought he was slimy, oozing corruption from every pore, but his hate and fear campaign seemed to be working. He was pulling ahead in the polls.

Nothing I could do about that, but just as the news ended and they were getting back to playing music, I arrived in Torrance. On the drive from downtown, I went through the Negro section of North Compton, said to be a battleground as overcrowded Negro tenants attempted to move south where there was more room.

Once out of Compton, though, the area became entirely white as I cruised through Gardena and then into Torrance. The address Sandra Chung gave me was right in the middle of town on Post Street, in what looked to be its oldest section. The houses were well maintained, but there was a look of sameness about them, with white exteriors over what looked to be very roomy three to four bedrooms and generous, lovingly manicured, lawns in front. The stores on nearby Cravens Avenue, pharmacy, toy store, real estate office, were composed of a red brick exterior giving the impression of Anytown U.S.A. and looking a bit like a Hollywood movie version of what a small town should be.

Number 34, though, which was to be Sandra's new home, was perhaps a little more honest about what small towns really were, showing me why I lived in the big, evil, corrupt city which at least had the saving grace of displaying its gaudiness openly.

On the lawn in front of this more modest two-bedroom house, stood a gathering of "folks," some of them carrying picket signs, or rather wielding them in a threatening manner, with slogans like "Keep Our Town Clean" and "We Don't Want Any." The signs didn't take much translating. "Clean" meant white and "Any" meant, in this case, Chinese—or "Mongolians."

There were angry looks on the faces of the twenty-odd neighbors who weren't being very neighborly. I parked my car a little way down the block and found Sandra and Lyn huddled in their car a little closer to the house but far enough away so the crowd had not seen them.

"Let's go," I said, rapping on the window and motioning for them to get out.

Lyn was up to the challenge and again assumed an open stance with her hands, palms down, spread out in front of her, but her mother calmed her and made her put her hands at her sides.

"Why did I want to do this, Mr. Palmer?" she said, grabbing my arm.

"Yesterday you wanted a better life for you and your daughter," I reminded her. I'm sure that hasn't changed."

We reached the house and started to walk up the sidewalk to the front door. It was a nicely constructed two-bedroom with a fence surrounding it and all kinds of bushes growing along the fence.

The crowd parted but some of them started yelling at her in unison for her to "Go Home."

"She is home," I said, wanting to add flame to the fire. "This is her home."

The women scowled and one or two of the men spit on the sidewalk directly in front of Sandra.

They had parted on either side of the walkway as I pushed us through. As we reached the steps to the porch and as I escorted Sandra up onto the landing with Lyn following, one of the men pulled me back. He looked to be mid-40s, dressed in cotton shirt and gray slacks.

I brushed him off, but he wanted to make his case.

"You see that tree over there," he said, pointing to an adjacent lawn with a mammoth structure with a huge brown trunk and green leaves budding out of it.

"That's Cork Oak. It's rare in Southern California. It's a sign of strength and stability. And that's what you're threatening here, our strength and stability," he said.

"She's a dentist," I said. "You oughta let her move in, she'll make the community stronger and more stable."

He looked a little stunned, but behind him another man, with pockmarks on his cheeks and looking to be a rougher customer, chimed in.

"We don't want Chinese hordes taking over the neighborhood."

I wondered if he was the one who left the flyer Sandra had found.

"What's your name, bub," I said, reaching out to collar him.

But two other men and a couple of the women stepped forward to push me back and I decided I had better get in the house before this went any further.

Inside I found a short man in a suit sitting at the living room table, sweating, though it was still morning and we hadn't yet got what was promising to be sweltering afternoon heat.

"I don't know why I'm doing this," he said, as Sandra sat patiently waiting for him to sign the deed of sale. Lyn, meanwhile, was up and pacing behind her mother.

"This is Mr. Barnum," Sandra said, motioning for me to sit. She told me the lawyers had already approved the sale and she was ready to write a check for the total amount.

"I just want to get out of here," the short man said, now practically cowering and folding himself into a bundle. "They're calling me a 'race traitor,' and I get all kinds of threatening notices and mail."

I had a feeling this might go badly, so I decided to divert Mr. Barnum.

"What's that flower?" I said, pointing to a vase on the table with a mix of pink, white and blue leaves sprouting from a jar.

"It's called a Hybrid Delphinium. It's our city flower. I used to be in the flower business, shipping them all around the country, but now I just want to retire and live in peace."

"And who's that?" Lyn said, pointing to a photo of a Japanese man on Barnum's wall, standing in front of a flower shop.

"He's the former owner of what was my shop before I sold it," the tiny man said.

"But he's Japanese, did you take it from him when he was sent away during the war?"

Barnum blanched. So much for trying to brighten the mood. Lyn was just too bold for her young britches and she wasn't finished yet.

Barnum signed the deed silently and uttered a sigh of relief.

Given Lyn's accusation, I wondered if he was also selling to an Asian owner out of some sense of guilt over whatever had gone down in his acquiring the shop.

It was now up to Sandra. This was her big moment.

Except it was not to be.

Instead, Lyn, who was standing behind her, startled all of us. Lyn grabbed Sandra's pen. Then she pulled a jackknife from her pocket and slammed it down on her mother's copy of the contract.

"Grandfather would not want this," she said.

Sandra quietly but firmly removed the knife, which had made only a small perforation in the contract. She handed it back to Lyn, admonishing her in a tone that was more patient than punishing.

"We don't know what my father would want," she said. "We haven't seen him for almost a year. But we have to assume he wants the best for us. Now, let me have the pen."

Lyn reluctantly turned it over, and Sandra signed the deed.

It's typical in these situations to raise a glass, but with all the tension both in and outside the room, a celebration didn't seem appropriate.

Barnum told Sandra she could move in immediately. He would be gone in a day, just as soon as the deed was turned over to the city officials.

She thanked him, and we got up to leave.

I thought of something and turned back to question Barnum, who at this point was preparing to go upstairs to his bedroom probably to sleep the whole thing off.

"Who called you a race traitor?" I asked.

He didn't reply but instead went to a drawer in a desk near the table and pulled out some scattered pieces of paper.

The words on the one he showed me were spelled out with letters drawn from different newspaper headlines. He had missed it, but I noticed that at the bottom of the page was a tiny inscription drawn from different newspaper articles. It read "KKK."

The Klan was very active in these contested towns and had caused a lot of trouble in border areas in L.A. County where new populations were trying to move.

He then showed me another letter in what looked like newspaper linotype. The letter was short, sweet and to the point. It read simply, "If you sell, things will not go well for you."

I thanked him, wished him luck, and led Sandra and Lyn out of the house.

When we got out onto the porch, the crowd had thinned, probably realizing there was nothing they could do at the moment to stop this.

As I led Sandra and Lyn down the sidewalk to their car, a few stragglers snarled at us. Sandra let it slide off her back, but Lyn turned to them and tightened her thin frame into what she thought was a fighting machine.

"None of this would be a problem if we had a revolution here and private property was confiscated like in China," she said, glaring.

Sandra collared her, leading her to the car, and I heard her say, "The revolution will do nothing for us except get us kicked out of this country." She then ordered Lyn to get in the passenger side.

The few remaining protesters just had a blank look on their faces after what they had heard. I think they got "Yellow Menace," but I don't believe they were well informed about the finer points of what was going on in China.

Sandra thanked me and asked me to keep coming by the house to check on them. I agreed but noticed Lyn rolling down the window and poking her nose outside the car.

"Who are those two men?" she said.

When I looked, whoever they were had gone.

"I saw two men at the side of our house in dark suits, looking over the place," she said, looking at me for confirmation. "And it's not the first time I've seen them."

"I didn't see anything," I said, "but I'll check."

I walked around the corner of the house, but there was no sign of anyone. When I got back, Sandra had pulled away, and I saw her and Lyn speeding back toward Chinatown.

I decided to stay on the grounds for a while and see if the two men, if Lyn had really seen them, would return or if anyone else would show up to protest.

What I saw instead was, two houses down, a beautiful young blonde in her late 20s with hair flowing down onto her shoulders in a dress which was designed to show off two magnificent, somewhat outsized breasts. She was getting out of her car and meeting what appeared to be a client, a single man on the front lawn of another house with a FOR SALE sign.

I decided to check out the show.

Her dress was also tight around two equally proportioned buttocks. As she saw me approaching, and before reaching her client, she gave me the full view as if I was in a 3D movie theater with objects popping out at me.

First, she leaned over in front of me, ostensibly to pick up a pen which I'm pretty sure she dropped on purpose. The view was stunning.

"Oh, I'm so sorry," she said, as I approached.

Then she got up and leaned over to close her car door in a way that purposely stuck out that exquisitely tailored posterior.

And the show was not over yet.

"Hello there, mister," she said. "I'm just showing this house, but if you're in the mood to buy you can come along because there's plenty more where this came from."

I wasn't sure what the "plenty more" was but I was certainly eager to find out.

The client was an older man who seemed to be as taken with her as I was, although he was somewhat agitated about me moving in on his territory.

"I'm Diane Chestnut," she said, holding out her hand first to him and then to me.

"You're both gonna like what I have to show you."

With that she turned away from us and sashayed up the stairs onto the porch, making sure to accent every turn of her behind as she shimmied away from us, turning her head to make sure that we were dazzled.

We were.

I wasn't sure if I was being sold a house or propositioned, or if there was any difference, but either was okay with me.

She led us inside, describing the features as she led us through the three-bedroom, single-floor, spacious interior.

"I work for William's housing," she said, "and this is one of our finest homes, though it's typical of the quality of all of our homes."

She pointed out the oak flooring, the "genuine lathe and plaster construction," gave us a peak at the "two custom baths," the brightly colored tile in the kitchen with its cedar roof, and let us have a look out the window at the equally spacious two-car garage.

She wound it all up with her summary pitch.

"A home," she said, "is a place of privilege, a place of happiness." She pronounced each of the words slowly with almost a breathless whisper. She had turned real estate into pillow talk.

Hey, maybe the suburbs are not so bad.

And then she ruined it.

"A home," she said, "is also an investment which must be guarded and preserved against 'infiltration.'"

I didn't think she meant bugs. I think she meant "infiltration" by those who were not as she might put it, "seemly," the way Sandra and Lyn were not "seemly."

She gave us each a card with her business phone, and, when the older man left and I lingered, she went to her car. As she was getting in, she turned and blew me a kiss.

The contrast between one population being lovingly seduced into entering a neighborhood and another being rudely repelled was striking and it seemed arbitrary. I marked Miss Chestnut in my mind and wondered who or what was behind her. There were so many threats on the horizon for Sandra, who really only wanted a better life for her and her daughter, I hardly knew where to begin.

5

Don't ask me why, but of all the threads that I could have pulled on in this case, I decided first that I would try to unravel what that little fireball Lyn might know, which was certainly more than she was telling. She was aggressive in trying to keep her mother from signing the deed, and who knows what was swimming around in that waterlogged mind of hers spouting talk about "revolution."

So I decided to tail her and see what a day in the life of Lyn Chung was like.

Sandra had given me her Chinatown address. They lived in a modest, some would say tiny, house on Bernard Street, almost at the edge of Chinatown, but on the northern tip of the area, far away from their move to the South of L.A. County.

It was the next day, a Saturday, when I parked on the other side of the street. The front door was open and I could see Sandra inside busily packing. Lyn walked out the door, and Sandra followed her and grabbed her arm, wanting her to stay put. But Lyn angrily pulled away and sauntered down Broadway as her mother shouted after her, "We're moving today and I want you home this afternoon."

Lyn shrugged and continued her walk, pausing in a bakery to buy a bun, then resuming while munching on it. She next entered one of the many herb shops on this crowded street. I saw her talking to the old Chinese woman, probably the owner. She and Lyn seemed to know each other. I could hear them sharing a laugh. Lyn then asked for something and pointed to the back of the shop. In reply, the old woman parted a bamboo curtain, disappeared for a moment, and came back clutching what looked like grass. She wrapped the package, and Lyn exited cradling the concoction.

I went into the shop after her, and the old woman, in a faded blue one-piece outfit, welcomed me as I perused the amazing variety of herbs displayed in jars on a number of shelves.

"You are looking for what?" she asked, noticing I appeared awkward and out of place.

"I need something for my health and state of mind. I've been very nervous lately and need to calm myself down. I noticed the girl who just left looked very calm. Can I have what she bought?"

The old woman was a little suspicious, but nevertheless, a sale was a sale, so she went to the back and returned with the same grassy herb.

"This is *mugwort*," she said. "Good for high blood pressure."

"Strange, would a young girl need to take this?"

"Best to mind your own business and your own troubles," she replied.

She told me the herb is to be brewed like tea and swallowed.

As I was leaving, she added, "It's also good for warding off evil spirits."

That was more like something that might interest Lyn. I thanked her and returned to Broadway, hoping I had not lost her trail.

I spied her in the distance, continuing down Broadway, past more herb shops, vegetable and fruit stands, and bakeries. She stopped this time at a huge open portal with red beams and pink tiled roofs. This was one of the four gates that bounded Chinatown. She didn't look at the gate though. Instead, she walked through the arches and stood just behind the gate.

She was lost in thought so I moved a little closer to get an idea of what she was looking at.

All of a sudden Lyn came out of her trance and turned quickly in my direction. I'm pretty good at tailing suspects but she had spotted me.

"Come over here, Mr. Palmer," she said. "You might learn something."

The jig was up and there was nothing to do but admit it. I felt sheepish, like a sheep. What was I doing tailing a teenager? But I regained my composure.

"This gate honors our mothers, Mother Meng and Mother Ow, two strong women in Chinese history. But I was thinking instead of our fathers. When I come here, I think about Doctor Sun Yat-sen, the founder of our country. I imagine him behind the mothers sitting on the chair from where he governed. He was the first to make China a republic and free it from the tyranny of the Manchu Dynasty.

"He visited Los Angeles in 1905, was smuggled in on a potato boat and took part in a fundraiser to get money and troops to fight for the republic. Over 2000 Chinese men went back to China to battle the Manchus."

I thought I would try drawing her out so at least I got something out of this morning.

"So, are you a revolutionary as well, carrying on in his path?" I said pointing toward where she imagined the leader to be sitting.

She laughed.

"Me, hardly. I may talk a good fight but I'm much more into the teachings of the Tao, that we should all live in a state of harmony with Tao, or you might call it 'the universe,' the source that underlies everything. I believe in passive mindfulness."

I wasn't sure I was buying this new passive Lyn.

"Now," she said, "there are probably much better ways to spend your time than following me."

She turned, but before she left gave me a glimpse of the old Lyn I had come to know and, not exactly love, more like fear.

"Stop following me or things will not go well for you."

With that she walked away and headed back up Broadway.

Rather than a warning though, this just piqued my interest, since I remembered the phrase "things will not go well for you" appeared on one of the threatening letters sent to Barnum, warning him not to sell the house.

I decided to keep trailing her. I just needed to be more discreet and follow at a greater distance.

She walked up Hill Street, where the gate was located, in the direction of her house. I thought, having honored Chinese mothers, she was then going to help her mother pack.

That was not the case.

Instead, she turned left and walked to the next street over, Yale Street, where she stood again lost in thought before what looked to be a school. It was Saturday, but there were still some kids in the playground. I guessed that Lyn had gone to school there.

She kept going, but I paused to talk to what was probably one of the teachers who was out in the playground with the kids.

She told me this was Castelar School, the second largest in L.A., unique because teachers taught in Cantonese, English, and Spanish. I asked if she had seen Lyn gazing at the school, and it turns out the teacher knew and remembered her.

"She was a pretty rambunctious child, full of energy, hard to forget. I liked her spirit. I think she's going to do great things."

I thanked the teacher, but was not so sure of her assessment, since one of the "great things" Lyn might currently be up to was threatening the man who was selling her mother the house.

I saw her now near the end of Yale Street, again heading toward her home. I thought that all she was doing was taking a farewell tour of the places where she grew up, and maybe there was nothing more sinister going on here than that.

But I persisted, maintaining my distance.

Instead of going home, she turned left on West College Street, but before she did, she looked left and right as if she was afraid of being followed.

At first, I thought she was wanting to make sure I was not still on her trail, but then I saw something which made me wonder again what she was up to.

Two Chinese men in dark ourfits suddenly came out from a nearby shop and seemed to trail behind her as well.

There were now three parties in our little parade.

Off in the distance I could see Lyn entering one of the side streets off College. The two men followed cautiously, as did I.

This was the poorer section of Chinatown, more like old pre-war Chinatown. This area was made up of tightly packed buildings with split-level, what looked like tiny apartments. A small park at the near end of the street was filled with men, playing mahjong, reading newspapers, and talking to each other. They were old and haggard and barely hanging on but each wore a tattered suit and projected a quiet dignity. I wondered what their story was.

Farther down the street, Lyn had now entered one of the tiny apartment buildings. The two men then stationed themselves just to either side of the entrance as if to grab her when she came out.

I had to get in to see why she was there.

I hated to do this but I was desperate. One of my favorite movie sequences was Fred Astaire as a doomed Chinaman in the song "Limehouse Blue," set in the Chinese section of London. The sequence was part of a film I had seen five years ago called *Ziegfeld Follies*. Astaire's costume was a long black one-piece with black fedora pulled down over his head. It gave me an idea.

I went into the park and made enough sense to one of the old men who spoke a smattering of English and who looked to be not too much shorter than me to offer to trade clothes with him. He was wearing his own black one-piece and had a replica of Astaire's black hat. We went into the washroom in the park and traded clothes. I tucked my hair under the fedora and noticed the old man was the talk of the park with what were his new threads. I had just bought that suit but I was going to bill it as expenses.

I crouched a little bit, bent my head down, and inched into the open apartment door past the two men on either side. They let me enter and didn't seem to notice me.

I had gotten in but I had no idea where I was going.

Several of the doors in the tiny apartments were open, probably to ward off the day's heat and try to take advantage of any breeze. There were more old men inside, but on the first floor there was no sign of Lyn. Where had she gone?

I climbed the stairs to the second floor and again no Lyn, but at the end of the corridor on the second floor there was a window looking out on an alley where someone could easily jump from the first floor and reach the building next door.

I went down the steps and made the short leap into the alley. There was a back entrance to this adjacent building and on the first floor I struck paydirt.

That Lyn was one smart cookie.

Halfway down the corridor, I passed one of the apartments which, like the last building, had open doors, peered inside, and saw Lyn sitting at the base of a bed in a tiny studio. Stretched out in the bed was a frail man with white hair and white beard who was sipping what smelled like medicinal tea.

That's the mugwort, I thought. Made much more sense than if she was buying it for herself.

I peered around the corner and further into the apartment. It was covered with books, both Chinese and American, and the floor was strewn with all kinds of newspapers.

This had to be her grandfather, the former editor and publisher.

I was able to dimly make out tiny snippets of conversation which was in Chinese but with English phrases inserted.

"Up to no good," I made out her grandfather saying, to which Lyn responded, "and a threat to us all."

I didn't know exactly what they were talking about but at that point losing my new suit seemed worth it.

Suddenly the conversation ended and Lyn got up from the bed and started to exit. As she did, the old man handed her a leaflet. She bowed to him and started to leave. I ducked for cover by heading down the other end of the corridor.

She went out the back door. Through an open window I watched her return to the alley and enter the next building, the one she originally came from.

But no sooner had she entered it than she was dragged back out into the alley by the two men who had apparently decided that they were through waiting for her to come out.

They were not tall, really almost about her size, but they were lean and agile.

They pushed her against the wall and seemed to be interrogating her in Chinese.

They searched her, found the leaflet, snickered, and started shouting at her.

One of them finally used an English phrase.

"Where is he?" he said.

It was time for me to enter the fray.

They didn't see me coming, presuming that nobody would come to help their victim, that the men in the building would remain silent.

I grabbed one of them, spun him around and punched him smack in the gut, direct hit to the solar plexus. He was surprised, but recovered quickly. He bent over with the blow but used his head as a battering ram and came at my mid-section. Fortunately, I sidestepped and he crashed into the building behind me.

Out of the corner of my eye, I watched Lyn grab the other man and use his own weight against him, pulling his shirt over his head and then delivering a kick to his nether regions.

Both were down and out but looked to be reviving fast.

I grabbed Lyn and pulled her out of the alley and out onto the main sidewalk. We fled into the park with the old men who recognized me in my Chinese threads and instinctively formed a wall around us: When the two men, now fully recovered, walked past the park they did not see us.

In the melee, Lyn had grabbed the leaflet and I pulled it from her hands.

It was in English, not Chinese, and was about the corruption of the Chinese Nationalist Party, the Kuomintang.

We were both exhausted, and as we watched the two men stride down the street I wanted to know more.

"So, you found your grandfather, the editor," I said.

"Yes," she replied, deciding to trust me a little. "He's my Sun Yat-sen. While I honor my mothers, I revere my grandfather who fights for freedom."

"I'm assuming he also still has access to linotype and helped you send the threatening letter to Barnum.

At this she grew cautious.

"Maybe, maybe not. But I want to work to make Chinatown better, not to leave."

"And who were those men?"

"They were the Tong. Enforcers. Defenders of the established business interests and big supporters of the Nationalist government which lost the war and fled to Taiwan. My grandfather has been putting out leaflets about the corruption of that government and they want to stop him. Luckily, they still don't know where he is."

"That was a pretty good kick you executed back there. I thought you were a Taoist, a proponent of passive mindfulness?"

"I'm also a proponent of Revolution," she said. "I combine the two. I'm a Taoist and a Maoist."

"You're a very complicated teenager."

"Thank you, Mr. Palmer," she replied, bowing to me in what looked more like a challenge than a bow.

The girl had many talents and might be of use in what was also becoming a very complicated case.

6

My first undercover assignment. Crysal was excited. Harry thought Diane Chestnut was a fairly suspicious character and needed looking into because either she or whoever was behind her might pose a threat to Sandra and Lyn.

He wanted her to cozy up to the real estate agent and see what she could find out.

"Flattery will get you everywhere" was something she learned in her time in the Hollywood studios, and she thought that principle would probably work in real estate as well.

Crystal decided not to pose as a would-be homeowner because that would only be a short encounter and Harry had already done that. Her tack would be different.

Harry gave her Diane's card and, when she called the number, she got an answering service that apparently Diane changed frequently, making sure her whereabouts were known to anyone wanting to be shown one of the properties listed in her Torrance office.

That day, the receptionist told her, Diane was out showing a home on Cabrillo Avenue, one like many of the others she was selling. The receptionist added that, though that home would probably be bought by her client, there was no harm in Crystal going out there to see what the house looked like.

So, she got in her car, left her North Hollywood apartment, and made the 40-minute drive to Torrance, which at midday was a lot less crowded and faster than rush hour.

Her first impression of the town was that it was the opposite of Los Angeles, clean, orderly, and inviting, though on the way to Cabrillo she also drove past the oil derricks which still dotted the town and spewed a hazy mist into the air.

She also drove past the Dow Chemical plant, whose sign out in front said this was the national headquarters. She didn't know much about the company, but given the name she couldn't imagine that a large chemical plant amid the oil derricks would add to the health of the town.

She parked her car on Cabrillo near 220th Street in front of one of several spacious white homes with picket fences and green lawns. On the sidewalk, Diane, in a low-cut pink dress wrapped tight around her derriere, as Harry had described, was going into her spiel. A man of medium height in thick black glasses was listening, raptured, but Crystal couldn't tell if it was about the house or about Diane.

I'm gonna crash this party, Crystal thought, jumping from her car, crossing the street, and joining the two on the sidewalk.

Diane looked startled that her lecture was being interrupted, so Crystal decided to put her at ease.

"I'm looking for a place in Torrance, also," she said. "I called your office and they said I could tag along and get the lay of the land."

Crystal had decided that if she was going into real estate she too needed to dress for the part and today had selected a yellow dress which also showed off her décolletage. The man in the glasses couldn't believe his luck as he kept shifting his gaze from one woman to the other.

"Okay, honey, you can tag along, but don't cramp my style," Diane shot back, grabbing the arm of the man, and leading him into the house with Crystal trailing behind.

She then took "Mr. Bennett" on a tour, describing each room in advance as if from a brochure so that, when the client looked in on the room, he saw it through her eyes.

"Notice the oak flooring," she said as she guided him into the living room. She then pointed upward toward the "hand-split cedar shake roof" and then below to one of the "custom fireplaces." Crystal had no idea what "hand-split" meant but Mr. Bennett seemed enthralled at both the house and Diane.

They then made their way toward the "dream kitchen," with its "multi-colored superamic tile."

What the hell is superamic? Crystal thought but kept that to herself.

Diane paraded herself in front of the "dream kitchen" installations, motioning her arm as she pointed out the "gas range and oven," the "natural ash cabinets," garbage disposal and the pièce de resistance, "the built-in dishwasher."

This sure beats my tired old tiny apartment, Crystal thought.

"My wife is going to love that," Mr. Bennett said, and Diane smiled, grabbed his arm, and led him to what she said was one of two custom bathrooms with "imported tile," beige shower curtain, and multicolored fixtures. Before he could catch his breath, she grabbed his arm again and led him toward what she said was the master bedroom, one of three bedrooms in the house. The room was huge, its centerpiece a monstrous bed with pink bedspread and covers.

Diane sat on the bed hoisting one leg over the other, rubbed her hand softly over the bedspread and whispered, or more accurately, Crystal thought, *cooed*, in Bennett's ear.

"You're gonna love this," she said putting her hand on his and gliding it over the bed. "It's comfortable, warm and a lot of fun."

She's really spreading it on thick, Crystal thought, but I guess that's the game.

Diane kept her hand on Bennett's, got up and led him back out to the living room, where they sat on the couch.

Crystal had been following this show on all its sets because, having been on a movie backlot, that's what this seemed like. When they got back to the living room, she tried to sit on the couch with them, but Diane shooed her off and pointed to a chair alongside the couch.

This was clearly the big finale and Diane didn't want anyone messing with it.

Mr. Bennett seemed flustered as Diane now moved closer to him on the couch and pulled out a contract from a briefcase she had stowed on the side.

"I don't know how I can ever afford this on an accountant's salary," he said. "I would love to take it but I just don't think it's possible."

Diane was undaunted.

"It costs almost nothing," she said. "Our homes start at $25,000. You only need $1600 down and we start monthly payments. You can move in immediately."

Bennett brightened.

"That we can afford," he said. "I'll talk it over with my wife and get back to you, but I'm interested."

Diane had one more trick up her sleeve.

"We don't have to sign at the office," she said. "You and I can meet privately. There's a cocktail lounge on Crenshaw and Monterey. We can have a drink, celebrate, and our lawyers will go over this in the morning."

Mr. Bennett was flattered.

She's turned a signing into a date, Crystal thought. This reminded her more and more of her old life in the clubs where the currency was seduction, but that usually led to a dead end. This was different.

Bennett said he would call her, probably the next day. Diane led him out the door, patting his hand and offering a hug to seal the deal.

With the client gone, Diane heaved a huge sigh of relief and collapsed onto the couch.

She then glanced around and saw Crystal looking a little awkward in the chair.

"C'mon over here honey," she said, patting the couch.

"I don't know what it is you want, but I don't think you're a client."

Crystal decided to level with her.

"I'm not," she said.

"I'm trying to break into this business and I was told that you were one of the best, so I wanted to see you in action."

"And how did you like the show?"

"I had a front row seat and it was spectacular."

"Yep, takes a lot out of you but in the end it's worth it."

"So how do I get to be like you?"

"There's only one me," she said, proudly puffing out her chest in a way Crystal could not help but find beguiling. "You want me to help you break into the industry?"

"Yes, that's it. I want to follow you around. I can really learn from you."

Crystal hoped she wasn't laying it on too thick.

"Let's go get a drink," she said. "I'm through working today and I need a break."

Diane gave her the instructions to the lounge she had described to Bennett, only a few blocks away. Crystal parked her car and met Diane in front. The neon sign on top read "Dealmakers."

Everyone seemed to know her there. The host, whom Diane smiled at, led the two of them to a secluded booth, and they ordered two mai tais, Crystal taking her cue from Diane.

The waiter came with two orange drinks with multicolored umbrellas in an oversized glass.

"That's what I use to seal the deal with the client," she said, "and this is my booth. Usually makes them nice and comfortable. Most people in here," she added, "are working on some deal or another."

Without even seeming to, Diane brushed her hand against Crystal's as she was holding her drink.

"So, what can I do you for?" she said.

"For whatever you want," Crystal replied, unable to contain herself given the drink, the dark booth, and the suggestive crooning of a jazz singer on the jukebox.

Diane suddenly turned serious.

"Look," she said, straightening up in her seat, "if you want to be in this business, it's a lot of work."

Crystal put a look of intense interest on her face, not all of which she was faking.

"The state requires you to have over 100 hours of training in various real estate classes. You have to prove you're honest and truthful and have a fingerprint check, although, if it comes back positive and you have a record, you can still be considered for the job."

"I have no record," Crystal said, thanking her lucky stars that though she had courted the underworld, she had never been mixed up in any of its schemes. She had come closer to breaking the law with her work for Harry, who always seemed to be straddling it.

"Then, after you get your license, you have to keep taking classes to renew the license."

She proceeded to wax eloquently about the profession.

"The Realtor," she said, beaming with pride, "is the way that land in this country is distributed widely and the way home ownership is promoted for all its citizens. It's a grave responsibility and a patriotic duty to see that everyone has their own home and is located in a friendly community. It takes integrity and honor."

Crystal was aghast at the contrast between witnessing Diane in action and then hearing her talk about how she actually saw herself. She decided this talk probably came straight out of a brochure from what she had read was the National Association of Real Estate Brokers.

The lecture continued.

"The real estate broker who promotes home ownership helps ensure the survival and growth of free institutions and of our civilization.

"The real estate agent," she concluded, now raising herself up in the booth, "is not a salesman taking orders, but a missionary, a pioneer with a vision."

Crystal thought she heard "God Bless America" playing in the background, but it was just the slow mournful crooning of the female Negro singer plaintively bemoaning her life of woe.

It was time to get down to business.

"And who does this missionary work for?"

Her speech concluded, Diane relaxed.

"I work for Dan Williams. He's transforming this town, changing it from a frontier oil town to a model community. He has big ambitions. He wants to build 30,000 homes in the next decade, all of them affordable for ordinary people."

"That's my next question," Crystal said. "How ordinary? Are they for everyone or just 'respectable' people?"

Harry had told her about the rough reception Sandra Chung had received and the way "the community" was threatening rather than welcoming her.

"I see what you mean," Diane replied, leaning back now as if she felt Crystal were grilling her.

But she quickly regained her composure, finding solace in the Realtors' handbook.

"A realtor should never introduce into the community any individual whose presence would be detrimental to property values in that neighborhood.

"If the individual is not respectable, 'destruction of value' can occur and that would be against the Realtor's code. We're not only selling a home, we're also selling an investment, and we must protect our client's equity."

So that's how you keep non-white people out of the neighborhood, Crystal thought. The whole enterprise suddenly seemed a bit shadier, and a bit more like being back in the mob bars.

If any doubt crossed Crystal's face, Diane didn't seem to notice. She just continued her rhapsody.

"We're always about ensuring 'highest value,'" she said, glowing. "The greatest value at the lowest cost with that value preserved and passed on in perpetuity."

And that's why white people own this town, Crystal thought.

Crystal decided that the official talk was at a dead end and it was time to get personal.

"So, where do you come from and how did you get into the business?"

Diane initially brightened at this less intrusive questioning.

"My father was a carpenter," she said. "He built homes by hand and he owned a lumber shop where he got his material."

But then she grew morose.

"My parents died when I was a teen. After that I was on my own. It was a hard road and I don't like talking about it much."

"That must have been difficult, but you overcame it and are now highly successful."

"Yes, it wasn't easy breaking into the industry, but Dan took a liking to me and helped me, and now I'm his best salesman."

"And is that your real name, Diane Chestnut?"

Diane laughed.

"No, not at all. It's part of the act. I introduced myself in a bar that way and this guy muttered, 'I'd like to have your chest rubbing against my nuts.' I hauled off and kicked him and he fell off his barstool. But he wasn't far wrong, and the name seems to work."

"Is your real name Crystal?"

"No, not at all. I'm a Southern girl. I came to big, bad Los Angeles to be an actress, but it never quite worked out and now I'm on the lookout for something else to do."

"If you work hard you can succeed at this," Diane said. "But you have to take it seriously. The seduction is a shell game, but behind it is real money if you know how to work it."

"I'm hooked," Crystal said, not entirely untruthfully. "Can I follow you around?"

"Honey, with your looks, if I don't watch it, I'll soon be following you."

With that they finished their drinks and, Crystal thought, sealed the deal, as Diane again casually rubbed Crystal's hand in a gesture that might have been more than just friendly.

Crystal had a lot to tell Harry. She left the bar, filled with all kinds of swirling emotions, a mixture of attraction and repulsion that she couldn't quite figure out.

7

As the old saying goes, "Don't come to me with your troubles, go to City Hall." I decided that in my two cases on Bunker Hill and the Mexican hamlet of Palo Verde that statement had merit. So I found myself walking the 15 minutes from my downtown office, up Hill Street, across 1st and then up Spring Street. On the way I had time to think about what exactly I was looking for. I knew I would be paying a visit to "Mr. Beame," the official who had tried to strong-arm Rosa Morales, and I was also looking for anyone else who might help me.

It was a Tuesday morning and the council was in session. The session was public, but they still wanted to see my credentials and the sergeant at arms at the door was curious about what I was doing there.

The sign outside said that today the council was debating a rent-control measure. I thought this might be very educational and presented a card identifying myself as "Harry Palmer, Reporter At Large." I didn't know what that meant, but it looked official enough that the sergeant let me enter and pointed to where a group of reporters were sitting.

There were now about six of us, five of them following the debate and myself following both them and the debate. It turns out the council had recently been rebuffed on a fairly onerous piece of legislation it had passed, and the members were weighing in on this defeat.

Last year, apparently, from what I could make out, the council had voted to cancel rent controls put in place during the war, when there was a housing crisis because of an influx of workers in the L.A. factories making war supplies.

Esperanza's boss Roybal was speaking when I came in. He testified that the cancellation last year was opposed by civil rights groups, labor leaders and unions, and tenants' groups, and that he for one was glad that the measure was rejected by the Federal Housing Authority, adding that for these workers there was still a housing crisis in the city.

Cheers went up from a small group seated at the back of the room, which I gathered was a tenants' group. The chair pounded his gavel and ordered the rowdy crew in the back to be quiet, pointing at the sergeant and telling them no more outbursts or they would have to leave.

"But this is an open hearing," a woman with salt and pepper hair and a slightly tattered gray shirt yelled back.

"Open doesn't mean incendiary," the chair shot back as the sergeant approached the woman and ordered her to leave.

"I'm Mariela Hernandez. You're not forcing me out of my home with your high rents and you're not dragging me out of here," she said, as those around her closed ranks.

"Alright, you can stay, but no more outbursts," the chair conceded.

A roly-poly council member, whose gut extended out onto the table in front of him, then addressed the group, calling the federal rejection of the council's measure the work of a "tin pot dictator." He said that the way to combat the housing crisis was not to employ these "Gestapo tactics" but to encourage private developers to build single-family homes. Anything else, he added, such as the public housing being proposed on Bunker Hill and the Moraleses' area of Palo Verde, was "destroying the freedom of private ownership" and a "major step to Communism."

As he was speaking, most of the reporters were just taking notes, but one of them was more active, motioning thumbs up at various parts of the speech. The councilman kept checking with him and seemed to be encouraged by his signals.

When the session was over, I asked one of the other reporters who this fellow was.

"Him, he's not really even a reporter," said this scribe, who worked for *The Daily News*.

"He works for the *Los Angeles Times* and thinks he runs this place. Rather than a reporter's hat, he should be wearing a ringmaster's top hat and costume and carrying a whip. He's the Chandler's representative at City Hall."

Norman Chandler owned *The Times*. He and his wife Buffy, or Buff, ran the paper which was read and advertised in by most of the city's heavyweights.

I thanked the reporter and followed our friend as he left the City Council chamber and got on an elevator that stopped on the 25th floor.

I got on the next elevator and when I got off on that floor, I looked at the names on the offices and found the one I was trying to locate. "Albert Beame, Housing Administrator" was painted on the outside door, and, though the glass was nearly opaque, I could still make out the outline of two men in the office. I pressed my ear against the door and heard snatches of a conversation.

The reporter was barking at the man behind the desk, telling him he had better get a move on. "We need that place cleared," he said, and then abruptly got up and made for the door. I was just able to avoid a collision with him. As I stepped aside, he burst through the door, impervious to anything and anyone. He brushed me aside, practically pushing me out of the way, and headed to the elevator without looking back.

I looked inside the office and there behind the desk was a man whose appearance epitomized that of a lifelong bureaucrat—balding with a thin black mustache. He was trim, dressed in a gray suit. His only sign of personality was a pink carnation pinned to his lapel. He was sitting behind a mauve oak desk which seemed to press his wiry frame against the wall of his small office.

Since the door was open, I decided to enter. He looked up, surprised by my presence.

"Can I help you," he said, though what he meant was, "Who are you and what on earth are you doing here?"

"Obediah Johnson," I said, handing him a card I had picked up the other day from the owner of my hotel. "They're trying to take my place and I want to know why."

He didn't quite know what to do with me.

"Come in, Mr. Johnson," he said, "let's talk about this."

On a bookshelf behind Beame's desk, which took up more than half of his tiny office, were all kinds of manuals about city land appropriation and one I noticed titled *Uses of Eminent Domain*.

"I run a respectable hotel, have never been any trouble to the city, and don't know why I'm being pressured to leave," I said. Maybe a quarter of that was true.

"Respectable" was stretching a point since there were all kinds of slightly shady customers, myself included. The hotel was thought of as a trouble spot for years and was raided once in a while. But this expenditure of city funds usually didn't turn up much. Nevertheless, we had a right to live where we wanted and in the way we wanted.

"I'm sure there's been some mistake, Mr. Johnson," Beame said, fidgeting with a pencil which he brushed against his mustache lengthening it. I must be making him very nervous.

"And I'm not the only one," I said. "My gardener who lives in Palo Verde also told me you had visited his parents and that there were two very tough customers with you who threatened them. They may have been the same two who showed up at my place."

At this he seemed to flinch, but then he gained a bit of confidence as he pulled the pencil away from his upper lip.

"Tell your gardener not to worry about those two men. The truth is I don't know who they were either. They strong-armed me as I was entering the home and forced their way in with me. The city wants this land but only in order to build low-cost public housing that will make your gardener and his family very happy, and they would never seize it by force."

"And who is it you work for?" I asked in a way that indicated I didn't believe him.

"Why, I work for the people, of course," he replied, motioning to a series of photos on the wall of him attending various dinners and public events.

I looked closely at the photos. The reporter I'd followed into his office was at his dinner table in one of them.

"And who's this fellow?" I said, pointing at the photo. "He was just coming out of your office and he didn't look happy, that is, if he ever looks happy."

"He covers City Hall for *The Times*," he said. "And the reason why he was unhappy was that I wouldn't give him an exclusive scoop. You know reporters."

I knew some, and the guy in his office didn't act like them. The way he threw his weight around both the City Council meeting and Beame's office was unlike any reporter I'd ever encountered.

Beame got up from his chair and extended his hand. Once on his feet, he looked even smaller than he had sitting at his desk.

"No one is going to lose their property who does not want to sell," he said. "Rest assured Mr. Johnson, all is well."

"And the two men?"

"My office is looking into that. We'll know who they are in a little while. You can check back with us if you like and we'll let you know."

"Thanks, Mr. Beame," I said. "You're a credit to the community."

I didn't believe a word he said, and he was equally suspicious of me. I guess that was most people's experience of City Hall.

I lingered outside his office after I exited. He made a call almost as soon as I left, but I couldn't hear who he was talking to or what the subject was.

I decided it was time to head home for the day. I walked from Spring Street downtown and then up the hill to my hotel. I didn't have anything to do that night and decided I would take a nap and then, before visiting Esperanza, go the library to look up "eminent domain," how it had been and could be used.

I was napping when suddenly from the hallway I heard some screams. I looked out and saw men and women scurrying to get out of the rain. The sprinkler system, which had once prevented a fire in the hotel from spreading, had been activated and was spewing water everywhere. I heard cries from the floors above and below me.

I didn't see any sign of fire and quickly assumed someone had systematically lit a match and tried to drown the hotel in water.

I went down to the lobby and found the real Obediah Johnson frantically ordering the clerks to grab whatever plastic they could find to put down on the floors.

"This could ruin me," he said when he saw me. "There's going to be a lot of damage to the carpets and floors and some may even have to be replaced. Get on the job, Palmer. I need you to find out what's going on."

I left the lobby, which now looked like a hospital emergency room with people scurrying back and forth, most of them wet.

Outside, I looked across the street and there were two men in black suits leaning against a red Chevrolet Bel Air and watching people scurrying out of the hotel. One of them had binoculars and was scanning the upper floors to see if people were still hustling out of the rooms there. I pulled out my camera, which I had luckily snatched from my room, and snapped their photo.

The camera I used was a miniature spy camera from Japan, about to go on the market, and obtained for me by the soundman Kelly I knew from my first case. He had contacts in the Japanese film industry. Because I had used him in the past, he gave me as a gift this gem of an instrument, which was barely visible and produced high-grade images.

After snapping the two men, I crossed the street and ran towards them.

They saw me and got in the car. The taller of the two was driving. I reached the car just as he was entering and tried to pull the door open. I noticed he had huge oversize hands and burly arms, and he used them to, instead of closing the door, throw it open to try to knock me away.

I noticed there was a car coming, but in the distance. Though it was dangerous, I pulled a maneuver I'd had some success with in the past. I staggered back and hit the ground, praying there was some time before the approaching car would be on top of me.

The two in the Bel Air assumed I was down for the count and possibly that they even had finished me. The burly driver waved to me as they pulled out, feeling themselves free of any pursuit. The driver in the approaching car swerved to avoid me, and when I watched the Chevy roll some distance away, I got up.

I wasn't hurt. I exaggerated the effect of the fall to throw them off and make them think they were in the clear.

I had parked my car in front of the hotel as well since I was going to use it that evening to visit Esperanza. None the worse for wear and tear, and needing to know who these men were working for, I climbed into my beat-up, old sloppy jalopy in as hot pursuit as its tired engine could muster.

The Chevy ahead of me, fairly visible with its red exterior, was heading south down Broadway at a leisurely pace, good for me, since their car, which looked to be this year's model, could easily outpace me if they knew they were being tailed.

We went through the town of Florence, then through Compton and Gardena, and I began having an eerie feeling about the whole trip. I had done this drive before.

They stopped for a moment in a no-man's land just before Carson, a strip full of bars, tattoo parlors and a few run-down hotels. The smaller man got out, ran toward the bar, pulling an envelope from his pocket and handing it to the security guard or bouncer standing outside the bar. The name of the bar was Last Ditch—same as on the two cards that I had found. *Probably gambling debts*, I thought.

But that was not their ultimate destination. The smaller man then ran back to the car and it took off, once again heading south, but then turning west and rolling into Torrance.

I followed them down the main street, Torrance Boulevard, to a complex of city administration buildings. They ducked into a parking lot behind one of the buildings and I had no choice but to drive past them to make sure they didn't see me.

I cruised around the block and then past the parking lot, but they were gone. They must have spotted me and waited until I drove past.

I thought the parking lot trick was just a ruse, but still I wanted to see whose lot it was. I turned into the lot myself and was met almost immediately with the smiling face of a man in an official uniform who told me this was the property of the Torrance police and that I could not park there.

Curiouser and curiouser, I thought as I pulled out of the lot. I was shooed away but my two friends in the Chevy were not bothered by the police.

Were these cases getting simpler or more complicated? At this point, I really couldn't tell.

8

I slept in the next day. I had had enough of all three cases, though the one closer to home was getting harder to ignore because some of the water from the soaked carpet in the hallway had seeped through the door, and the small carpet by my bed was soggy when my feet touched it mid-afternoon. Outside was soggy also. It had rained that night and it was still ominous and overcast when I looked out the window. A perfect day for sleeping in.

I turned on the radio and it had more bad news. The U.S. adventure in Korea was escalating. MacArthur, the decorated World War II general who was in command, had decided to "stick it to" the Koreans and was invading the North. He was a cocky son of a bitch and declared that he planned to defeat the North Koreans, their Chinese Communist allies, and bring the troops home by November 11 for "an Armistice Day Parade." The Chinese, though, had warned him not to go near the Yalu River, the border between Korea and China. MacArthur's troops ignored the warning and were advancing rapidly toward the river. The latest news was that the Chinese were crossing a bridge on the river and now engaging the UN troops, which were mainly U.S., in what might be a full-scale war. MacArthur seemed to welcome the conflict, claiming that anything short of victory "would be the greatest defeat of the free world in recent times."

Why did I care about this? I was still on retainer by Sandra, and if it looked like suddenly the U.S. was at war with China, it was possible Torrance might join the war on the side of the U.S. and against the Chungs.

Still, I didn't figure much would happen during the day, so I had an afternoon breakfast, courtesy of Johnson who hadn't reneged on our agreement despite the latest attack. I told him what I discovered about the two men and the Torrance police and he was convinced at least that I was working on the case.

There is nothing like scrambled eggs, bacon, toast with peach marmalade and two cups of coffee with cream to convince you that all is right with the world.

So, I was feeling better as evening approached and I started the drive out to Torrance.

That feeling was quickly quashed when I arrived at the Chungs. Sandra answered the door as night was starting to fall, looked around furtively, and pulled me inside. There were boxes strewn everywhere, but also piles of cardboard indicating they had had a busy day moving in and unpacking.

"I'm so glad you're here, Mr. Palmer," she said.

Lyn was nowhere to be found. Sandra said she had snuck out but didn't know exactly where. She was worried about her.

"Lyn can take care of herself," I said, remembering how she had dealt with the much bulkier and taller member of the Tong.

That didn't seem to allay her fear.

"I'm worried because of this," she said. "It was tacked to our door when we arrived last night."

She handed me a paper. Again, as with the threat to Barnum, the message was made up of various newspaper headlines, and this time I knew the threat was coming from outside and not from Lyn. The paper read "**THE KKK IS LOOKING AT YOU.**" It was a much bolder announcement than the small letters at the base of the warning to Barnum.

"What does it mean?" she said. "What should we do?"

"It means you should be careful, lock all doors at night, pull down the shades and keep a low profile until I can find out who is behind this."

At that point Lyn entered. She was wearing a sweatshirt with a hood, pulled up over her jet-black hair and partially over her face. She looked in the approaching shadows like a phantom.

"Look what I found," she said, waving another piece of paper. "It was tacked to a bar a few blocks from here."

This notice read, "If you are interested in keeping this town Caucasian and the type of community that you can be proud of raising your children in, then you will get on the band wagon." Nothing else was said but the notice seemed to be an invitation to a meeting possibly taking place in the bar that evening where the notice was attached.

"I'll be back in a while. Don't let anyone in in the meantime," I said.

"Be careful, Mr. Palmer," Sandra said. "Where are you going?"

"I'm going to find out who's on the bandwagon."

I decided to drive the few blocks to the bar Lyn had found.

When I got there, I found a sedate crowd, a few men at the bar, a few couples at the tables arranged around a jukebox and Hank Snow's "I'm Moving On" booming from the machine.

Nobody seemed to be at all concerned about the Chungs. I thought they might be taking Hank Snow's advice and "Moving On."

That hope went up in smoke when I saw the pock-marked man from the signing enter the bar, give a nod to the old, grizzled bartender who motioned him to a room in the back, near the toilets. The only other server in the bar was a young kid who was taking orders and bringing drinks to the tables.

I knew I had to get back there and figured it would be easy. I approached the bartender and ordered a Scotch, straight up. "I want to whet my whistle but first I need to use the restroom," I said.

"It's closed, mister," he shot back. "Out of order. You'll have to use the café across the street."

He wasn't going to let me pass so I took his advice and went outside.

I crossed the street and went into the café so if he was watching he wouldn't suspect anything.

As soon as I entered, I went right back out the front door, down a few buildings and crossed the street again, this time circling back through an alley behind the bar.

Sure enough, there was a back entrance surrounded by garbage cans and a lot of beer bottles, but it was locked.

I banged on the door, hoping to get lucky.

The kid came to the door, irritated that he had to interrupt his job and put a crimp on his tips.

He opened the door and I stepped inside.

"Got a delivery for you," I said. I had taken off my suit coat and left it and my hat in the alley, rolled up my sleeves and did my best to act like a trucker.

"Those come in the morning," he shot back suspiciously.

"We got delayed. Are you gonna let me in or do I cancel the order?"

"Okay," he said, "but be quick."

He took off down the corridor, not scrutinizing me too carefully, and mainly relieved to be back to work.

That left me alone. About halfway down the hall, I heard loud men's voices from behind a closed door.

"I don't want to do it. I don't think it's safe," one of them said.

"It's perfectly safe. No one's against us," said another, this time gruffer and deeper voice.

"When do we go?" a third chimed in.

"Tonight is our best chance of stopping them," the gruffer voice said.

He seemed to be their leader, and the others fell in line behind him.

"Let's get to it," he said, and I heard a rustling in the room as if they were all getting up to leave.

I barreled out of there, unlocked the back door, and just managed to close it before they exited.

I reclaimed my coat, went around the corner, and reentered the bar just as they were exiting. I pulled my hat down and shuffled past them.

"Let's hurry," said the gruff, irritated nasal voice leading the way.

It was the pock-marked man who motioned his fellows—I counted five of them—forward and to their cars.

I went back inside the bar, downed my Scotch which I figured I would need for strength in what was promising to be a long night, paid the bartender, and got out of there before the kid could notice me.

It was pitch black outside as I followed the three cars–two of the men had gotten into a car with their companion–south on Crenshaw in the direction of the San Pedro Port. They parked in a deserted lot not too far out of town and I drove past. I could see about a half dozen oil derricks next to the lot, still pumping in the middle of the night.

They were handing out something to each other and one of them retrieved two pieces of a heavy object which I could not clearly make out from a trunk of his car.

I parked within sight of the lot and watched them at work.

They assembled the object and bolted it to the top of the car belonging to the pock-marked man.

They got back in their cars and streamed north toward the town, with me following at a safe distance behind them.

They turned right off Crenshaw, and now I had a perfect idea about what they were up to.

As if to confirm my suspicions, a few blocks later, I saw them turn right up Carillo Avenue, take a left, and park around the corner from Post Street.

Now there was no doubt where they were heading.

They worked quickly and efficiently at what they were doing. I guessed they had practice at this job and had done it before.

They were assembling a cross on the Chungs' lawn and pouring gasoline over it.

I ran up on the lawn just as they set fire to the cross, and not in time to stop them. They were all wearing white hoods.

On the side of the cross they had painted in red the words "Go Back to China."

They were very surprised to see me and, before they could make a move, I grabbed the hood of the one seeming to give the orders and pulled it off.

It was indeed the pock-marked man. He shuddered when I exposed him, and he and the others ran off the lawn.

As they were bolting for their cars, I kicked the cross over and rubbed it against the grass on the lawn, which luckily was still wet from the rain the night before.

Sandra and Lyn came running out of the house, terrified.

"This isn't safe. I'm getting us out of here," Sandra said, grabbing my arm and holding on for dear life.

Lyn seemed to brighten at that thought.

"No, you're not," I said. "I'm going to find out who these men are and turn them over to the police. They'll be punished and you'll be safe."

I didn't have the faintest idea where to look for them. All I had to play was a hunch, but it seemed worth trying.

I was going on the idea that they might have a meeting place to reconnoiter if their plans went awry, or even if they didn't.

A perfect place would be the parking lot near the oil derricks from where they launched their attack.

I drove past the empty lot and saw two cars leaving as I arrived.

One car remained. Leaning against it was the pock-marked man, smoking a cigarette with an angry look on his face.

I decided he would need looking after. I was parked next to one of the oil derricks, waiting for him to exit. I realized I knew almost nothing about him and I thought I could start by finding out who owned the lot he was parked in since he and his gang seemed to feel they had the run of the place. He had the car door open and by the light of his car I snapped his photo, figuring it would be useful later on.

Adjacent to the lot, next to the derricks, was the Dow Chemical Plant, which Crystal had told me was the company headquarters. This site was, according to the label outside, used to manufacture rubber. Next to the building was a huge, exposed area that looked like a swamp, which I assumed was where they were dumping the waste from the plant.

My pock-marked friend was likely an employee of the plant. It was something to go on in identifying him.

At that point, his car barreled out of the lot, back up Crenshaw, and toward the center of Torrance with me in hot pursuit.

I think I might have followed a bit too close, because he took a sharp right, as if to try to lose me, and headed in the direction of the no-man's land of bars, strip-joints, and tattoo parlors that I had seen earlier. I figured that was where he was going and I could ease up and just look for his car parked outside one of the bars when I got there.

No such luck.

I couldn't find the car anywhere. I figured he probably went home and I decided to do the same.

But I thought I'd have a look-in on the Chungs before I left.

As I pulled up, I was astonished.

There was another fire coming from the direction of their house, but this one was not on the lawn.

The house was going up in flames and the fire was spreading fast.

I had a blanket in the trunk of my car. I rubbed it on the wet grass and burst through the front door, which fell over easily when I kicked it.

Inside, the wood in the living room, where they had done the signing, was going up fast.

I ran down the hallway, and the first bedroom I came to was Lyn's.

She was just starting to stir as the fire surrounded her bed.

I grabbed her, hoisted her on my shoulders, and had her breathe through the wet blanket.

I ran up the corridor with the flames in hot pursuit and jumped through the front door which was now lying on the floor just ahead of a whoosh of flames on our tail.

"Where's your mother?" I said, as I laid her down on the lawn.

"I think she's still inside," Lyn replied. "She was so anxious she took a sleeping pill."

I wet the blanket again and ran back inside. There was a narrow path toward the room in the back which I figured was Sandra's bedroom.

When I got there, though, the room was a mass of smoky embers. It looked like this is where the fire started.

The thin linen bedspread had probably enabled the flames to speedily crawl up her bed.

She was moving, but just barely, and badly burned.

It was all I could do to grab her, lift her out of the bed, break down the back door, and get her outside.

I was carrying her out to the front lawn where Lyn was struggling to stand up when I felt the last breath ooze from her body.

I laid what was left of her at Lyn's feet.

Lyn grabbed her inert body.

"Māmāmā mā wǒ ài nǐ," she said as she hugged her close.

I guessed it meant something like "Mama, I love you."

She looked down at the charred body and then up at me, and her next words were in English.

"I'm going to kill whoever did this," she said.

At that moment, I couldn't blame her.

Act 2

You Can't Go Home Again

9

This case had just gotten as messy as it could get, and I had my own share of guilt. I was off following a suspect when, after the burning cross, I probably should have stationed myself on the Chungs' front lawn.

The aftermath was messy also. There wasn't much left of the house by the time the fire department showed up. I gave Lyn a ride back to Chinatown that night. She was going to stay in her old house since Sandra had paid the rent until the end of the month.

It was probably too soon, but I visited her the next day and brought up the subject of insurance. She was in line to get a hefty payment for the house and I wondered what she would do with it.

She was beside herself with grief and all she could think of at that moment was her mother's funeral, which she was getting some help from friends and her mother's patients in arranging. She invited me and I agreed to come. You never know what you can learn at funerals. Lyn wanted me to stay on the case, saying she would pay me when the insurance money came. I told her that her mother had already paid me for a month, and trying to find out what really happened at the house was included in my pay.

And then she said something surprising, given what I knew about her.

"I'm going to rebuild the house. Those bastards are not keeping me out. I'll be 18 at the end of the month and in my mind, whether it's true or not in California, I can do what I want. I'm going to move in there and transfer to the school mother wanted me to go to. I'll show them and I'll avenge my mother."

I was with her up until the last part. I wasn't sure what that meant and didn't particularly want to find out.

The next step for me was to check with the police and see what they had discovered about who or what was responsible for the fire.

It seemed obvious it was the Klan, but I didn't want to take anything for granted and I needed to see the results of the police investigation.

I had not had any encounter with the Torrance police, but I had heard some suspicious rumors about them.

Before I went to the station, I decided to check with my contact on the force, Captain Luis Nader. Nader, an often-besieged homicide squad leader, had been my boss and helped me with cases in the past.

I went down to L.A. police headquarters and popped my head in the door of his office, unannounced.

He greeted me warmly.

"Get out," he said, as I entered. "I don't have time for this."

And it looked like he didn't. There was a half-smoked cigar in his ashtray perched on top of a desk laden with all kinds of files and papers. I don't know how he kept track of it all, but he did.

"I'll just be a minute," I said. "I need to get the lowdown on the Torrance police."

At that he brightened, looked up from behind the pile, stopped leafing through whatever folder was on his desk, picked up the cigar, and lit it.

"That thing stinks to high heaven," I said as he started to blow smoke rings my way. "What the hell brand is that?"

"It's not really a cigar," he said. "It's actually an aerosol spray. It's called 'Harry Palmer Repellent.' It's to get rid of bugs."

He thought that was very funny, and after his little laugh he was ready to talk.

Nader was an honest cop and there weren't many of them around. We had gotten along okay when I was working for him. We only clashed a bit over some of my methods. He particularly didn't like a skill I had cultivated from my years on the burglary squad that involved breaking and entering. But he was in a forgiving mood.

"I'm only going to say this once and then I want you out of here, and don't steal anything on your way out."

I was all ears.

"What is it with you and cops, Palmer? Last year you were in here asking about the Wild East and Boyle Heights, and this year you're tangling with the police in Torrance? You have some kind of a death wish?"

He wasn't far off. The two sergeants in the Mexican neighborhood nearly did me in.

"That's a tough force. This is what I know. They have a reputation of shooting first and asking questions later. Last year there was a manhunt in L.A. County. This soldier home from the war had been on the force, got himself kicked off, and decided to go on a one-man rampage against cops. He shot at several of them all over the county.

"We were looking for him everywhere, but two cops in Torrance took the chase to extremes. We had a make on the truck he was driving, but the cops in Torrance stopped what they said was a suspicious vehicle and noticed what they thought was a gun in his pick-up. They surrounded the truck and shot him dead before he could reach for the rifle."

"Brave boys," I said, shaking my head in disgust.

"It gets worse. The driver was a Negro, shorter than the man we were looking for—who was white. The truck was a different make and color. And the gun was a bb gun, that his kid had left in the truck."

"And what happened to the cops?"

"The usual, one's doing desk duty and the other got off scot-free, though the victim's family is suing the town and will likely collect some money."

Nader took a long, last puff on his cigar.

"And that's all I know, and now it's time for you cowpoke to be moseying along."

I took the hint, got up to leave and was at the door when he looked up from his pile of reports.

"They're very protective of their town and they keep it very clean, so don't go poking that bear. You might get mauled, and then I'd have no one to annoy me."

I patted the brim of my hat. I didn't know he cared. I also figured that "clean" meant white and I remembered that the two men I had trailed had gained easy access to the police parking lot.

The Torrance station was small. There was only one officer at the desk when I entered. I had to be careful because I had a bit of a reputation surrounding my being mixed up in the death of the two officers in Boyle

Heights last year and my having left the force in what to outsiders looked like mysterious circumstances.

The man behind the desk was reading one of the popular men's crime magazines and chuckling to himself.

"What's so funny?" I asked as I approached the desk.

He was stocky and sitting on a stool so he towered over me, and with his big hands and puffed-out chest was an intimidating presence.

"Why do you want to know?" he said, angry that I had interrupted his reverie.

"I like to have a good laugh," I said and held out my hand. "Name's Harvey Prince, I'm an insurance inspector looking at the fire in the town the other night. Looks to me like a case of people trying to crowd in where they don't belong getting what's coming to them and we don't want to pay for that."

"You got that right," he said, relaxing and releasing his monstrous hands that had been pawing the magazine. "It's a police magazine," he said. He showed me the cover. It had a pulpy drawing of a woman in torn shirt and pants being rescued by a dashing officer who was shooting out the lights of a truck streaming down at them." Emblazoned across the top in bold red letters was the title, *Manhunt*.

"What I was reading," he said, "was a story about a cop who was asked what to do if he caught his girlfriend skulking around with a black. What they told him on this Southern force was to break the guy's taillight, so his buddies on the force could stop the guy and shoot him."

"That's a good one," I said. "Though I'm not supposed to be hearing this."

I winked, indicating to him that it was our secret. I also wondered if this was the cop who had taken part in the shooting last year that Nader recounted.

His badge said "Sergeant McGinty" and I wanted to see if I could get him to open up a little further.

"What else is in there, McGinty?" I asked. He didn't mind me calling him by his last name.

"Just another joke. This one's good. What's the difference between a candy cane, a Christmas tree bulb, the star on top of the tree, and a slave?"

"Got me," I said.

"You don't hang the star." This was followed by a big laugh and I had to follow suit, though the joke didn't make much sense except as a pure expression of hate.

"You know," he said, "it reminds me of a saying in the department about our history. Last century, when they were putting together the police, somebody said, 'We don't need the police, and courts and jails. All we need in Torrance is a tree and a rope.'"

He started laughing again, louder this time, but was interrupted by an officer coming out from the back and silencing him.

"What's going on out here, McGinty?"

"Just having a laugh with this insurance dick," the burly officer replied.

"I'm here to get the report on the fire for the company files," I said.

He motioned for me to follow him to the back and as he was leaving shot a piercing look at the officer behind the desk, who appeared embarrassed and went back to his reading.

He led me to his office, one of a few in the back of a small station. His was neat and orderly, the opposite of Nader's. Not a file or a paper out of place and an almost empty desk.

He looked to be a bright man in his early 40s. The title on his office read "Jack Lance, Police Investigator."

He motioned me to a seat.

I gave him one of my "Harvey Prince, Insurance Accessor" cards. He looked at it and threw it aside.

"What happened the other night was tragic," he said.

Before I could even agree, he went on.

"Unfortunately, from what we can determine, it was their own fault. We had an electrician in to look at the wiring, and it appears that the wires got crossed on the fuse box and sparked a flame that just took off. The tragedy is that those people didn't have the wires checked before they moved in. It appears to be their own fault."

That's how they're going to play it, I thought, but there was a chance it could be right and I needed to verify their version.

"Can I see the electrician's report?"

"Oh, there was no real report. We trust him and he seemed very certain that was what happened so we're in the process of closing the case."

"One question, and I know this is going to sound like I'm making trouble, but we have to look at all sides of the case before we deny a claim."

Lance fidgeted in his seat, leafing nervously through the trim file on his desk.

"There has been some talk about the Klan being active in the town, and the Chungs, according to their daughter, had received some threatening letters, to say nothing of the fact that a few of the neighbors reported a burning cross on the lawn the night the house caught fire. Is it possible they could have been behind this?"

Lance closed the file and looked me straight in the eye as if he was taking my question seriously and was going to level with me.

"There are some Klan members in the town, you're right," he said. "But the farthest they've ever gone is a burning cross, and apparently that night, some private muscle the family hired put out the flame a few hours before the house caught fire. So, no, nothing on that end."

He decided to "level" with me further.

"This is a very peaceful town," he said. "We don't like trouble and we don't like people showing up where they aren't wanted. We run a very clean operation and if undesirables come into the neighborhood, we have ways of moving them out. We spend a lot of time ticketing those who don't belong here. They sell unlawfully on the streets, try to ride the city buses for free, and congregate on the public sidewalks. We get them to move along and make sure they know they're not welcome here."

"I'm guessing also that the more upright, respectable citizens you have living in town, the higher the property values and the more money the police can argue is needed in the budget to keep 'undesirables' out."

He didn't like that at all and I could see my nice welcome was coming to an end.

It was then that a commotion arose from outside.

I heard McGinty bellowing, "That's funny. We got a fellow in the back who says he's also an insurance investigator."

It was time for these bootheels to be wandering.

I got up abruptly, thanked Lance, who from deeper in his office had not been able to make out McGinty's words, ducked out of his office, and raced down the corridor.

As I filed past McGinty, he yelled "Hey there. Hold on."

I waved to the man in the tweed suit who was standing next to his desk with a look of confusion on his face.

I got in my car and tore out of the parking lot. In my rearview mirror I saw Lance race out the front door, but it was too late and he didn't see which direction I was driving.

Could the cops have been involved as well?

Nader was right, sometimes they shot first and asked questions later. Or sometimes, in the case of the Chungs, they hardly asked any questions at all.

I had run into a blue wall and I couldn't help thinking that the very orderly Investigator Lance was just a slightly more buttoned-down version of the crudeness of McGinty. One was upfront about his hatred and prejudice, while the other was more secretive about his. I reckoned they could each do about the same amount of damage and I needed to be wary of both of them.

10

The next day was to be Sandra's funeral. On the phone, I told Lyn about the police report saying the fire was the result of faulty wiring. She just said "No," but refused to say anything more. She said she was busy with the details of the funeral and told me she would talk about this afterwards.

I invited Crystal, who was eager to see the spectacle. We both wore black, one of the traditional Chinese funeral colors, but I noticed Crystal's dress was cut short in the back, was plastered tight against her, and cut low in the front displaying her ample breasts.

"If you can't have fun at a funeral, where can you have fun?" she said.

Okay, the girl was young and had not met Sandra or Lyn. I just hoped she behaved herself.

The procession was to start at the funeral parlor on Broadway, wind its way up Broadway to Sandra's office on Yale Street, then return to Broadway to stop at Sandra and Lyn's home, and then on to the cemetery in East Los Angeles. Lyn had given me the itinerary so I could follow the procession.

Crystal and I stationed ourselves along the route on Broadway, near Sandra's office. The Chinatown streets were lined with spectators, all eagerly trying to get a glimpse of Sandra's coffin. The death had been well covered in the Chinese papers, and it looked like the whole community had turned out for her.

When the hearse bearing the coffin stopped, Lyn, who was riding in front, got out. There didn't seem to be much family besides Lyn, but Sandra apparently was well-liked in the community. Since, as she said, she was one of the few dentists, she must have had a number of patients, and it seemed like they were all there.

Lyn, dressed in black, waved to the crowd, threw open the door of the hearse and pulled it a little way out for onlookers to file by the corpse. Lyn had told me something of the customs which were largely about making the deceased comfortable as they started their journey to the spirit world.

There was food on the side of the open coffin, a cooked pig's head and chicken, along with bowls of rice and fruit. Sandra was dressed in traditional Chinese garb, a red long-flowing costume. Her body was wrapped in blankets, multicolored and carefully sewn fabrics which apparently were designed to keep her warm as her spirit migrated. There looked to be about 20 of these, wrapping her from waist to toe.

At the side of the body lay an extra set of clothes, again to insure comfort on the trip. As Crystal and I ambled by the coffin we saw inside it also what looked like a small department store—cameras, watches, automobile models, fish, and mahjong kits. All meant as creature comforts to ease her journey to the spirit world.

There was something else too, a miniature replica of what looked like the house that burned. The reconstruction included a lawn and a fence around the house with wild plants and other flora growing on the fence. It was a miracle of minute detail.

I introduced Crystal to Lyn, who smiled approvingly at her dress and presentation. Lyn herself was wearing a one-piece black outfit which looked both delicate and sporty. It was loose enough so she could maneuver gracefully, but also, I thought, use her martial arts skills if needed.

Lyn saw me looking at the tiny house and said, "This was her dream and I'm going to honor it."

Suddenly a look of fear crossed Lyn's face. I followed her gaze and saw two men who looked like the two we had fought in the alley near her grandfather's place.

She abruptly shoved the coffin back into the hearse, climbed into the front with the driver and it took off again, this time up Broadway in the direction of Lyn and Sandra's old house.

I told Crystal who the two men were and we followed them as they followed the hearse. They apparently did not recognize me owing, I hoped, to my being in disguise the last time they saw me.

We were late arriving in front of the house and we lost sight of the two men in the dense crowd. We saw the hearse stop outside the house. But this time there was no Lyn to welcome the crowd, just an old man who announced himself to be a patient of Sandra's and invited the crowd to file past the casket. Next to him, what appeared to be the funeral director, guided the crowd in single file past the coffin offloaded from the vehicle.

The two men also had disappeared.

What I did see, though, was an old man with a black hat pulled down over his forehead who I thought I recognized as Lyn's grandfather. He was near the edge of the crowd, but he cowered and bent over in a way that made his appearance almost indistinguishable.

I felt sorry for him, for losing his daughter and for having to skulk around at her funeral.

A brass band played in front of the house, creating a very loud ambiance, beckoning those from the surrounding area to come out to watch the show. It worked. More people began streaming out of homes and joined the crowd around the hearse.

An enlarged photo of Sandra in her white dentist's coat was mounted on the top of the car of what was probably a former patient now driving alongside the hearse. People recognized the photo and scurried to tell their neighbors. The crowd was growing larger by the minute.

But where was Lyn?

At that moment Sandra's father turned and made his way to the back of the crowd. He had seen something which made him afraid.

The hearse was now about to start the long journey to the cemetery, and as it turned around and started back down Broadway another old man—and former patient?—riding in the front starting throwing money at the crowd. This, someone told me, was the "devil's money" and was being gotten rid of to keep demons from molesting the spirit as it went to the gravesite.

Crystal and I scanned the crowd for any signs of Lyn, but there was no sign of either of them.

I didn't know what to do, but figured it was best to follow the funeral procession and see what turned up.

The hearse wound its way to the dilapidated burial ground, badly kept, with a maze of graves and vines growing on them. To add to the mysterious atmosphere a thick mist, even in late morning, hovered over the graves and made visibility difficult.

The hearse stopped before an empty plot, which had an open hole. This last part of the ceremony began with the funeral director burning the items scattered next to the coffin. He said this was once again to send these comforting objects along with the deceased to the next world which both would now inhabit.

While many Chinese were cremated, Sandra had apparently chosen the more American method of burial.

As the casket was being lowered from the hearse, with Crystal and me standing near it and the brass band blaring, there was a commotion from the back of the crowd.

Someone was trying to break through. It was Lyn. She was frantically pushing her way through the onlookers, and behind her we saw the two men in hot pursuit.

Lyn ran to the casket and threw herself on it. "They killed my mother," she said, pointing in the direction of the two men. "It was the Tong. They murdered her." She then collapsed on the coffin, crying, and wailing.

The crowd looked at the two men, who quickly slunk away.

I went to follow them and left Crystal with Lyn.

The crowd was too thick, though, and by the time I made my way through it, they were gone, disappeared in the mist which still had not cleared.

I got back in time to hug Lyn as they closed the casket and lowered her mother's coffin into the ground. Crystal grabbed her other shoulder and held her tight. They seemed to have become fast friends within a matter of minutes.

The plot they had chosen was near the entrance of the cemetery. Lyn told us this was so her mother would have an easier time leaving the graveyard and making her way to her new home.

I wasn't able to question Lyn immediately. After the burial she was busy handing each person who attended a white and a red envelope. Inside the white envelope was a quarter and a piece of candy, and she presented it to everyone, saying, "I wish you good luck and good fortune."

The red envelope contained money. Mine had a five-dollar bill. I tried to refuse it but Lyn told us this was not a tip or payment but simply another wish for good luck and good health and we could not refuse. She then gathered white ribbons from each of an abundant display of flowers. The ribbons identified the sender so Lyn could thank them.

It was then time to go to the burial dinner, where I hoped I would get a chance to talk to her.

The dinner took place in a meeting hall in Chinatown with huge tables and plates of noodles, alongside what I was told was bean curd, a host of Chinese vegetables, and various kinds of fish.

Crystal and I were seated at the table with Lyn, and while we ate, an array of speakers got up and told stories about Sandra.

One of them was familiar to me. He was the old man with whom I had traded clothes in the park, allowing me to enter the building and get past the Tong.

Like many of the old men, he wore a deep-brimmed black hat which for the occasion he had pushed back from his forehead, as well as khaki pants, a dress shirt, a gray vest, and a long coat. He told a story, which Lyn translated for us, of how he had come to see Sandra at her office and did not have money to pay.

She had said, "Never you mind," and given him a filling for free, which stopped a painful toothache. He said he approved of Sandra being buried in America, though in his generation, where few Chinese, and almost no women, were allowed in the country, the custom was for the bones to be dug up from the graveyard, packed in cans, and sent back to the family homes in China.

He then shared a memory of growing up in Guangdong, a province where many of the Chinese in California came from. He was from a village called Toisan, and he described riding a water buffalo during a kite festival just before he had to leave his village to come to America because he was told, "You can never make a living here."

"*Tow-gee jai mon,*" he said, and everyone laughed. Lyn said this means American-born Chinese have no brains and are often accused of being lazy, petty thieves and constant gamblers. To counter this impression, he launched into a story about a Chinese entrepreneur who started with nothing and opened a small factory delivering ten sacks of roasted peanuts every day to the circus, and built a thriving business from there.

"But you weren't born here," somebody yelled from the tables.

"Me, I'm longtime Californ."

Everybody laughed, and Lyn told me this was a designation that Chinese, many of whom were forced to enter the country illegally because of immigration restrictions which only allowed wealthier Chinese to enter, used to ward off those who asked too many questions about where they came from.

He ended with an ominous note. "Things are changing now in Chinatown. People are going to school and becoming prosperous, and some people are standing in the way of those changes. They will be cursed."

The old man's tale and warning drew a muffled sigh from the crowd.

Crystal had spied Anna May Wong, the actress, at one of the tables, and had gone over to talk to her and probably to see if she could drum up any additional work. The two of them seemed to be getting along famously, and I watched Anna May patting Crystal's palm and Crystal smiling in a way that made me wonder what else was going on. I also thought that, given her flair for the dramatic, Crystal should introduce the Chinese actress to Lyn, who with a similar flair often seemed to be in a film of her own.

With the two of us alone at the table, this seemed as good a time as any to find out what had happened to Lyn.

"It was the Tong," she said. "I spied those two who had come at us the other day. I wondered what they were doing there so I snuck off and started following them. I couldn't find them but suddenly a hand reached out from the crowd and grabbed me.

"They tied me up, threw me in the back of their black coupe and barreled out to the gravesite. On the way I caught snatches of their conversation. It seemed that they and the merchant association behind them are very worried about a mass migration out of Chinatown, the center of their power. One of them said they would do anything to stop this and, apparently, they were ordered to monitor the funeral procession and the burial to take down names of anyone who seemed approving of my mother's moving out.

"They're part of an ancient order and they think that with this move to the suburbs their order will be dissolved."

"So how did you get away?"

At that she smiled and showed me a little knife she kept in the pocket of her robe, the jackknife that she had threatened Barnum with at the signing.

She had sawed through the rope, and after they parked the car at the edge of the cemetery, they locked the doors and left her there.

She had broken the back door window with her elbow. She showed me a trace of blood, barely visible on her garment. And she had crawled out the back.

Unfortunately, they had heard the noise, and when she leaped out of the car, they came back for her. She sprinted into the cemetery and started yelling to get away from them.

That's where we came in.

"Do you think they could have been responsible for your mother's death?" I asked.

"I'm not sure, but I did find this in their car," she replied, pulling a vial from her dress pocket that I had seen on the arson squad.

It was a bottle of acid, which I told her was often used as a trigger device to start a fire.

"Good work," I said. "We have to follow this further."

"You mean I have to," Lyn answered.

That didn't sound good either for her or for me, but it was useless to try and stop a rambunctious teen on a mission, I hoped, of justice rather than of vengeance.

11

There was certainly a lot of pieces in this puzzle, and it seemed like the puzzle, rather than coming into focus, was just getting larger. While I knew I had to take a long look at the Tong as well as at the pock-marked man and the Klan and whatever else was going on in Torrance and with the Torrance police, at the moment, after the funeral, I just needed some sleep. The last time I tried to get my beauty sleep at the hotel it was interrupted by a mini flood. I hoped I would have better luck this time.

I did, or so it seemed. I got up refreshed and early the next day and was eager to get to the restaurant for my free breakfast. I sat down at one of the tables and as I started to put in my order, the lone waiter in the place shook his head.

"I can get you whatever you want, but you gotta pay," he said.

"What's going on?"

"Johnson wants to see you in his office pronto."

I was looking forward to that breakfast and eager to get our deal going again. I knocked loudly on Johnson's door, and from inside I heard a frail, low voice saying, "Go away. I don't want any."

"It's me," I said. "Palmer."

This time the voice got stronger. He was making an effort.

"Then I definitely don't want any."

I had enough, I opened the door, and not sitting behind his desk but rather lying across it was the owner with a bandage on his head. I could practically hear the throbbing from the other side of the room.

"What happened?" I said.

"Where were you last night?" Johnson spit out accusingly, slowly trying to sit up.

I didn't want to tell him I'd gone to bed early.

"Out working on a case," I said.

"Yeah, but not this case."

He began to unfold his tale.

"It was late. The desk clerk had retired for the evening and it was just me alone in the office going over the books, trying to see if I could keep this place open a while longer.

"The door opened and the two men in black entered. They told me my time was up. The shorter one held my arms and the bigger one with the stocky arms began wailing on me, he then walloped me with something right across the head. They told me they would stop if I agreed to vacate the place and let it be levelled.

"What could I do? I agreed. I'm turning the place over to the city. They'll probably bulldoze it like the place next door but I can't put up with these threats and sabotage anymore. I'm getting out."

That wasn't good either for him or me, and especially for me.

"Give me a day. Let me see if I can do anything," I said.

I did a quick search of the room to see if there was any trace of them.

Johnson had already questioned the staff and the neighbors, and nobody had seen them enter.

But I wasn't starting from scratch. I had trailed them to the bar on the strip and also watched them gain easy access to the parking lot of the Torrance police.

What I found, though, was another piece of the puzzle.

On the floor at about the place where the tall man would have stood to assault Johnson, were some wet and fine pieces of what looked like what was once silt but was now dirt.

I asked Johnson for an envelope and scooped the granular pieces into it.

I didn't know what to make of it but I knew someone who would.

On the force we frequently came across traces of mud and dirt which had fallen or been knocked off a shoe in a scuffle.

The LAPD had a geologist on retainer who could look at these particles and possibly identify where they came from. I had met him once. He was an odd duck but good at his job.

When I called, I got his service and they told me "the professor" was in his office on the Occidental College campus in Eagle Rock. It meant a trip to the Valley but it might well be worth it. I drove through the now battlefield sites of Chinatown, Rosa's settlement of Palo Verde, and then north out near Pasadena, known as the center of old L.A. wealth.

The campus was a stately structure, built in the 1920s but already graying though covered with trees and benches in its square. Made me wish I'd gone to college or rather stayed in college. I dropped out of community college after a year. Needed to support myself, so instead I attended the college of hard knocks, kicking about on the street until I joined the force where I found I was an eager learner.

I went into the main hall and asked for the office of Professor MacGregor.

"That one," the pert brunette secretary said. "Good luck with him."

"Why do you say that?" I asked.

"There's eccentric and there's his kind of eccentric, which is way beyond and sometimes bordering on mad."

I thanked her for the warning and she told me where to find him.

I went out the main entrance and over to a side hall. From the first floor I heard a commotion. It sounded like a landslide, falling rocks. I figured this was the right place so I ran down the corridor in the direction of the noise.

I threw open the door, and there sitting in the midst of a pile of brightly colored stones of all shapes and sizes was MacGregor, not in a professor's suit but in khaki short pants and brown short sleeve shirt.

I helped him up while he explained what he was doing.

"Rocks," he said, "stones, pebbles, boulders, that's the way people think of them but to me they're God's creatures, composed of unlimited kinds and varieties.

"I piled them up in my office in a kind of sculpture, but sitting at my desk, one of them just called out to me and I went over to pick it up. When I did, the whole thing collapsed."

He then showed me the rock which he had extracted from the pile. He said it was zoisite, and the sample he held up was purple, green, and pink.

"Used for jewelry," he said, "I decided I wanted it on my desk without realizing the whole thing was like Lincoln Logs and I had pulled out the foundation log."

I helped him tread across the rocks now strewn all over his office and sat him back down in his chair.

"Going on an expedition?" I asked, since his costume suggested he was preparing for a safari.

"It's my day off and I'm going rock climbing," he said.

What else would a geologist do on his day off?

He dusted himself and straightened up in his chair.

"Thanks for your help, young man. What can I do for you?"

He didn't recognize me from the force, and I didn't want this to seem to be police work.

"You're not going to believe this, but I think my wife is cheating on me. I was away for a week. I came home and she was nowhere to be found. What I did find was two empty wine glasses in the sink. I combed the apartment and came up with traces of this dirt on the living room carpet and in the bedroom next to our bed. I live around here, came to the campus, and they told me you might be able to help me track down the philanderer."

"Let me see that," he said.

I poured the particles out on the ink blotter on his desk. He stared at them for a short while and then snapped his fingers.

"That's basalt," he said, "a common stone used for gravel. What's uncommon is that most pits also use limestone and sandstone but there are no traces of those two elements here. There is a pit out here in the Valley, maybe not so far from your home, a little further north at Porter Ranch. That's likely where this stone comes from. I don't think there's another pit in the county that uses pure basalt. It's possible your man works there."

"Thanks very much, professor," I said.

As I left, he was rising from his seat and starting to reassemble his sculpture.

I turned back and I heard him say, in a soft voice, amid the rocks, "Give the guy a break, son, we're all God's creatures."

Maybe the old coot wasn't looney. Maybe he was wise even beyond his years.

I found the quarry just outside Porter Ranch, a short drive from the college.

I parked on a road above the quarry and looked down on it. I saw two trucks rumbling out of the place filled with gravel, made, as I now knew, from basalt.

I then watched a group of men on the far side of the pit approaching a mountain of rock and planting something at the base of the rock.

They retreated, and a few seconds later there was a boom, an explosion, and a whole side of the rock tore off and collapsed. The men ran to the site of the explosion, shaking hands and slapping each other on the back.

I decided I had to go down there.

I followed a narrow winding road down to the pit and parked a short distance from it.

There was a guard at the entrance.

"Can I help you?" he said, in—what else?—a gravelly voice that made him an appropriate guardian for a rock quarry.

"Here looking for work," I said. "Who do I see?"

"Alright," he barked, "I guess you can talk to the foreman. He's in that trailer over there."

I ambled in the direction he pointed and knocked on the trailer door. There was no answer so I let myself in.

The trailer was deserted, giving me a chance to prowl around. A folder open on the desk told me this was the Phillips Gravel Yard, but didn't say much more.

At that point, the door swung open and a huge man with a raging red beard entered, saw me just closing the folder, and grabbed me from behind.

"What are you doing here?" he said.

"Sorry, just looking for work. Wanted to know who I might be working for."

"You won't be working here at all. You're too curious. Get out, and if I see you around here again there will be hell to pay."

With that he pushed me out of the trailer, pointed toward the entrance, and went back inside.

As I was leaving, one of the men I had seen setting the dynamite approached me.

"Sorry, buddy, I assume you're just here for work and that you're not getting any. Noggins is a tough customer to deal with."

He seemed to have a minute so I asked him if he wanted a cigarette. I didn't smoke but I kept a pack for occasions like this.

He agreed, and I backed him out of sight of the trailer so we could talk.

"He's certainly got a rod up his ass," I said. "What's driving him? Who's his boss?"

"Oh, you don't know? This pit has its own name but it's rumored to be owned by the Chandlers. They're big promoters of automobiles and highways and this gravel is being used to build a new highway system that's supposedly going to allow more people to live outside the city and still get to work inside."

He seemed to really want to talk, but I only had him for as long as our cigarette break lasted so I had to get to the point.

"Is there any kind of security work here? Any need for any tough guys or do you ever see any mugs around?"

"There were two guys out here the other day. Had a big bulge in their dark suits. Might have been packing. I don't know what they were doing but they went into Noggins' trailer and were in there for a while."

At that point, the trailer opened and Noggins burst through the door. I put out my cigarette, thanked my friend and scurried through the gate, not wanting to get him in trouble.

I got back in my car and lit out for home, wanting to tell Johnson I was making progress with the case, that I was beginning to locate the source of his troubles, and that source was pretty far up the food chain. If he would just give me some time, I might have some leverage for him to use to keep his place.

He wasn't having any of it. I found him still crumpled behind his desk, only this time there was someone in the office with him, whom he introduced as his lawyer.

"You're too late, Palmer," he said. "I'm giving the place up. Let the city demolish it. I don't care. It's not worth getting beat up over."

Ouch, that was no good. I was losing my place to live, and, just as important, I was losing those free, any time of the day, breakfasts.

I went to my room and took a nap. It seemed the only way to deal with this.

When I got up, I started looking for places. I decided to start a little way west of downtown around Sunset. I found two places, a house for rent and a hotel that was a mirror image of mine. On east Sunset were Hollywood hangers-on, day workers who got piecemeal labor, and the unemployed who haunted the streets, sometimes selling themselves at night.

I told Esperanza what had happened and she wanted to come with me to look at the two places. She liked the house, located between Sunset and Western at the base of the Hollywood Hills where the streets were just starting to slope upward.

The hotel meanwhile was right off Sunset and near all the woebegone street traffic that shadowed the area. She didn't much like the hotel and at one point she even offered or asked if I wanted to stay with her.

I thanked her for her offer, though I thought it was a little scary and saw the look of disappointment on her face as I politely brushed aside the agent showing the house and then accepted a month's stay at my new digs at the hotel. It wasn't a four-star place, that's for sure. If I had to rate it, I'd say "Just Above Fleabag," but that was okay by me and where I was at the moment. It afforded me minimal upkeep and maximum concentration on a case that was becoming more dangerous by the minute.

I had never done much with the old room anyway. There was a design style, which still enjoyed some success, called "early modern." My style, with few wall hangings and even sparser furniture, might be called "late ancient."

That I chose the hotel didn't bode well for our relationship, but we had weathered a bigger storm when last year she caught me cheating and I was hoping we could get through this mild downpour.

12

I spent a day packing and moving my stuff to the new hotel. I said goodbye to Bunker Hill even as I watched the bulldozer next door go about its work. I could easily imagine that was my residence being demolished and there was little I could do about it. Johnson was not going to fight back, so my hard work had gone for naught.

But I was still on retainer now to find out what really happened at the Chungs.

I had to start by verifying the police report. They told me an electrician had found faulty wiring and blamed the fire on the Chungs' lack of diligence when they moved in. There couldn't have been that many electricians in the town, so I looked in the yellow pages, and what they said was the oldest and apparently most reputable firm was Stevens' Wiring and Home Fixtures.

When I walked in the office, there behind the desk in blue coveralls with a cigarette dangling from his lips behind a desk strewn with bills and open manuals was, I presumed, Stevens.

He was about 35 with some sandy locks in his hair, just short of handsome, the "just short," I figured, being the pressures of running his business.

I don't know why, but he looked as honest as they come, and I decided to level with him.

I told him I was a PI investigating the Chung fire and I showed him my license. It seemed strange to actually be telling someone who I was instead of making up some cock and bull story. I was so used to the other thing that the truth almost felt like lying.

He didn't much care. He had handled the report but he was very busy and said his two helpers were out that day.

"There's just so much work to be done here," he said. "Dan Williams has us all running around like madmen wiring up his new homes."

I had heard that name from Crystal, who told me Diane worked for him.

"And can anyone move into these homes?" I asked.

"You mean, is he trying to keep anyone out? Not that I know of, but you'd have to ask him," Stevens said with the cigarette burning down to the filter but still dangling from his mouth. He had apparently managed the difficult trick of never having to take it out of his mouth, so he could keep working and smoking at the same time, a sure sign of how pressured he was.

Now for the $100,000 question.

"So, what did you tell the police and are you convinced the fire was the result of faulty wiring?"

"Is that what they told you? That's not a really good assessment of what I said."

Now I was all ears.

"I looked over what I could make out of the electrical lines the day after the fire but the place had been burned badly. I told them the source of the fire could be faulty wiring or someone could have started the fire. The basement was smoldering and could have been where the fire started by someone crawling inside. I said either was likely and I couldn't say for sure which."

"Wow that's very different from what the police said."

"I'll tell you something else which they also didn't pay much mind to. When I went down into the basement, there was a wooden stairway leading up to the main floor which opened up just outside the two bedrooms. There were bits of the stairway on the basement floor and I found traces of kerosene on one of the bits."

"So, if someone started a fire in the basement it might have gone up those stairs very fast?"

"I thought it was a possibility, but the police didn't think so."

"Thanks, you've been a big help."

The cigarette had now burned down to the filter, but he hadn't noticed and still kept the damn thing in his mouth. As I was leaving, he said, "I think you're on the right trail, Palmer. I want you to know that not everyone in this town is as close-minded about who lives here as some."

I took that as real encouragement. Now I was getting somewhere and, at that moment, all roads were leading to Dan Williams, who had the lay of the land and might be able to tell me who would and who wouldn't want people to move into the town he was building.

Williams's office was on Arlington Street in the town center. There were cars everywhere on the streets surrounding his office, and Torrance by day was different from what I'd seen at night. The streets were bright, and it was the very image of what in the Old West they used to call a boom town.

Williams was certainly at the center of it. The office was not huge but busy, with people going in and out and a very cute secretary, a redhead, juggling the phones and directing traffic.

She looked to be in her early 20s and was the very image of efficiency. I wasn't sure I could get past her to see the great man.

"Have you an appointment?" she said briskly, ready to usher me out if the answer was no.

"Dan will see me," I said. "There's a pyromaniac in this town burning down houses and I'm on his trail. I'm sure he wouldn't want any of his new places to go up in flames."

It worked. She got on the horn, or rather the intercom, and a few minutes later she ushered me back to his office. She waved me in, turned briskly and went back to her station.

The man who greeted me was tall and gangly with a slightly chiseled face and brown, loosely tousled hair. There was a charm in his lanky good looks. Like his secretary, though, his desk was the model of efficiency, an array of neatly arranged manila folders in a tall bin.

I gave him my card. He looked at it and directed me to a chair across from his desk.

It was only when he was seated that I noticed a slight paunch starting to extend out from his belly, a sign that in Dan Williams land things were prospering.

He knew about the Chungs' house burning down but was surprised to find out what the electrician had told me about the possible origins of the fire.

"What happened to that woman was a tragedy. We've got to get to the bottom of this," he said.

He got up from his desk and began pacing. He was a can-do guy, and I could see he attacked every problem with a resolute sense that it could be solved. My old pappy—or rather one of the men my mother brought home who probably wasn't my pappy—used to say that a man like that had "gumption." I could never figure out what gumption was but whatever it was, it was sitting across from me.

"The town seems awfully white and unwelcoming," I said. I told him about the pock-marked man and the Klan's burning cross on the night of the fire, no trace of which had made the local newspaper.

"I'm trying to change that. I'm not only building in Torrance but also in Compton, where I'm trying to provide affordable housing for Negroes wanting to move south out of their crowded quarters. I believe in giving everyone a chance to own the home of their dreams."

He then showed me an article in the *Los Angeles Times* where he described his "experimental interracial tract," where all races lived in harmony.

"You see," he said, "I'm building the city of the future and it's a city where everyone has space to grow." With that he sat back down and "leveled" with me, man to man, I'm sure he would say, though I felt it was more like salesman to client or conman to mark.

"We get a bad name out here. Some people say that what we're doing is raising the drawbridge and keeping the medieval peasants in the city, but that's neither true nor legal. With the Supreme Court decision two years ago, restrictive covenants, used to enforce conformity, were outlawed so it would be foolish to try to go against that. The Chinese, many of whom served in the war, can now use the GI Bill to go to school. They will become middle class workers, civil servants, accountants, engineers, even doctors and, of course, businessmen. They will be good working members of this community and we want them."

And, of course, I thought, good purchasers of Williams homes.

"I support you, Mr. Palmer, in finding out who did this to the Chungs. This kind of violence threatens our whole plan for remaking Torrance as a model American city of the future."

He then launched into his "vision." I didn't know the guy from Adam, but he seemed to delight in presenting his master plan, and judging from the *Times* article, he shouted it from the rooftops to whoever would listen to him.

I wasn't pressed so I let him go ahead.

"Torrance," he said, "was once a wild and woolly town, but I'm helping to turn it into a model bedroom community. With the new highways, people who settle here, away from the noise and bustle, will have easy access to the city without having to live there."

I liked the noise and bustle but I didn't want to interrupt him.

"Torrance is the perfect American town. It's known as the city of churches with over 28 denominations. If you choose to live here you have clean access to the beaches and none of the smog of L.A. because the air is clear due to the cool sea breezes."

That wasn't the Torrance I saw and that Crystal described with its oil derricks and chemical plants, and 28 denominations means they're all Christian, so there was variety but in the same product line. He was on a tear, though, and I was hardly about to interrupt his reverie.

He was so excited he got out of his chair again and paced around the room with his hands waving back and forth. I thought maybe he was going to build a house in front of me.

"We're erecting better quality homes more efficiently and we're a one-stop shop for the new homeowner. We handle accounting, keeping deposit and tax payments in escrow, taking the property from vacant lot to furnished home. We're also planting thousands of trees on these new lawns. We plan to build 5000 homes in the next five years. This is enough lumber to string a fence around the state of Texas. Now that's really something to be proud of."

So, he was going to cut down trees from one population and plant them for another. I wasn't buying the spiel but I never liked Texas much and wouldn't have minded seeing a fence built around it.

He then pulled out a full-color brochure and showed it to me as he described the homes with their variety of five fireplaces to choose from, made from what he called "Palos Verdes stone," as well as brick, hardwood floors, decorated shower doors, "cedar shake roofs," and oversize double garage for the homeowners' two cars.

I never realized how real estate was so linked to Madison Avenue advertising. I had no idea what "cedar shake roofs" were but suddenly I wanted one.

As he talked, he pointed to the photo emphasizing each of these in the brochure, and I realized where Diane had gotten her presentation, though the hard sell was different. She used sex and he used his enthusiasm and dynamism.

And then he came in for the kill.

"Williams homes," he said, "handles everything under one roof, assuring buyers a high-quality home, with excellent construction, a land value that will increase their investment, and all at the lowest possible cost, $1600 down and $25,000 for the whole deal. It's your best home buy by far, a bold new concept in living that is secluded, private and desirable."

He was exhausted and nearly collapsed in his chair. I got tired just listening to him, and I figured it was now time to talk turkey.

"You don't have to convince me any further, Mr. Williams, the whole thing sounds great. I just moved into a new place but I'll certainly keep Torrance in mind."

"Not Mr. Williams, Dan," he said. I guess anyone who listened to his talk got to call him by his first name.

I decided to be blunt.

"So, Dan, who's financing all this building?"

"I've been in this business for years and have saved some capital but there's an investor or two behind this concept and why not, the idea is affordable housing for middle- and working-class owners. Who wouldn't want to be in that business?"

"Sandra Chung's daughter claimed to have seen two men in dark suits loitering around their house after the signing, and I tracked two characters matching that description who had threatened a hotel owner in L.A. They stopped in a run-down area just north of town which is nothing but bars and then disappeared into the Torrance police lot. Know anything about them?"

"Nothing at all, but one thing I can tell you is that the place they stopped, The Strip, is a blight on this town, and one day we're hoping to remove it. If those characters are hanging out there, they may be dangerous and you'd best stay clear of them."

I thanked him for the warning and was getting up to leave when his office door burst open and a young man in his early 20's ran in. In appearance he was a match for his father, gangly with loosely combed hair and a handsome face, untouched by the realities of life. But his manner was completely different. He was waving his hands wildly and his whole body was jittery. In some ways the apple didn't fall far from the tree. But in others there were whole orchards between them.

"Father, I've got the construction company ready to sign on the dotted line, but suddenly they're hesitating. I don't know what to do."

"This is my son Dean. He's new to the business but very bright, a real go-getter."

Then he turned to his fidgeting offspring.

"I'll be with you in a minute. Just let me finish up here."

"Fine," he said, suddenly angry at being turned away. "I'll see you later. I need a drink."

Then he stormed out of the office.

"He'll learn, but he'll do anything to establish himself in the business, and right now he's a little reckless."

I was on my way out when Williams stopped me with a wave of his hand.

"While you're here, Mr. Palmer, you could do me a favor."

"Are you hiring me?"

"Yes, let's call it that. My protégée Diane, my best saleswoman; I'd like you to keep an eye on her and report back to me on what she's up to. She's still young and a bit sex-crazed and too devil may care. I wouldn't want to see her, or for that matter any of my employees, get hurt."

"I can do that," I said, and as I waited in the outer office for the redhead to draw up the contract I had almost the same feeling listening to him as I did to Diane. Both in their own way were seductive, but it remained to be seen what else they were selling and how far they would go to sell it.

13

I was prowling around a town I knew almost nothing about. These small but growing towns usually had someone who kept track of them, not funded, but someone who took an interest in the town's history.

I figured the best way to find that someone was to go to the town square and see who was hanging about. It was late morning and I assumed the old men would be meeting, having coffee, and amusing themselves before going home in the afternoon to watch television, eat an early dinner, and get ready for bed.

I figured right. There were a couple of old coots in the square. One had a cane, another supported himself on what he called "a newfangled invention," a walker. They were having a heated argument as I approached.

"It was 1912, I tell you," the one with a long beard said, pointing to make his point or perhaps threatening the other with his cane.

"11, it was 11," the other shot back, warding off the cane with his walker.

"Who will you get to solve this argument?" I said, stepping between them.

"Gerald Macready," they both said at once. "That's his hobby, he's the local historian," the one with the cane said, rising and pointing his weapon north of the square.

They told me he lived on Maricopa Street. I went back to Arlington, picked up my car and drove to Maricopa, which was on the edge of the city but close to the police department and bounded by a couple of the "denominational" churches Williams had mentioned.

Number 850 was a comfortable one-level house painted white with a white picket fence. Nothing out of place, I thought, but when I rang the bell the fellow who answered was anything but bland.

Macready was wearing a Hawaiian shirt with a multicolored print pattern, and that wasn't the half of it. Emblazoned on the shirt were different images of what I assumed were different eras of the town's history. That wasn't even his most distinguishing feature. He sported—with these kinds of characters you always say "sported"—the biggest, bushiest handlebar mustache with both ends roped around in what looked like long cords. A former girlfriend had shown me a photo of an eccentric artist named Salvador Dalí who had the same look. Macready's "handles," though, were more flamboyant and made Dalí's look more like the tame, trim mustache of a William Powell.

He had music going in the living room, sounded like Artie Shaw's "Begin the Beguine," with horns blaring. He had a drink in his hands and yelled over the noise.

"Can I help you?" he said, eyeing me suspiciously.

"I think so. I understand you're the local historian. I'm from *The Daily News* and we're doing a feature on 'Boom Town Torrance and How It Grew.' I wonder if you had a few minutes."

I brandished my card but didn't need to. I had him at "local historian," and he immediately invited me in.

His living room was cluttered with old newspapers, a few books, and all kinds of what I guess he would call memorabilia: buttons, pins, brooches, and artifacts from what looked like a factory floor.

He cleared a pile of papers from a chair, that also had a silk bathrobe draped over it and that looked like a relic itself, and motioned for me to sit.

"Just have to clean up in here, things just get out of hand," he said, smiling and offering me a drink which turned out to be vermouth and water. It was too early for me and I was still, on past advice, trying to lay off.

"What can you tell me about the town, how it grew and how it got to be what it is today?" I said.

"Big question," he said. "But you're a big boy."

I didn't like where that was going, so I set him right. "Just here for the story, Mr. Macready," I said.

That was fine with him, he really just wanted an audience. He relaxed into his tale.

"The city," he said, "was founded in 1912."

Score one for the crotchety old man with the cane.

The land, he recounted, was originally inhabited by the Chumash Indian tribe before the white man arrived. In that year, one Jared Sidney Torrance decided he wanted to build what Macready called "a workingman's paradise," an industrial city with all the comforts of modern living between the city of Los Angeles and the San Pedro Harbor, which was becoming the main seaport of the city.

Torrance spent $1 million and bought 3,533 acres from the Dominguez family, whose ranch took up a huge portion of the South Bay, stretching from San Pedro to Redondo Beach.

I was beginning to think maybe I was wasting my time, but after that his tale started to get interesting.

Nine years later the town was incorporated, because its residents feared that it would be swallowed up by Los Angeles.

This was about the time that the county became flooded with white Midwesterners who had read, mainly in the *L.A. Times*, about the abundant opportunities California could offer. The town saw itself, he said, as a place that could produce maximum efficiency in both its factories and its workers, who would be happy to live in a place free of the "troubles" of Los Angeles.

"They didn't want all that dirt and filth out here," Macready said, and by that it was getting clearer what he meant was the mingling of the races that in some parts of the city was common.

Once the town became its own entity it gradually began absorbing land around it.

He told me a main goal of the town, if it was to grow, was to secure access to the beach, which it did not have. It gradually annexed or, from the way he described it, "stole" a mile and a half of beachfront that now, with Torrance expanding, the town was hoping to develop. I remembered that Williams had mentioned closeness to the beach as an asset in the Torrance he was building.

The earlier fortunes of the town, besides manufacturing and chemical plants, were tied up with oil. Macready, who had read widely about Los Angeles County, told me that in 1922 one L.A. suburb was called the "Gusher

Field of America." That promo, which I dimly recalled, was part of a huge swindle, but Torrance did have abundant oil and hence the very prominent derricks at the edge of town.

"But I heard the town advertises its clean air coming from cool sea breezes," I said, quoting from Williams's brochure.

"Yes," Macready countered, reaching over to pour himself another vermouth, "the two don't fit together and one of them will probably have to go. But there is oil everywhere here, even under the houses."

He then went back to talking about the making of modern Torrance.

"We did our part in the war," he said, showing me a headline from a local paper pasted into one of a series of scrapbooks scattered around the room.

"JAPS LICKED IN TORRANCE," the headline read, and the article, which he let me see, went on to support something called the Alien Land Law which was, it said, "the most complete repudiation of the Japanese invasion of California, even to renting them land."

Another article in the same part of the scrapbook, which Macready let me leaf through, was especially interesting. It said that in 1942 there were 42,000 Japanese living in Torrance, and in response a petition circulated promoting "burning them out."

He was also extremely proud that an oil tanker used in the war was named the *USS Torrance.*

But I wanted to return to the petition, since it was likely my Asian clients, the Chungs, had been burned out.

Macready pooh-poohed the idea of actual violence but he did say that during the 1920s Torrance was a center of Klan activity, and from what I had seen was still a center today.

"We're very tolerant here," he said, explaining that the petition to burn down Japanese homes was defeated by the City Council.

"Yeah, that's very tolerant," I said, not bothering to conceal the sarcasm in my voice.

That made him nervous, and when he got nervous, he took to twirling the handlebars on his mustache.

Now he wanted to convince me of the town's good intentions.

"This is a perfect middle-class city, utterly free of the sins of Los Angeles," he said, though from his earlier come-on it seemed likely he might have indulged in some of those "sins" himself.

"After the war, Torrance became a chartered city. Do you know what that is, Mr. Palmer?"

At this he leaned forward and patted me on the knee.

"I don't," I said, attentively, as I straightened up in my chair. I had to tread a line between wanting to hear more and not wanting to get involved in whatever he might envision for the two of us.

"It means that the town, already free of the city of Los Angeles, follows its own city charter rather than California general law. In that way we can go our own way. It's been very helpful. We've built up, for example, an excellent school system, in which we now have 20,000 pupils.

"And because we're independent, the population is booming and will continue to grow. In the last ten years it's more than doubled, and we're expecting it may triple over the next six years."

He went to another of his scrapbooks, and this one held letters from the kids in the "excellent" school system. For him, the letters were part of what made Torrance an "All-American" city. I had a different interpretation. To me All-American was just code for "white."

One kid loved the city, he wrote because it was "clean, nice, healthy" and because "people are polite." Tell that to the crowd outside the Chungs' house, I thought to myself. Another liked the city because "there are no Indians that climb over your fence and steal things" and because Torrance "has a good police force." Good, I thought, at making sure there are no Indians. Finally, another wrote that "the oil wells in Torrance are the best wells in America." And how does that help to keep the city, as Willliams's brochure described, smog free?

Macready closed the book, literally, on the kids with an admiring, "These youngsters are vaccinated with good books and immune to horror comics and lurid television programs."

That was the latest scare, that somehow comic books were corrupting the youth who, by what the Torrance kids were writing, were already, it seemed to me, pretty corrupted, or at least narrow-minded.

I needed to be a bit more confrontational with the town's historian.

"Does the town have a history of racism?" I asked, point blank.

He was a taken aback that I would even ask but he recovered quickly.

"We've never had a problem with other races," he said. "In the 1920s the town had a foreign quarter outside the city, and that worked well. A former mayor once said, 'Torrance has no Negro problem. We only have three Negroes in the city.'"

Finally, he covered this all up with language that concealed this exclusion. "To be successful, as we are becoming, you have to have the 'right kind' of people. Some classes of workers have better character than others. Therefore, it is desirable to attract the one and discourage the other."

I could tell he was getting restless. He had given me what I needed to know and I wasn't going to play along with anything else he might want.

But I wasn't finished.

"What about the strip?" I said. "Just outside this paradise there's Sin City."

That was an area, as he described, that big bad Los Angeles created and then left to rot.

"The city needed a piece of land to be contiguous to the San Pedro Harbor so they could incorporate it, or rather, swallow it up. Once they got the harbor, they didn't care what happened to the land connecting it with the city, and it has developed as a den of iniquity."

He shivered as he said those words.

"There's a petition now to turn that foul piece of land into the 'Harbor Highway.' Good riddance to bad rubbish, I say. We don't want people with those proclivities in this town."

Macready was a strange character, invested in chronicling the history of a town which, if it knew fully who he was, might have exiled him to The Strip.

I had to ask.

"How is it the town accepts you with your 'proclivities?'"

At this he blanched, at first caught off-guard, but then he accepted the challenge and sat straight up in his chair.

"Dan Williams knows there is a need for someone like me in this town. I do good work as a private town historian, and he's told me that someday there may even be funding for a historical society which I might run. He's very open-minded and doesn't care to know anything else about me."

I thanked him for his time. He walked me to the door and hugged me as I was leaving. I didn't pull away. I just figured everyone deserved their own happiness wherever they could find it.

On the drive back, once again I had the radio on just in time for the blasted news.

The story was all about Nixon, who was on the attack again. His Democratic opponent. the New Dealer Helen Gahagan Douglas, was advocating for peace with the Soviet Union instead of ramping up the Cold War. She also wanted to regulate offshore oil drilling. She had called him "Tricky Dick" and described him as a tool of the oil industry. In return Nixon was running a complete smear campaign, based on one principle. He persistently called her a "Pink Lady," and passed out a "Pink Sheet" naming those who supported her.

Nixon kept explaining how he came from the small, clean town of Whittier, with good ordinary folk, while Douglas was "the darling of the Hollywood Pinks and Reds."

Having listened to Williams, Macready, and Nixon, I had had it with "clean" towns and what that messaging really meant. I started to wonder if what lurked underneath the "clean" towns was not the opposite but maybe an even more violent version of dirty towns like The Strip.

14

I thought I was finished with this kind of work but no such luck. Harry had assigned Crystal once again to tailing duty, which he dressed up by calling it "surveillance." On the last case that was about all she did. She was sick of it and much preferred the undercover work she was doing with Diane. He told her that since he was known to this "pock-marked man" he couldn't follow him, but that it was likely he had something to do with Sandra's death. So, it was up to her to keep tabs on this suspect. She much preferred keeping tabs on Diane, or maybe it was that she just preferred Diane.

Harry guessed that he worked at the Dow Chemical Plant at a site called Del Amo because he and his Klan cronies had parked in the plant lot.

If that's true, he's certainly not the brightest bulb in the lamp, she thought, sitting in the company parking lot near 5 o'clock, quitting time. They had let her onto the lot where, with what looked like a host of wives, she was waiting for the men exiting the factory.

They were friendly with each other and seemed to be having their own tailgate party, though with no football team in sight. Crystal went up to a smaller gathering of three of them who were having a laugh between them.

"What's going on, girls?" she said.

They eyed her suspiciously. Everybody in this town seemed to know everybody else, and nobody recognized her.

"And who might you be?" asked the most talkative one, wearing tight yellow pants, a red shirt tied at her waist, sneakers and a kerchief binding her short brown hair.

"I'll show you a picture of my honey," she said, pulling out the photo Harry had snapped.

"Him? Oh, my God, we were just going on about him," the talkative one said, and the other two laughed.

"I'm surprised he's got a honey because we've never seen him with anyone," said the leader, who this time held out her hand.

"I'm Dolores, and sweetheart, if that's your man you must be able to put up with a lot."

Crystal was not dressed like a housewife. Her pants were if anything tighter than Dolores's and the pink pullover she selected gave anyone who wanted it a look at her bounteous cleavage. The whole package was topped off with not fancy but plastic orange high heels.

"He's worth it for what I'm getting from him," she shot back, sticking her chest out.

"But why do you say that? I really don't know him that well."

Now they were more sympathetic.

A second one spoke up. She was dressed similarly but had a spatula and a pot in her hand. She said she was making cookies and had to stop to pick up her husband, so she brought the batter with her.

"Frank Chase is always stirring everyone up, getting them to go out on 'mysterious missions' at night. He's a pain."

"Have any idea how he got those lumps on his face?" Crystal asked. "He won't tell me."

Dolores again: "One of his 'missions' went wrong, my husband told me."

Alright, this was going somewhere.

"And what are these mysterious missions?"

"They're a complete waste of time," said the third. "We've got a lot to worry about out here. Don't know if you can tell, but there's three plants all right next to each other, and we live near all of them. What they manufacture here is used to make synthetic rubber for plastic packages, cups, and containers. My husband Fred says they're building the new America and helping change the world.

"But if you look over there," at this point she gestured to what looked like a soggy marshland, which Harry had described to her, and which was located behind the three plants, "they call that the waste-pit. It's where they dump the run-off from the plant and we're not at all sure it's safe for our kids."

Crystal needed to bring the conversation back to Frank.

"So, what do the men do when they're out at night?"

"They're up to no good," the third one started to answer. "The other night—"

Suddenly the factory whistle blew.

Dolores gathered the other three around.

"To our post, girls," she said, as the three of them started waving as the men poured out of the factory.

Their three husbands approached first. They waved goodbye to Crystal, got in their cars, all three driving the men home.

Frank then came out of the factory almost dead last, with the rest of the parking lot practically empty. He looked at her suspiciously and was about to question her.

Desperate, Crystal shot her hand up, puffed out her chest, smiled, paraded around in her heels, waving frantically to a lone straggler behind Frank.

He smiled and walked past her.

The man she was waving at approached.

"Hello, sweetheart," he said. "What to go for a ride?"

"Not in a million years," she said. "Beat it."

He frowned, walked to his car, and drove away.

A man dressed more formally than the rest—instead of blue coveralls, he wore black slacks, a white shirt and tie—ran past her and up to Frank, trying to get his attention.

I'd like to be a fly on the wall listening to that conversation, Crystal thought and then decided she would be.

They were having a heated discussion, both yelling and waving at each other.

Crystal crept up to the side of the car and stationed herself behind it, amazed at how daring she could be.

"Listen," the man in the white shirt was saying, or rather screaming, "I don't know what you think you're doing here, lurking around the parking lot, but the factory guard saw you the other night with some of your buddies. We don't want any of your Klan nonsense here. It could damage our reputation and the plant. Watch it, Chase."

Frank was nonplussed, Crystal thought. *Where the hell did that word come from?* Probably from those damn novels she and Harry had been reading and exchanging in their down time. *We've just got to get busier.*

Frank was a lot more than nonplussed. He made two fists and threatened the other man.

"Oh, yeah," he said. "You want to talk about my activities after the job, what about yours? I saw you the other night out taking samples in the waste-pit, and I'll bet what you came up with was something you don't want anybody to know."

"Those samples don't mean anything," the plant official said.

"So, you don't deny it?" Frank shot back.

"I think we both better keep our mouths shut."

The man in the white shirt threw up his arms and marched back into the plant, not forgetting to add, "Don't let me hear about this again," as he walked away.

Frank just shook his head, but he did look around and for a moment focused on one of the few cars in the lot, Crystal's.

Crystal had anticipated this, and as the foreman walked away, snuck back into her car.

She got in the back and climbed over the seat into the front as Frank eyed her.

She tore off her panties, waved them to him as she drove away, nodding toward the back of the car and saying loudly, "Behave yourself back there, and put your pants back on." She drove past him fast enough to be sure he didn't get a look in the back seat.

Please, please, Harry, get me back on Diane duty, Crystal thought as she drove out of the lot and back to her more sheltered home in North Hollywood.

While Crystal was investigating the pock-marked man, I thought I would do something the cops probably hadn't bothered to do, and that was to canvass the area around the Chungs' house and find out if the neighbors had seen anything.

The first five places I went to on the block had only seen the fire burning and hadn't come to the aid of the Chungs but rather stayed inside their homes and just watched the place smolder. A couple of them I recognized from the group on the lawn when the Chungs did the signing.

On the sixth I hit pay dirt, but not the kind I was expecting.

A woman came to the door, a not unattractive brunette, holding a boy in her arms, who was probably about four and looked a little old and heavy to be held. She threw open the door and invited me inside. The outside of the house was a bit shabbier and run-down than those surrounding it, and the inside was smaller, clean but with none of the custom features of a Williams abode.

She got me coffee and we sat in the kitchen as a girl, probably about six, came timidly into the room and positioned herself behind her mother, peeking out to look at me. I told her mother the truth, that I was a private investigator trying to find out what had happened in the fire.

She said that was a tragedy and was sorry for the family and for the daughter losing her mother.

"Yes," I said, "well, at least she'll get the insurance money and she wants to rebuild the house and move in again. She's a brave girl."

"And lucky." The woman, who said her name was Mrs. Fran McCordle, sighed and allowed as how "some people are just born lucky."

"She's not that lucky. She lost her mother," I said.

"Yes, but she's got a good start in life with the kind of money I'll probably never have, not given my situation."

"And what is that, ma'am?"

She then let loose with an incredible tale of woe which I began to suspect was for the purpose of enlisting my services.

It turns out that "Mr. Fran McCordle," her husband, was in polite language a bigamist, a two-timer who had fooled both families with whom he claimed to have set up a home.

Her family, family number two, was in central Torrance, while family number one was on the eastern edge of Torrance near Carson.

She found out his real name was Stan Cardiff and that he had been using a phony name and identification with her. He was an engineer at Dow, near the oil derricks, where Harry had sent Crystal to research the pock-marked man.

Family number one lived out near the plant. Fran told me they were a matching two-kid family, but that on his salary both families did not have what their neighbors had.

She had only recently discovered his second life and wife, though from her story it was amazing that he'd carried on the deception for so long.

The kids went to different schools, but one day, when Fran was scoping out schools in the area which her kids might attend, she saw Stan coming out of one of them with a woman on his arms.

She followed them, crawled up to the kitchen window of the house they'd entered, looked inside and found him happily at home bouncing two kids on his knees.

"How did he pull it off? He must have been away a lot?"

"Yes, he told me his work for Dow required a great deal of travel and he'd be gone a lot during the week but home on most weekends. He kept to that schedule, and like a ninny I never questioned him about it."

"This is incredible. How did you guys meet? Why did he want two families?"

"We met at the beach one afternoon. I was wanting to start a family and he seemed bright, eager, had a good job, and was more than willing to go along. It happened pretty fast. The only hitch was I had to accept him being away."

She pointed to a bunch of photos on the wall of the happy couple.

"Why he wanted both of us, I don't know. I think it was something about proving what a good provider he was. It wasn't for the sex, I'll tell you that. We indulged, but it was nothing spectacular or adventurous. Mainly it was, well, workmanlike, sort of methodical."

"Well, you did say he was an engineer."

"Exactly. He didn't prove his masculinity in the bedroom but rather in the supermarket checkout line. We always had everything we needed, though as you probably noticed, the house now could use some repair."

"Why are you telling me this?"

She pulled out a cigarette, which she took a drag on while sipping her coffee.

"Because the next part is up your alley," she said, releasing a puff of smoke and suddenly seeming more confident.

"I gave the best years of my life to that man and I want my reward, for me and my kids."

"Doesn't he just go to jail?"

"No, the whole thing's legal. After he met me, he told me, he tricked his wife, unbeknownst to her, into signing divorce papers, which he filed but never told her. The whole time we were together he was legally married to me."

"And where's he now?"

"That's the thing, he's disappeared. When I found out about the other family I had him make out a will saying that I would inherit the house near Carson. But now he's gone. No one's seen him for a few days and the will has disappeared too.

"I went to the other family, told them the story, but they haven't seen him either."

"But I don't understand. What do you care? Is the other house better than this one?"

"That's the thing. He's an engineer and he'd done some tests on the ground underneath. It has a fairly rich oil deposit and will make a great well. He told me it's worth a million.

"He also blabbed it all around his job. He seemed to really have a need to show the world what a winner he is.

"But the other woman has put in a claim on the house as well. She maintains she had never legally granted a divorce and the house should be hers. Without the will, I'll never be able to have my house and collect the money that's owed me."

"You want me to find the husband and the will?"

"To tell you the truth, I'd prefer you just find the will, but do what you have to."

As she said this, she crushed her cigarette in the ashtray, practically stomping it out. She had a lot of anger toward that husband, and I wasn't sure she hadn't done him in herself.

"What do you think happened to him?"

"Who knows, maybe he went to start a third family."

"Do the police know he's missing?"

"Yes, but little good that will do us. They did a preliminary search and found nothing. They're great at harassing people and ticketing but not great at actual police work. So, if you take the job, you're probably on your own.

"I can't pay you up front, but if you find the will, especially if something has happened to him, I'll soon be a rich widow and you'll get paid handsomely."

She was all business, but I guess she had to be. It probably wasn't easy raising two kids alone.

"Alright," I said. "I'll see what I can do."

I didn't like to take assignments on spec, but this one could have a decent payoff, even though that payoff meant another family would be homeless. I'd cross that bridge when I came to it.

After I got paid, maybe I could get her to split the profits.

She gave me the address of the house of family number one and added that they hadn't seen him at the plant either.

The more I prowled around this town, the deeper I got stuck in the mud. Torrance was a many-splendored thing alright, with murder, betrayal and deceit lying just under the surface of the "All-American City."

15

The case on spec could wait. Crystal and I were still being employed by the Chungs, and that was my priority. Crystal had done great work at the plant and we now had a name, Frank Chase, to go with the description of the "pock-marked man." He seemed to be a local Klan leader and likely set the fire, but I still felt I didn't know enough about the activities of the Klan and who might be behind them. There was a strong possibility that Chase, or Chase and his buddies, had not acted alone but rather had the backing of someone higher up.

I called Dinitia. She was busy recording her second album but she did still take my calls. I told her about the Chungs and what I was up to. I could hear her shaking her head across the phone lines.

"Harry Palmer, you always gettin' in a mess o' trouble," she said. "When you gonna live like ordinary folks?"

I took that as a kind of invitation on her part, since her career was taking off, but I couldn't take her up on that offer because there was already Esperanza and because I liked living on the edge of my seat.

"Probably never," I said, and that put an end to that line of conversation.

"What you want?"

I told her I was trying to find out more about the Klan and their relationship with local big wigs. I knew that when she moved north from Central Avenue, she had gotten some aid and support, and she might be able to help me.

Dinitia was always grateful for my getting a payment for the death of her mate Horace that helped her buy the house, and she could be generous when she wanted to.

She told me that the person to go see, known throughout the Central Avenue community, was the editor of *The California Eagle* and the local keeper of the flame about the history and struggles Negroes had trying to better themselves by moving out of the territory where they were confined.

When Dinitia moved, she told me, there were some threatening letters put in her mailbox, and one day, when she returned home from the studio, she found her couch and two chairs spread out on the lawn. She called *The Eagle* editor, Charlotta Bass, and she arrived that afternoon with a small army of Negro women who helped her move the furniture back inside and then stationed themselves on her lawn, until late in the evening the police, whom Dinitia had called that morning, finally arrived.

Once the police had shown up the trouble stopped, but it was mainly the presence of Bass and her little army that turned the tide.

I knew where to reach *The California Eagle* because I had advertised there before, but it was nightfall before I had time to take the drive south from my new digs on Sunset to Central Avenue. The place was just starting to hop. I drove past jazz clubs where the frantic sound of swing and the peals of horns belted from the rafters and, more to my liking, past the new rhythm and blues clubs where guitar, bass and drums were echoing in insistent and catchy beats.

I parked near the newspaper's offices and was on my way there on foot when I saw something that made me realize I had definitely come to the right place.

The light was on in the front office, and a woman I assumed to be Charlotta Bass was sitting at a typewriter. She seemed to be finishing whatever it was she was working on. She removed the paper, laid it on the desk, grabbed a black shawl and was putting it over her brown dress when a commotion occurred outside.

A group of hooded figures, I counted six in all, approached the office, and threw open the front door, which for some reason was unlocked.

I wished I had brought my gun.

None of the figures in the white hoods were tall. They were likely a group of kids. Together they could probably handle me, but I needed to see if I could intimidate them.

I pulled out a fake police badge and was about to confront them when something miraculous happened.

The editor, smaller than even these boys, reached in her desk and pulled out a gun, a .45, which she waved at them. Their courage faded fast. They backed out the door and disappeared into the night, but not before I'd seen the strange symbol of a distorted face on one of their hoods.

She had noticed me about to come to her rescue brandishing my badge. She collapsed in her chair and motioned for me to enter.

"Who would you be," she said, "and what are you doing here?"

"I am just here to ask you some questions about the Klan and, in a way, I guess I came at the right time."

She didn't think that was particularly funny but she did ask me to sit.

"That was very brave," I said.

"You don't know the half of it," she said, exhaling and patting my hand, glad to have me there. "I don't even know how to use this old thing," she said, picking the gun up gingerly and putting it back in the desk drawer.

"Listen, mister," she said, taking long deep breaths and trying to regain her composure, "I don't have much time. I'm late for a woman's social and tonight we're celebrating the second anniversary of Nat King Cole moving to Hancock Park which *The Eagle* publicized."

She pointed to a front-page headline announcing the move that was one of several editions of the paper pinned to the wall behind her desk. She beamed with pride as she said this, and I vaguely remembered the moment when the popular singer was able to purchase a mansion among the other mansions in what was an exclusive part of Wilshire, home to established stars and titans of industry. Also posted on the wall were buttons of an organization called CORE which I guessed was an anti-segregation outfit.

"Can you give me a few minutes?" I asked.

I told her about the case with the Chungs, the burning cross and involvement with the Klan, and the hostile atmosphere in Torrance. She perked up at that and agreed, telling me she had much to say about Klan activities. She pointed again to the clippings on the bulletin board behind her.

"Okay, you're serious. You earned a little bit of my time.

"As you can see, we cover their neighborhood terrorism often in the paper. And while you would think that after the Supreme Court decision forbidding racial covenants, which by the way a former writer for this paper argued, that activity would cease, it hasn't been the case."

She told me the latest battlefront was in the San Fernando Valley and other suburbs where the terrain was much like I was describing in Torrance.

She recounted an incident of a twelve-foot-high burning cross in Eagle Rock, where I had been recently, watched by 75 people. Then she told the story of a Negro family in Glendale threatened by phone calls while Klan members threw milk bottles on the lawn as they sped by in their cars. She finished by describing the case of a mob of 150 people threatening another family and leaving the lawn and driveway strewn with tacks.

"And how do you fight back," I asked, figuring the answer would probably not involve the police.

"We have a network of women's groups who are always ready to help, and we cover their activities in the back of the paper."

I guessed just like the group that showed up at Dinitia's.

I perked up when she told me that in one case there was a hand-painted sign on the lawn of a new Negro homeowner that said, "If you're interested in keeping this town Caucasian and the type of community you can be proud to raise your children in, get on the band wagon." The wording was almost exactly the same as the poster that Lyn had found in Torrance.

It was not so long ago, she pointed out, just six years ago, when there were 18,000 Klan members in L.A. and Long Beach. These included, in the past and probably still today, public officials and police. One of the fiercest battles during the war had been in Culver City, center of both the arms and movie industry, where Klan propaganda warned that, if Negroes moved in, property values would decline by 50 to 75 percent. The Klan marched under the banner "God Bless America with Life, Liberty and Justice For All."

"They want this place to be a super-paradise in the Paradise of the Pacific," she said. "An exclusive home of blond-haired, blue-eyes Aryans, 99.44 percent pure for at least seven generations, for addicts of *Little Orphan Annie* and life-long subscribers to the Klan paper *The Cross and The Flag.*

"The answer," she said, and she was now off and running, and who was I to stop her from waxing eloquent, "to your question 'who is the Klan?' is that a high proportion of them are property owners and have a huge stake in the value of that property. There is also a phobia about Negroes in public spaces 'at all hours of the day and night' that they just can't seem to deal with."

She sat proudly in her chair, this small woman, frail in appearance, who was actually anything but. Before we went on, she wanted to tell me briefly about the difference between *The Eagle*, her modest paper, and the gigantic, but for her monstrous, *L.A. Times*.

"That paper's founder, General Otis, was always in a fight with someone, his own workers, Filipinos, city reformers. He had led the charge," she said, "against the revolt in the Philippines, declaring those who wanted independence from the U.S. to be 'ignorant, misguided, bumptious natives' much better off accepting the government 'we will give them.'"

Otis had led a slaughter of Filipino women and children, then returned home to lead "campaigns" against his own printers, minorities, and reformers. He viewed the world, she said, as being in a constant state of war, naming his L.A. homes The Bivouac and The Outpost, riding around the city with a machine gun mounted on his vehicle, and organizing the *Times* staff into a "phalanx" with rifles and shotguns.

"This is the history of what we are dealing with," she said, slumping a little in her chair.

I had heard enough about the horrible past. I needed to talk to her about the horrible present.

"What do you think is going on in Torrance with my Chinese clients?" I asked.

In answer, she described a larger battle for the soul of the city. Coming out of the war with the defeat of Nazism and its theories of racial superiority, there was, she said, on the one hand a concerted effort not to stem the tide but to take on those values and make 95 percent of Los Angeles "*verboten*" to Negroes and other minorities. She described a city that on one side was made up of the Klan, the National Rifle Association and property restriction organizations, and on the other the labor movement, the Negro, Jewish, Mexican, and Chinese minorities; "those people who do the work in the city and who are fighting against the threat of a new fascism at home."

I wasn't sure how this was relevant but, as she continued, I finally got it.

"In your case," she said, starting to reach for her shawl, indicating she now really had to be going and our interview was coming to an end, "property owners are always talking about 'encroachment' by both the 'Negro' *and* 'Mongolian' races.

"The long-term strategy perhaps for both is to concede land but not wealth, so that rather than achieving integration and equality, the poor conditions that both groups are living under simply spread."

I flashed on something Williams had said about building homes in Compton and wondered about the connection.

"The segregation is not going to go away with the Supreme Court decision," she said. She explained that the California Real Estate Association was claiming that private discrimination was not only lawful but that the board could discipline a member for selling property that violated its racial restrictions.

"The rise of professional real estate agents and associations is not something that lifts all boats but rather one that promotes different size boats in the same unequal water," she said, and now she was exhausted.

But not quite finished.

"In your case, Mr. Palmer, with the onset of the Cold War and now a hot war against the Chinese, there is animus and hatred against all those who want change and who want a peaceful and more collectively organized world. That goes back again to the *Times* and General Otis who called reformers who campaigned against city corruption 'socialist freaks.'

"The new Cold War policy of containment is now being applied in our cities as well, and used by those who want to perpetuate their wealth as an excuse for 'containing' neighborhoods.

"It's why *The Eagle* opposes the Cold War against both Russia and China, instead championing the world living together in mutual respect and cooperation.

"On the other hand, there is a new demagogue on the horizon, Senator Joseph McCarthy, who is looking everywhere for communists and who the *Times* supports saying he 'speaks softly and carries the big stick of logic,' just like General Otis's big stick used to annihilate the Philippine people."

I looked again at the bulletin board behind me and saw a banner for the Progressive Party, which had hired me two years ago to find the leak in the

Henry Wallace campaign and which I remember espoused—the local papers would say "spouted"—the same line.

She saw me looking at the banner.

"You know," she said, "I won't be working here forever, this wave of terror has to be stopped and who knows one day I may run for national office with that party."

I told her I thought it would be a good idea.

She gathered her things and as she was leading me out and locking the door, issued a warning.

"Things are changing," she said, tapping my hand, "but as they do, the violence is increasing. There's white youth gangs all over the area, the most notorious of which is called the Spook Hunters. I believe you saw them in action tonight. They come into our neighborhoods and attack us. Besides the derogatory name, their emblem, which they wear on the belt of their jackets, is a garish black face with its neck in a noose."

That's what I had seen on the hood of one of the fleeing boys.

I thanked her very much for her time, and in return she left me with a final thought.

"They always talk about Negro and Mexican violence, but in reality, and it's true in your case with the Chinese as well, the real fear is white violence."

16

Before I could use what I had learned from Charlotta Bass, I got a call from Esperanza telling me things were heating up in Palo Verde, and she needed me out there.

After what Mrs. Bass had told me about the Klan and the way I had seen them threaten her, I decided I needed to be armed, and that from now on for this case I was going to carry a gun.

I drove up to Rosa's house to find Rosa and Esperanza outside with a few other tenants from the neighborhood. Esperanza was pointing to the house next door to Rosa's.

"They're coming today to take her home away," she said. "Can you do something?"

There was Beame and another man, looked like also from City Hall, another bureaucrat with the same washed-out, neutral look and dress.

The house the residents had surrounded was not a shack but rather a modest, small family home, again with garden and fence to hem in the goats in the front yard.

"What's going on here?" I asked Beame and his partner.

"Unfortunately, we need this place immediately and the city is claiming the right of eminent domain to remove the residents," Beame said.

His companion added, "They're standing in the way of progress."

Directly in front of the house, barring the way to Beame, stood a man, his wife, and their school-age son.

"We don't want to move," the man said. "There's no reason to. We're perfectly happy where we are."

Beame threw up his hands at what he obviously thought was their unfair resistance.

"We've already offered them more than the place is worth," he said.

The man stepped forward and piped up. "That's not true, they offered more money to a couple in La Loma, the next village over, last week for a similar home."

Esperanza stepped forward and backed him up. "It's a tactic to spread fear. They want these owners to panic because they're afraid they will continue to get less if they hold out."

"There's nothing much we can do about it," Beame said.

His partner added, "Yeah, it's the city and the feds that are claiming the land to be used for public housing for all these people."

Esperanza had done her homework and again confronted the men.

"That's a scam also. Edward's office has been looking at a scheme where, in the end, the city buys back the land from the federal government for far less than it's worth. They're just trying to cheat these people in whatever way they can."

Beame had the last word.

"Sorry to have to do this. But this document says we can legally seize the place so, if you won't move, I have no choice but to call in the authorities."

At that point, as if on cue, two sheriff's cars barreled up the hill and into the driveway.

"No, no, please don't do this," the man's wife cried. "Raul, stop them."

But the deputies, four in all, grabbed the man, and when he tried to resist handcuffed him. They pushed his wife aside and went into the house and began removing the furniture and dumping it on the lawn to the cries and protest of a crowd that had gathered around.

There wasn't much I could do except watch this spectacle, but I noticed that stationed on top of a nearby hill were two familiar figures, the two men in black whom I'd last seen disappear from the Torrance police parking lot.

They nodded in approval at the spectacle below. I knew I needed to try to corral them. They appeared too often at the wrong place at the right time. They had already threatened Rosa and her parents, and I figured they would be back to threaten her if the state could not seize her house through eminent domain. As I was trying to catch up to them before they saw me, I saw one of them pointing at Rosa's house, which confirmed my suspicions.

But as I was making my way on a path over to the hill they were occupying, they spied me and immediately disappeared from sight. When I got to the top of the hill, all I could make out was the red Chevy disappearing, vanishing in a cloud of dust off in the distance.

"What now?" I said, as I returned to Rosa, Esperanza, Raul, and his family watching their house being emptied. Up the hill climbed bulldozers. As soon as the sheriff's deputies had cleared the lawn of the family's possessions the machines began to level the house.

"Now we go to City Hall and let them know what we think about this," Esperanza said. She was hopping mad and wanted me to drive her to the City Council meeting currently in session that she said was addressing this issue.

On the way, she described similar events taking place on the East Coast. Puerto Rican residents on New York's West Side, on San Juan Hill, were just starting to be cleared to make way for a cultural complex that would be built on top of their homes.

"What do you think's going to happen to Chavez Ravine?" I asked.

That made her very angry.

"Don't call it that. That name is a real estate gimmick to erase all trace of the real residents in La Loma, Palo Verde and Bishop. What will happen to it finally? Who knows? Anything from a parking lot to a baseball stadium, but I doubt the proposed public housing which they're calling Elysian Heights will ever be built."

I held her hand while I was driving to try to calm her.

The City Council meeting was as raucous a sight as I'd ever beheld at a public gathering. In the crowd was the woman who had been threatened with being thrown out last time I was here, Mariela Hernandez, leading a highly vocal group of tenants, many displaying signs from where they lived, including the three villages we had just left. There was even a much smaller contingent from Bunker Hill, and I was at least glad to see my former neighborhood represented.

The rotund councilman, with balding hair and a gut that had if anything enlarged since I was here a few days ago, was speaking, again cheered on by the *Times* reporter I had seen last time.

"The area these people are defending is blighted. It's an eyesore, a scar on the landscape. They claim it's a country setting but it's really just a slum and blight and needs to be cleared."

Boos went up from the tenants' council. A thumbs up from the *Times* reporter.

The councilman ignored the boos and seemed cheered by the thumbs up.

"The city is proposing public housing be put in its place, but I'm against 'socialist housing,' imposed by a 'Gestapo housing authority.' It's a major step toward Communism which we are at war against abroad."

He then went on to rail against what he called an attack on "the freedom of private ownership," urging the Council to vote against a "socialist public housing measure" and nodding to a small group of supporters on the right side of the aisle, opposite the tenants. This group waved signs reading "Committee Against Socialist Housing."

The hearing then got more raucous as Esperanza's boss Edward Roybal addressed the Council. Mariela stood up and cheered as he began to speak and was warned as before by the Council chairman. Esperanza also waved to Roybal, cheering him on as he began.

Roybal conceded that if the plan went through to build the public housing complex, which he described as two dozen 13-story buildings and 160 two-story townhouses with schools, parks, and playgrounds, it could be a boon for the neighborhood. Then he pointed to his fellow councilman with the paunch.

"These people don't even want that. They only want private buildings, complete with tax breaks for real estate developers. They're proposing a $17-billion-dollar tax subsidy, only not for tenants or local residents chased from their homes, but for landlords and developers. They say they're against socialism, but that's not true. They're in favor of socialism, alright, for the rich!"

Thumbs down from the *Times* reporter, big cheer from Mariela's group whose leader was told that one more outburst and she would have to leave.

Roybal wasn't finished. He then launched into a spirited defense of places like the three villages and Bunker Hill. He was outraged, he said, about the way that clearing these areas and selling them to private developers amounted to "stealing space from workers and remaking their space as spaces for private profit." For a certain group of workers—which I took to mean white workers—the time devoted to their trip to work would decrease, as they could afford these new private spaces. On the other hand, he said, the colored people already living in these areas were characterized as "outsiders in their own homes," forced to move farther away from the city where their time to get to work would increase.

"Los Angeles," he concluded, "would become a place only the rich could afford."

In a surprise move, Roybal then asked the Council to listen to a special witness, a professor from San Jose State University, which he said was the first public education institution in California, and who, Roybal announced, was also in line for an appointment to the City Planning Commission.

The chair gave this new speaker five minutes to address the Council over the loud objections from the small but boisterous "Committee."

"Go ahead, Professor Gonzalez," Roybal said.

The professor, a tiny and frail, elderly but scholarly presence in a well-worn blue suit and tie, read from a prepared statement.

His statement attacked the idea of private home ownership and was met with boos by The Committee.

His claim was that "owning your own home was a scheme promoted by money, real estate and newspaper interests" meant to "undercut labor organizing and destroy communities."

I noticed that as he was starting to talk, two new figures entered the hearing room and positioned themselves at the back. They were my old buddies, the two men in black. I was lonesome for them. I hadn't seen them for hours. The *Times* reporter nodded to them and then pointed to the professor. The smaller of the two nodded back.

Gonzalez then launched into a measured speech which, coming from such a small, meek man, was received with unbelievable hostility by many of the members of the Council who openly booed his words.

"The history of private property in the United States is one of dispossession, colonialism, and racism. To turn wage earners into homeowners is a scheme to put them in debt to the banks and make them fearful of losing their jobs which would result in losing their homes."

He called the whole organization of the city a "real estate conspiracy," developing a major industry to rope families into buying homes in California, "the land of milk and honey," some of which he said were "no more than shacks which it would take them years to pay off."

"The plan," he concluded in his quiet but incendiary manner, "was to break up communities and instead have people live as isolated individuals in "a world run by the Chamber of Commerce and real estate interests."

When the professor concluded his speech, Roybal thanked him for his wise words as Mariela stood up and cheered.

That was it for the Council chairman. He ordered the bailiff to remove her from the hearing. She was led out just ahead of the professor, and that seemed to be fine with her, as she turned and patted him on the shoulder.

Trailing the little procession were the two men in black and, when I saw this, I figured I should bring up the rear.

Out in the corridor, Mariela was congratulating the professor, who seemed a bit taken aback at the commotion his words had caused.

The two men approached. The taller one rubbed his coat against Mariela, and when she felt what was inside it, she snapped back in fear.

I wasn't surprised he was packing, but I was surprised he would threaten someone in such an open manner. They must have felt this was a friendly space in which to operate.

They hadn't seen me, and as the smaller man was whispering something to Mariela, I came up behind them and pushed the taller one into the smaller man.

They both fell forward and, when the taller one recovered, he pulled his pistol from his suitcoat pocket and brandished it at me. I think he was about to use it when suddenly the bailiff, who had lingered in the corridor to make sure Mariela did not reenter the chamber, came up behind them.

"Here, here," he said. "We'll have none of that in this hall."

He also looked at me suspiciously.

"What do you have to do with this?"

"I was just helping the little guy up. He seems awfully clumsy and I wanted to make sure he didn't hurt himself," I said.

The duo gritted their teeth at me and shuffled off.

The bailiff didn't think that was particularly funny and he had had enough of our whole little group.

"Make yourself scarce," he shot back over this shoulder as he ambled back down toward the hearing.

I asked Mariela if she was okay and was relieved to see that Esperanza had come out of the hall and was comforting her also.

I saw the two men enter the elevator, and this time I decided they would not elude me.

I watched the elevator ascend and realized that once again they were making for the floor with Beame's office.

I followed on the next elevator and decided I would wait for them to come out.

When they didn't exit after a few minutes, I tried the door. It was locked, but I had to get in.

My old boss Nader was right. I had in my time on the burglary squad become an expert locksmith and safe cracker. It just went with the job.

In a few minutes I jimmied the lock and was inside the office.

I wasn't sure they were there but I thought it likely.

As I entered, I heard a rustling in the back and thought this time I had them. I pulled out my gun and hid behind Beame's desk waiting for them to come back to the front office, thinking to surprise them on their way out.

They didn't show up.

I began to suspect I had been outwitted again as I headed to the back room. Sure enough, there was an exit out into the corridor. The sound I had heard was of them leaving the office.

By the time I got back out into the hallway, the elevator was on its way down.

I lost them, but not for long, I thought, fingering the card that my former landlord Johnson had given me with the location of the bar on The Strip that they probably frequented.

I went back downstairs, picked up Esperanza, and we headed to her house. Perfect for me because I needed a break from a case that was becoming more dangerous by the minute.

17

It was about 20 miles long but only about a quarter of a mile wide. It ran from L.A. South to the San Pedro Harbor at various points bisecting several of the towns in the South Bay, separating Gardena from Compton, and Torrance from Carson. A big part of it was now somewhat unused farmlands or drained oil fields. Its purpose for being was to connect the city of L.A. to the harbor so the city could legally annex the port and move its sea traffic farther south from the older harbor of Santa Monica. It was at first called the Shoestring Corridor, later the Shoestring Strip, and finally just "The Strip."

The part I was speeding toward, though, as I headed south on Figueroa, had nothing to do with farmland or oil derricks. It was a wide-open, Wild West section of bars, tattoo parlors, gambling halls and some even shadier and more audacious after-hours places where all manner of things and people were bought and sold.

I remembered that in my time on the force, these places were mostly off-limits for the LAPD, hardly patrolled at all, with the law barely enforced. There were just too many fish to fry elsewhere, so that in this little piece of heaven, or hell, depending on your perspective, those frequenting the joints were allowed to run free, possibly on the idea that if they got it out of their system here, they would not bother "good, clean, decent" people elsewhere. Though from time to time, when some kind of violence would erupt in one of the joints, the police were called in, not to stop the violence but to make sure that the "good, clean, decent" people who had found their way there never made the papers, leaving with their reputation intact.

The Last Ditch bar sat right in the middle of this, as the Torrance historian Macready described it, "den of iniquity." It was a Tuesday night when I entered, normally not a busy bar night since there was still a lot of the work week left and nobody could afford to get too plastered. But on this night the place was packed. It looked like an old Western saloon, with a long bar against the side wall running the length of the place, tables in front, and a stairway leading up to a second floor which I guessed were either offices or places where a team of scantily clad waitresses, if that's what they were, might shanghai the customers. The only concession to this century was the jukebox in the corner opposite the bar, which at the moment was filling the crowded tables with the mournful wail of Hank Williams's "Long Gone Lonesome Blues." Places like this were meant to nurse grudges, and country music was full of them. So it seemed a perfect blend of artist and mood.

I went up to the bar. Behind it stood a man who, like Macready, also wore a carefully trimmed handlebar mustache. He was dressed all in leather and looked to be in excellent shape. I ordered a rum and Coke. It appeared he had a minute in his busy night, so I asked him to give me the lowdown on the place.

"Last Ditch," he said, "is exactly what it sounds like. It's the place where you go when you're down on your luck and the bright shiny world out there is ruining you."

"That's quite the opposite of the way I heard Torrance just across the way described," I said. He smiled and let out a little grunt.

"I bet you've been talking to Macready. He's a mouthpiece for the 'new' Torrance, where everything is bright and shiny."

I nodded.

"I don't mean to be prying, but he didn't seem to totally fit into the 'clean, upright' Torrance he laid out."

The bartender, who said his name was Smith—Jack Smith—agreed.

"Yeah, damn right he doesn't quite fit in. Comes skulking around here sometimes, calls it 'slumming.' Comes onto me like I'm his best friend, but truth is, I don't like having much to do with him. I'm accepted for who I am here and that's fine with me. I don't have to hide who I'm attracted to on The Strip.

"People like me are being persecuted by the government in Washington, where they're claiming we're a security threat and so we have to hide who we are. I choose to be in a place where I can be myself but folks like Macready suck up to the very people who are persecuting them. Doesn't appeal to me."

To make his point, he spat on the bar floor.

I told him I agreed with him. This was a perfect moment for me to show the photos of the two men in black. He looked at them and said yes, they came in frequently and probably would be in later that night. Otherwise, he had nothing much to say about them and, since they sometimes looked at him suspiciously, he told me he kept his distance.

With that, Jack Smith left to tend to a busy bar.

I had some time to kill and ordered another rum and Coke. I looked around, and two stools down from me sat a Negro man who motioned for me to come over. He was slumping against the bar and looking dejected, but also like he wanted someone to talk to. He offered to buy me a drink in return for me being a ready listener. It was my third but who was I to turn down a free drink? I obliged.

His name was Horatio Everly. He was a little beyond middle-aged and, like most people I was meeting these days, he had a sad story to tell.

Before I let him get started, though, I showed him the photos of the two men. He recognized them, shook his head, and said, "Bad business," but wouldn't say more.

He pulled out a photo of his own and threw it on the bar. It was of a much younger Horatio, lounging at the beach in his bathing suit with a beautiful Negro woman folded into him.

"That was my wife," he said. "We got married on the beach at Santa Monica at Belmar Park. This photo was taken the day after as part of our honeymoon on the beach."

I said they both looked very happy.

"We were," he said, "but no more. She dead."

"What got her?" I asked.

"Them people," he said, waving his arms around the predominantly white crowd in the bar.

"The beach was generally off limits to our kind, but we had our own stretch of beach and our own beach house called La Bonita. The whites didn't like it and called our bay beach 'The Inkwell.' There was a whole settlement of Black folk there in the Belmar triangle with a Black Methodist Church,

Black doctors and dentists, and a trolley line that took people to and from work.

"But it's all under attack now. They want to close the trolley line, the city has started seizing the space, and it's getting much harder to open a Negro business in the area."

It was a sad tale, and to go through it he needed another drink. He was buying, so that meant I needed another drink too. What can I say? I'm cheap.

He went on.

"My wife and I had a janitorial business, cleaning local offices, but the city seized the land with our business office, and it was hard to find another space. That was it for Lula. She folded under the pressure and died last year of a heart attack. Me, I keep on tickin' just to show them they can't get the best of me."

"And what do they want to do with the land?" I asked. This was sounding too eerily like my other cases.

"Now that the beach is no longer a port, they want to develop the area and turn it into an upscale place for tourists. The term they use that gets them state and federal money is Urban Renewal, but, in our neighborhood, we call it 'Negro Removal.'"

He had a good laugh at that, and I joined him, a bitter laugh, but a laugh, nonetheless.

"I'll tell you something else," he said. He was talking a little louder now and I was getting worried we were attracting attention.

"What 'modernizing,' the other name they use for this, means is getting us out of neighborhoods that we built, and instead moving us to areas the white population has abandoned because the property values are low, in houses that are so rundown they're hard to maintain and show the traces of not being properly looked after and badly managed. They move us out of our homes and we get scraps and leftovers."

Now he was really on a pulpit. Everything he said was right, but I was getting nervous.

"To tell you true," he said, as he wound up, "in Belmar we were not an isolated group where everyone only looked after themselves, like they're building in the suburbs around here, but a whole community of folks who looked after each other."

Despite my fear of being conspicuous, I was cheering Horatio on and did not notice the two men behind us until one of them put a huge arm on my companion's shoulder, bearing down on him, and the other said, "Nigger, if you value your hide, don't let us catch you here again."

Horatio glared at them, nodded to me, and moved to a back corner of the bar out of sight.

That left them and me.

"We been seeing you around quite a lot," the bigger one of the two men in black said, as he now put the same huge fist and arm on my shoulder and held it tight.

"You got nothing to fear from me," I said. "My friend here was getting a little loud but he don't mean much by it. Just shooting off his mouth."

The smaller one blanched when I described Horatio as my friend and gave me a stern warning. "The Creator had a good reason for dividing humanity into various races," he said.

The big one added, "And you shouldn't oughta to be messing with that."

They were starting to crowd in a little tighter.

"Look," I said, "I'm just a low-level private dick, hired to help my landlord. You guys won that round and that's okay with me. I've already moved out. Can you just let me buy you each a drink and can we be friends?"

They backed off and took stools on either side of me at the bar. Friends might have been pushing it but they, like me, were in favor of free drinks.

My fourth round, their first, and I was trying to keep my wits about me.

"So, who might you guys be?" I asked.

The big man was going to start talking, but first he looked at the smaller guy who gave him a signal that it was okay.

"I'm an ex-cop, Torrance's finest," the big one, who said his name was Mick Blaine, began. That would explain their welcome in the Torrance police parking lot.

"I'm an ex-cop too," I said. "We had some real fun on the force, with Negroes and Mexicans."

"And Jews," Mick said. "Before I left, we impounded a car from this kike accountant and painted a swastika and a smiley face inside."

"And did the guy sue?"

That was the wrong question. He shut up. I imagined the city had to pay off for that, and it may have been why he had to leave the force.

But it didn't take him long to recover since I offered them a second round. He then told a story of how another officer, he wouldn't name him, used a choke hold on a vagrant sleeping in a Torrance park after it closed, and the bum died of a heart attack on the way to the hospital.

"So, what did you do?" I said. "How did you—I mean 'they'—get out of it?"

He didn't pick up my attempt at getting him to confess. He said, though, that "the cop" conveniently found a gun near where he had strangled the man and claimed it was an "officer-involved shooting." In court, he said, "They believed our lies" and "we all stuck to the script."

"We ended up laughing our asses off."

He didn't realize he had switched from "they" to "we" and probably implicated himself. I wished I had a recorder.

"And what's your story?" I asked the smaller one. He was smarter and more reluctant to say much to me, so I bought them another round. We were really getting quite chummy.

His name was Anthony, or Tony, Lomax. He grew up in Owens Valley, the place where legend has it, the *L.A. Times*' Harry Chandler and General Otis siphoned off water to irrigate the San Fernando Valley. Otis and Harry Chandler, in the swindle that created greater Los Angeles, bought up thousands of acres in the Valley of what before was desert but which with water would then be a fertile oasis, worth many times more than they paid for it.

On the other hand, Owens Valley, now with its water drained, was turned into a desert. Tony watched his father, a farmer, make plans to blow up the pipeline, which were thwarted as the Chandlers sent a hundred armed men to protect it. He left what he called "the valley of desolation" where his father deteriorated, but he decided, after being in the intelligence services during the war, that "if you can't beat 'em, join 'em."

"So do you work for these people now?" I asked gingerly, not wanting to upset the apple cart but taking the opening Tony offered.

"Never you mind," he said. "What I will say is that we're on the side of right. We're not trying to crush or humiliate the Black race which is much younger than our own. We're only following a law of nature which has been obeyed, respected, and fought for ever since time began—the right of living among our own kind."

"Sounds kind of Klanish," I said.

"Well, if the shoe fits . . ." Mick piped up.

What I didn't say is, it also sounds kind of dumb, and illustrates one of my most fervently held beliefs, that racists are idiots. The Black race was the first race on earth and human beings have always lived and prospered through their differences. As an old girlfriend used to say, that's how the world turns.

But now Mick was starting to get going and I was beginning to suspect that the two men in black may have had a lot in common with Torrance's pock-marked man.

Mick told the "hilarious"—or so he thought—story of how when a Black family moved into the area around Leimert Park in L.A., he had helped the "neighbors" there run a hose through the window of the house, flooding the kitchen and the cellar.

He also then started talking about a case of a family of four where a fire, as he said, "got a little out of hand" in the Klan stronghold of Fontana, which I had visited last year when I had a run-in with the Klan and a police officer I was trailing.

"And what happened?" I asked, now more curious than ever at hearing him talking about burning out a family.

But Anthony, the brains of the outfit, motioned for him to clam up and he instead interrupted Mick's litany to explain the righteousness of their actions.

"The Negro," he said, "is dragging the Caucasian race down to his level through his selfish and unnatural effort at self-advancement. Once one of them moves onto a street it's 'broke.' All we're trying to do is protect our families and our homes against this injustice."

Yep, racists are idiots alright. But the next part got more interesting.

I bought them another round. Mick downed his whiskey and soda in two gulps and started up again.

"And now we got the Chinese to worry about. There's 500 million of them in China and they all want to come here. If we let them all in, we'll be nothing here but a motley race of half-breeds."

Idiots alright, and me without a recorder.

We'd all had a lot to drink, me double what they had, and it appeared we were becoming fast friends, when suddenly the mood changed.

Who should walk into the bar but Dean, the nervous, fidgety son of the developer Williams, whose father had called him reckless.

He saw the men in black talking to me and seemed to recognize me from his father's office.

They saw him also and went over to talk to him. He then went to the other end of the bar where he flirted with one of the waitresses.

They came back and seemed friendlier than ever, though it was difficult for me to tell, since I was way over my limit and didn't know how I would drive home.

"Come with us," Tony said. "There's something we want to show you."

They say when you drink your guard goes down, and what they say is correct.

We went outside in the street with Mick's arm on my shoulder.

They pointed to another place across the street, Madame Thai's, which they said had all kinds of Chinese girls and where we could continue the party.

I was all for that, but when we I started to go up the steps of the place, Mick pulled me back down and Tony punched me in the gut and then let me have one across my face.

I collapsed.

They dragged me to their car and tossed me in the back. We drove for it didn't seem very long and then stopped.

Mick pulled me out of the back seat and threw me on the ground, which luckily was a sandy beach. I realized we were just south of Torrance.

Tony kicked me and said, "Stop asking so many questions, mister, and if we catch you around here again, next time we won't be so nice."

He was about to kick some more when a young man and his dog strolled along the beach, forcing him to stop, and beat a hasty retreat.

The man with the dog helped me up and got me to a run-down hotel along the beach where I could call a cab. He also issued a warning before he left.

"Stay away from those people. They're bad business, and this, despite what it looks like, is not a friendly town."

I started to sober up, realizing I probably needed to be back again the next day. I wondered, *Was I now smarter and wiser about what was going on in Torrance, or just dumber and crazier for not having enough of it?*

18

Sometimes my boss, or partner or whatever he is, can be a real jerk.

Crystal was once again called in for regular detective duty and unable to meet with Diane, who had called her to see if she wanted to go on a presentation with her to start her training.

Instead, she had to decline because Harry was in his new fleabag nursing a stomach ache and coming down from a hangover. She was glad she didn't drink like that and certain that she could never have survived her former life in the nightclubs if she had. Those fishing expeditions for contacts in the film industry required a girl to constantly keep her wits about her and they had forced her to learn how to hold her liquor.

Harry called saying the case might be too dangerous and that maybe they were going to withdraw from it. He had apparently been roughed up though it was unlike him to let that stop him. Anyway, he told her, there was an even hotter case they needed to be working on, also in Torrance. He said this one could have a big payoff though there was not going to be any money coming in yet.

Oh boy, a lot of dangerous work for nothing, she thought. And suddenly the idea of going into real estate seemed a whole lot more promising.

So, before getting back to Diane, Harry wanted her to interview the first wife of the two-timing spouse, who might have every reason to do in her husband and bury a will which would allow the second wife to claim her house and the oil buried beneath it, leaving the first wife homeless.

Crystal had spent the morning visiting an ex-actress wannabe who was now taking her act on the road as a Tupperware saleswoman, hosting parties to hawk the product.

She got her friend not only to give her a lesson in sales but also to loan her some of the plastic containers.

So it was that that afternoon she rang the door of a nondescript white house on Hawthorne Street near the border of Carson and Torrance and close to the Dow Chemical plant which had been the site of her last assignment.

Crystal was dressed "suburban" for the occasion, in white skirt and pink top with saddle shoes.

I look more like a plastic doll than a person, she thought, but had to admit, as she watched some female passersby, that she was not out of place.

A woman in a long, slightly frumpy housedress and an apron answered the doorbell, followed by a boy who looked to be about six, with blond hair, blue eyes, and an inquisitive air.

"Ma'am, I'd love to come in and show you this miracle plastic container that can be used to keep all kinds of foods from spoiling," she said.

"Sorry, not interested," the woman said and started to shut the door.

Crystal stuck her foot in the door so it wouldn't close and made her pitch.

"You can also make money selling this miracle invention," she said. "And you don't even have to leave your house."

At that the woman perked up a bit and motioned for her to enter.

"God knows I could use some money," she said. "That useless husband is gone and I'm stuck home with two kids and can't even go out to look for work. So how do I cash in on this?"

The woman, introducing herself as Lucy Cardiff, motioned for Crystal to have a seat, and before Crystal could answer went to the kitchen and returned with coffee and what she said were "freshly baked" oatmeal cookies which Crystal gladly accepted.

"You're already proving that you can be a Tupperware saleswoman," she said.

"To make money all you have to do is host a party. You start off the party by passing out plastic hats," she said, as she pulled one from her bag. "They get everyone in the mood for playing little games, like this one, my favorite."

She pulled out a string of brightly colored gift bags which she said Lucy could pass around, telling everyone to pass the bag to the right or left when she used either of two "magic words" in a little story she would tell. At the end of the story, everybody got to keep the gift bag they were left with.

Crystal then fished a pink plastic spatula out of the bag she was using for the demonstration.

"Then, when everyone is comfortable, you show them the product. I seal it, tap on it, and sometimes toss it across the room to show how resilient it is. They can't buy this product in stores, they can only buy it from you, and you get a percentage of every box you sell."

Lucy was interested, and this was going so well Crystal started to wonder if she might be a natural saleswoman herself.

Fuck Tupperware, I'm selling houses, she thought, and then she remembered she was there to do a job.

"Everybody can use some extra money," she said. "But if you do this full time, it could become not just a sideline but an occupation."

At this Lucy perked up and, as she refreshed her own and Crystal's cup of coffee, she started to tell her story.

"I could certainly use it. My husband's gone," she said. "He disappeared a few days ago and at this point I may need to assume he's not coming back. His car is in the garage but I haven't used it since he left."

"That's a terrible tragedy," Crystal said. "Is it another woman?"

She hated to be this blunt but she didn't want this to take all day and had to get to the point.

"Well, yes and no," the woman said. "There is another woman, a second wife in fact, but she doesn't know where he is either and she has put in a claim on this house. If she finds him or the will she says he left, we're homeless."

"That's horrible," Crystal said. "When was the last time you saw him?"

"He was at work at the Dow plant near here. Called the other night to say he was coming home late and never arrived."

Crystal decided she needed to have a look around the place. She asked for more coffee, told Lucy the cookies were amazing and asked for more of those too.

As soon as Lucy headed for the kitchen, Crystal scampered down the hallway and noticed a door that led out to the garage. Next to the door was a clothes hamper. She leafed through it and found a pair of coveralls that had a name tag that read "Stan" on them.

She heard Lucy puttering in the kitchen and skipped back to the living room just in time to greet her.

As she settled in, she asked Lucy about Stan's work in the plant.

"He's an engineer, so he doesn't usually get his hands dirty," she said. "But it's a chemical plant and sometimes they have to do inspections. The night he went missing was one of those nights and he had to wear his plant coveralls."

All of which meant it's likely he returned to the house that night, Crystal thought.

"You have a lot to worry about," Crystal said, patting Lucy's hand.

"You don't know the half of it. We're also under attack here. I do a bit of neighborhood work and have a list of the other girls involved—which will help me organize the parties!"

She then reached behind the couch and pulled out a sign that read *KEEP THE NEGROES NORTH OF 134TH STREET*.

"We want to keep them in Compton. We don't want them moving any farther south. We're trying to maintain the purity of our town for the sake of the children," she said. "And we don't want them breaking the color line and swarming in here."

Though shocked, Crystal covered her true feelings by tapping Lucy's arm and nodding in agreement.

After having told Lucy she would be hearing from her, she couldn't wait to tell Harry about what she'd found out.

Like to see her racist ass in jail, Crystal thought as she smiled and headed for her car.

———————————————————

The last thing I wanted to do was go back to Torrance. I had been warned off the place twice in the same night. Wasn't that enough? Certainly, the men in black, Mick and Tony, warranted a second look after what they had let spill in the bar. The pock-marked Klansman was still wandering around with the rest of his gang, and I did not want another encounter with the Torrance police.

So, I slept in. Part of it was the hangover. I tried getting up the next morning but that didn't go anywhere. I didn't even know if I wanted to continue on the case.

Late afternoon, though, after a hearty breakfast at 3 p.m., I stumbled into my, or rather our, office. My partner was there, with a face that conveyed both excitement and alarm.

She told me she had good news on the case of the two wives, that wife number one, who was concealing her husband's plant coveralls on the night he disappeared, looked guilty as hell. All I had to do was some routine skulking around and we might be coming into a good deal of money.

"It's not usually that easy," I told her, but she didn't care. She just wanted me to get on the case and for us to crack it.

"Meanwhile," she said, "I'm going back to keep an eye on Diane."

I didn't tell her I was thinking of pulling us off the case after what had happened to me, especially since she seemed so eager to pursue this lead. Made me wonder if there was more there than just an assignment.

"Go, child, with my blessing," I said.

She frowned, crinkled up her nose and sauntered out of the office, sashaying and working an orange dress that was the tightest thing I'd ever seen on her.

"So long, Daddy," she said. "And get to work."

She slammed the door and left me alone in the office to ponder.

It was just starting to get dark when I drove back again to the Torrance-Carson border and parked a few blocks away from Stan and Lucy Cardiff's house. To get there I had to skirt what looked like a swamp, but which I figured, since it was located between three plants including the Dow plant Stan worked for, was the waste dump.

Crystal told me that Lucy had two kids and I wondered what ill effects would be visited on them in the future for living and maybe playing so close to what was most likely a contaminated area.

When I got to the house on 204th Street, it was as silent as all the other houses on the block. It was a weeknight, and most of the owners probably worked in the nearby plants and had now marched off to bed where visions of sugar plums—or more likely rubber tires and plastic cups and containers since that's what the plants made—danced in their heads.

The easiest way to gain access to the place was through the garage. The door was locked but I figured I could crack it without much trouble. For some reason that was not the case. The lock refused to jimmy and so I found myself slinking around the back door and, lo and behold, it was not locked.

I guess Lucy trusted her neighbors, though from what Crystal said, that might be because she spent some time keeping anyone not "neighborly" out of the area.

The back door led through the kitchen into a long corridor off of which was a door to the garage. There, near the kitchen, was the clothes hamper that Crystal had mentioned. I rechecked it and sure enough it still contained, at the bottom of the hamper, covered by a whole lot of other clothes, Stan's plant coveralls.

I needed to get into the garage, and so I found myself tiptoeing down the corridor past Lucy's bedroom. I peeked in and saw her fast asleep, but I didn't need visual confirmation because she was also snoring, not loudly but softly, which I figured I could just monitor to make sure she didn't wake up.

Now for the garage. This was going to be easy, except it wasn't. There was also a lock on the door from the house to the garage which only made me doubly determined to get in.

As I was lining up the tumblers to open the door, I heard the snoring stop.

I leaped down the hallway toward the back door and hid myself behind the laundry hamper.

Lucy, in blue nightgown, came out into the hallway, looked around, then went down the corridor in the opposite direction, probably to check on her two kids to see if either of them had made a noise.

In a few minutes she returned. I peeked out from behind the hamper and watched her shake her head and go back into the bedroom.

Now I had to wait for the snoring to begin again.

About ten minutes later, it did.

This time I was quieter but had more luck with the lock. I got the tumblers to fall into place and entered the garage, being careful to close the door behind me.

In the garage was a green Oldsmobile, a family car with a huge trunk.

I had a weird feeling as I entered that I was not alone, maybe because a whole section of the garage behind the car was completely covered in darkness.

I shrugged the feeling off and opened the car doors but there was nothing inside.

It also looked like what Lucy said to Crystal was correct. The car was almost spotless and seemed like it hadn't been driven in days.

A slight smell came from the trunk, so that was my next project.

To jimmy it I needed a crowbar. On a tool shelf near the car I found what I was looking for.

This might be a noisy process, and instinctively I looked around to make sure I was alone.

I couldn't see anything moving so I inserted the crowbar under the lock on the trunk and with one motion, which I knew was going to be loud, pushed it upward, trusting that the door would muffle the noise and that Lucy would be in a deep sleep.

The trunk popped open and from it there floated a strong stench that initially blew me away. Then what to my wondering eyes should appear but a body, crumpled up and pushed toward the back of the hatch. I pulled a flashlight from the tool shelf and shined it inside. It was Stan, alright. I recognized him from the photos on Fran's, the second wife's, wall.

I don't know why, but my first impulse was to go through his pockets. It proved correct. Maybe I was a detective after all.

In his front right pants pocket, I found a folded set of papers. I pulled them out, unfolded them and there was the will.

This is the easiest money I ever made, I thought. *Can't wait to collect.*

My second thought was *Torrance police, what a bunch of idiots.*

That was my last thought, though, because at that moment I turned to dimly see the outline of a blackjack coming straight down on my skull at an angle that indicated whoever was wielding it was a professional.

The ground then rushed up and hit me, and I joined the other shadows in the garage as one more dark mass now lying in a heap on the concrete floor.

Act 3

Home is Where the Heart Was

19

I woke up with a huge headache in more ways than one. My head was throbbing as I lay on a living room couch. When I came to, though, the other headache was worse. There was Lance and behind him McGinty looking down at me. The burly sergeant, I guess, was now back on active duty, and he was holding a pair of handcuffs that he was anxious to introduce me to.

Behind them I recognized Lucy, now out of her bathrobe and in a gray frock and looking none too happy as well. I looked at the clock. It read 6 and it was just starting to get light out.

"Alright, Palmer, what's going on?" Lance said. He had apparently gone through my pockets and found my card.

"Should I cuff him, Chief?" McGinty offered eagerly.

"Let's hear him out. This should be interesting," Lance shot back, putting his hand out to restrain his overeager partner.

"Yeah, what was he doing in my house last night? I was sure I heard something, got up to look, went back to bed, and this morning the garage door was unlocked. I went out there, where I haven't been in ages, and there he was, sprawled on the floor."

Lance was losing patience fast, that is, if he had any to begin with.

"What are you doing in her house and what are you doing in Torrance, Mr. 'Insurance Accessor?'"

I tried to sit up but quickly slumped back down on the couch.

"That woman is a murderer," I said, pointing at Lucy. "Her husband's body is stowed in the trunk of her car, along with his will, leaving the house to his second wife. If you don't believe me, go check the garage."

Lance went to check, with Lucy unlocking the door to the garage. McGinty stared coldly at me, not liking my tricking him, and looking for some revenge.

Lance and Lucy returned. He was patting her arm to assure her all was well.

"There's nothing and no one in the trunk," he said. "Why would you think she killed him?"

I was not entirely surprised. Whoever hit me had all night to figure out what to do with the body and probably exited using the outside garage door.

"Check her hamper at the end of the hallway. At the bottom you'll find her husband's coveralls which she said he was wearing the night he disappeared."

Lance had Lucy remain in the living room with McGinty while he went to look in the hamper. She glared at me, probably realizing that Crystal had tricked her into giving herself away.

Lance came back with the coveralls.

"Your husband was wearing these the night he disappeared?" Lance asked.

"Yes, he was, but I have no idea how they got in with the dirty clothes. He must have come back here and dropped them off just before he left."

"That's possible," Lance said, seeming to accept her explanation, but then added, "If he came back, why didn't he take the car?"

"He couldn't if he was killed and dumped in it," I said, but Lance was more inclined to believe Lucy.

"I'm getting Palmer out of your hair," he told her.

He and McGinty lifted me up on their shoulders and dragged me where I told them I had parked my car.

"We're letting you go because you may have in some strange way helped our investigation, but we don't want you around here anymore."

Sheesh, if one more person wanted me out of this town, I would have to spend the rest of the time working on this case at home. Most towns had a welcome wagon. This one had a "Get Out of Town" wagon.

Why couldn't I take what was now an order and no longer just a hint?

One reason was I needed the money and I was so close to getting it, I didn't want to let go.

The thing I could be certain of was that whoever knocked me out then had a body to get rid of. I let that be my starting point.

It seemed to me that if you didn't want to go far and had to dump a body quickly, there was a natural place to bury it, and that was the waste dump near Lucy's home. If she was in on this, she may even have suggested it to them.

I decided to prowl around the dump, but to do that I first needed to get me a pair of high boots, like the green rubber-soled boots electricians wear when they go out to work on power lines.

I found Stevens, my friendly neighborhood electrician, hard at work invoicing customers, even though it was only 7 in the morning. He agreed to loan me the boots but advised against wading into the waste dump.

"Everybody avoids that place," he said.

"I know, that's why I gotta go there," I replied.

"One man's poison is another man's medicine," he said, shrugging and going back to his billing.

I didn't like him using the word poison, given where I was going, but I had little choice but to hope this turned out to be my medicine.

I parked near the Dow plant where Stan Cardiff worked and thought that if they had used the dump to conceal and then disintegrate his body, it might just be a speeding up of what the dump was doing to so many workers and their families.

I started wading out into the muck. It was indeed a swamp with who knows what chemicals swirling at my feet. The problem with using this place for body disposal was that the swamp wasn't deep. The murky waters never came up even close to the highest point of my boots.

I waded around for a while and was about to leave when I saw a piece of paper concealed in a clump of thick weeds. I reached down and picked it up, and lo and behold, there was some writing on it.

I made out the words "Last Testament," which seemed to be the heading of a page from which this little piece had been ripped.

I couldn't believe my luck. They had dumped him here. I was back in business.

Then my luck turned. I could find no other trace of the body. I stomped around the entire dump, and not a sign of the engineer.

I began to figure that whoever they were—and it was probably more than one person necessary to drag a body around—they had come to the same conclusion as me: The dump would not conceal the body.

I clawed my way to the edge of the dump and dejectedly plumped down on dry land.

Then my luck turned again.

Just to the left of me I noticed tracks, two pairs of footprints leading out of the dump and onto dry land. I followed the tracks a few feet, and they ended. But even more to my surprise the trail continued, only now the footprints turned into car tracks.

There was still so much mud, even on semi-dry land that the tracks were visible as the car pulled out of the swamp.

I couldn't believe my luck or their stupidity. It wasn't yet 8 o'clock and the muddy tracks had not been completely erased.

I got back into my car and was able to follow the trail.

On my way a Torrance police patrol car whizzed by. I ducked down slightly and kept going.

I followed the car in my rearview mirror and thought it had disappeared but, way off in the distance, it may have turned around.

Oh well, I couldn't worry about the incompetent police.

As the trail wound through the town, at first, I didn't know where it was going, and then it became clear.

The muddy traces wound past the Chungs' former house reduced to smoky embers, and a few streets beyond to where the tracks stopped. The house was at the end of the street and it had a good-sized backyard behind it.

How Fran McCordle, the second wife, was involved in this I couldn't figure, but there was no denying this was her house.

It was now about 8 in the morning and I needed to see if I could gain access to that backyard.

I was in luck. A few minutes after I pulled up near her house, she came out with her two kids. She piled both of them into her car parked in front of the house and was on her way to drive them to school.

I was in luck also because the mud was still coming off the shoes of whoever was dragging the body, probably because the weight of the body forced them to make a deeper footprint.

The new trail led, as I suspected, around the corner of the house and into the backyard. The yard had a swing set, I guess for the girl, and a ball on a string with plastic bats nearby for the boy.

Off to the right of the yard, though, were rose bushes, and just in front of them was where the tracks stopped.

I needed a shovel.

A small tool shed in the back of the yard wasn't locked, and I found what I was looking for, which I guessed was used to plant and spade the roses.

There was nothing to do with my new shovel but start digging.

I got about a foot deep when I hit something solid.

I kept digging around the contact and within a few minutes I had found a body. It was Stan, alright. He had been quite active last night, taking the grand tour of Torrance. Crystal was reading a popular novel which she said was very funny called *The Trouble with Harry* about a corpse that kept moving around. I was in a novel of my own called *The Trouble with Stan*.

I couldn't resist. I reached inside his pocket, looking for the will, but it was gone.

Whoever buried him didn't do much of a job of it, since it had taken me only a short while to dig him up. Was that because they were afraid of getting caught, or was it because they wanted him found?

I had no time to think further, though, because who should come waltzing around the corner of the house but Detective Lance. Not far behind, again with the handcuffs, was McGinty.

"Now we got him dead to rights, Chief," McGinty said. "Let me slap these on him."

"You idiot," I said. "I just found your body for you. Why would you think I'm the killer?"

Cooler heads prevailed.

Lance told him to put the handcuffs away and then turned to me.

"We know the story of the two wives," he said. "They might both have a reason to kill him, but it looks like this one did."

"But what does she get out of it?" I said. "She wants the house and there is no will for her to claim it."

"She's still the wife and maybe she gets revenge," Lance said.

At that moment we heard a car pull up next to the curb, and Fran, stunned to find a police vehicle parked outside her house, came around the corner and saw the three of us standing there.

"What's going on here?" she said, and then came closer and saw Stan's body.

"Oh, no," she said, and burst out crying.

"How did he get here?"

"Ma'am," Lance replied, "that's what you're going to need to tell us down at the station."

McGinty asked if he could finally use the handcuffs. He apparently just liked to see people in chains. Lance nodded okay, and as Fran was being led off, told her she was likely going to be booked for first degree murder.

I ran after them trying to tell them what had happened, but they didn't want to hear it.

I had done their job for them and presented them with an open and shut case that neither of them had any interest in disturbing.

As they were pushing Fran into the back of the patrol car, she turned to me.

"Some detective you are. I hire you to get me a house and instead you get me thrown in jail."

My luck had gone from good to bad and finished at worse.

I really didn't know what to do next, in a case or cases I couldn't seem to stop screwing up.

20

Things were not going well. I always hated football pep talks and so I made them my own. In this case, when the going got tough, this quarterback was going to the beach.

That's where I had been dropped by the two goons and where I had also gotten a warning by the young man with the dog.

I wasn't there to learn anything, though. I just needed to take a break.

The beach straight out from Torrance was covered with all kinds of tiny shells, what looked like little mollusks.

This can't do me any harm, I thought, and I was about to sit when I heard a shout in the distance and saw someone approaching me waving his arms.

It turned out this was the young man, he seemed to be about 25, who had helped me back to my car. Once again, he was with his dog, which this time I had enough wits about me to notice was a friendly, loppy-eared black and white collie.

He ran up to me.

"Just looking for a little peace and quiet among the shells," I said. "Don't need to be disturbed."

He smiled.

"You won't get it here. This is RAT Beach. Know why they call it that?"

I shook my head and remained standing.

"There is a creek just behind the beach which is never drained. It attracts all kinds of rats, and what you were about to sit in is not shells but rat shit."

I had started to sit down, but sprang up quickly.

"Just when you think you're safe, this town comes back and bites you," I said.

"That's right. That's its history."

"C'mon," he said, grabbling my arm. "Let's walk a bit."

He pulled from his pocket a folded-up plastic bag, and as we walked, he leaned down from time to time and, if he found a particularly shiny shell, he put it in his bag. He also stopped to dig out any coins which had been left in the sand by some bather and for which he had an eagle eye. He was a true beachcomber.

"What are you doing here anyway?"

He seemed friendly enough and I decided to trust him.

I told him about Sandra Chung and about the disappearing body which I had finally found.

"Who are you?" I asked. "And why the warning the other night?"

"I'm someone who knows what this town can really do to you," he said.

Still not saying who he was, he instead launched into a story about how the beach came to be part of Torrance.

From his account, and also from Macready's—and why would I even be surprised? —Torrance pilfered it. The area was part of a dispute between Torrance and Redondo, the next town south. Starting in the mid-'20s and continuing until the early '30s, Torrance gradually annexed a five-mile chunk that now makes up about a third of the city.

When the annexation, or the theft, was complete, there was still no path down to the beach. A path was finally built in 1931, part of a new members-only club that opened that year.

Sure enough, on a rapidly ascending path up from the beach rose a palatial structure that looked with its pointed arches like a boardwalk version of Xanadu, "the stately pleasure dome which Kubla Khan decreed," as my former English major girlfriend recited to me.

I looked around. The beach below was fairly wild with almost no stores or beachfront. I mentioned this to my guide.

"Yes," he said. "That's what makes it special. It hasn't been turned into a tourist trap, but if the wealthy developers from L.A. have their way this gorgeous open stretch will be made into 211 lots for a major housing development.

"Come back, Bill," he said as the collie took off, ambling down the beach and then frolicking in the water.

The dog returned and he patted her head—he told me it was a her.

He had long brown hair which grew wild. He rambled a bit ahead of me down the beach with the dog at his heels, and then let her go and we watched her race past us.

"It's nice to have this open beach where no one bothers you," he said.

I was interested and thought this might be relevant.

"So is the division into private lots going forward?" I asked.

"There is a competing project, much better for the city, of manicuring and trimming the brush behind us and building more stairways with lifeguard stations and a few small snack bars. The City of L.A.'s parks and recreation is also trying to rope off the area from developers, but it's not going very far because the city owns only about half of the lots in this area and they are divided up and not next to each other, so it's likely one day the place will be turned into private bungalows for the rich."

"How come you know so much about this?" I asked.

At first, he didn't want to tell me, but as we walked, he got more comfortable and finally related his Torrance tale of woe since everybody who wasn't a fine, upright citizen had one.

"My father tried to change this town and it cost him his life," was the way he started.

This was right up my alley so, since we were now away from RAT beach, I asked if we could sit, so I could hear the story with no interruptions.

Bill came back to us and licked his face as he began.

"My name's Sandy, and my father William Muller was once mayor of this town."

"That sounds more like something to profit from rather than something tragic," I said.

"You'd think so, but my father was a Socialist and the town powers that be hated him from day one."

"How was a socialist elected mayor of a town like Torrance?" I asked, stupefied.

I knew that there were some isolated towns in the U.S. where every once in a while this could happen. Once it had almost happened in L.A., but there was a convenient scandal and the candidate was defeated.

"This was before the mayor was elected directly. My father ran for the City Council many times and never won. But, in the Depression, he was elected to the council on a platform of reforming corruption and providing more city services. They then elected him mayor."

"That must have gone over well."

"The first thing he did was get rid of a corrupt police chief. He also proposed that Torrance remain part of the L.A. school system because he felt kids would get a better and more thorough education, and he campaigned for a town library. He was fiery and funny at the same time, a rousing orator."

"And how long did this last?"

"The more corrupt City Councilmen started recall elections immediately. The first one did not succeed, but about a year later, they were able to remove him from the mayor's office. They called him 'The Menace,' and accused him in their petition of a 'lack of dignity,' 'class prejudice' and 'behaving in such way that he could not serve the city efficiently.'"

"Was any of that true?"

At this point Bill came back to us and nudged Sandy, who patted him and rubbed his nose.

"Not as far as I can tell. It's just the way this town reacts to anyone trying to change anything."

"You said the town took his life."

Sandy got up, picked up a stick, and threw it down the beach with Bill in swift pursuit.

It was almost as if he did not want his father's namesake hearing this part of the story. He bowed his head and mumbled.

"My father, after all he'd done or tried to do for the town, ended up on a chicken farm just south of here in Lomita. He'd had enough. He tried to kill himself by running poison gas into his car and when that didn't work blew his brains out."

"I'm sorry. And is that why you warned me off the town the other night?"

"There's something else. Anyway, I decided I could not follow in his path. Those who control the town are too powerful and don't tolerate interference. I keep an eye on what they do but I don't get involved."

He was beginning to make sense. With that, he got up and started to amble down the beach.

He wasn't finished, though.

He turned, as Bill ran past him, and had another admonishment to make.

Where do I come up with these words? Crystal and I have to stop reading these novels.

"The power my father faced is far more powerful now," he said.

"Do you mean Williams?" I asked as he walked away.

"That man also has a son," he said, and that was it. He strode off down the beach after his dog, back to his work of plucking precious metals from the sand and quietly watching the ebb and flow of political life around him.

This was not what she wanted. Harry had pulled Crystal off of Frank Chase duty and put her back on Diane duty, but not as a budding real estate agent. Instead, he had her tailing Diane for a job that Harry was hired to do by her father.

Diane had given her an itinerary, asking her to join her when she would like. Crystal felt rotten using that against Diane. She didn't think this assignment was going anywhere, but a job was a job.

Diane was showing a house that morning on what looked like prime property on Normandie Avenue almost on the Torrance-Carson border. Crystal parked her worn out roadster, *a contraption*, she thought, *that looked almost as old as Harry's*, around the corner and waited for Diane and the potential buyer to come out.

She didn't have long to wait.

Diane was splendid today in yellow, tight blouse stretched over breasts that appeared to want to pop out of their loose corsetry. If that weren't enough, she was also wearing pink pants that clung so tight to her thighs and derriere that Crystal was afraid she might have trouble breathing.

However, it was not Diane that was having trouble. It was the client. He was smaller than her, looked in his gray suit to be a city official or another accountant, and he was fumbling behind her as she threw open the front door and they went out onto the porch.

She let him pat her butt as they came out. He tried to slide his hand into her pants, but she brushed it aside and instead offered him a contract which he took.

As he started to look it over, she pressed against him with those inviting breasts and he looked up and stopped his reading.

She backed up as he reached out for her, but she motioned for him to continue reading. At the same time, she made a sweeping motion with her arm, probably letting him know what an overall great deal this was.

As Williams had told Harry, she certainly was using sex to sell, *but,* Crystal thought, *who didn't?* That was what the Hollywood studios were about, selling their product through sex and totally aware that the screen kiss that seemed so chaste was actually just a substitute for full-on sex.

She's certainly got him eating out of her hand. In fact, at that moment, Diane brushed her hand against him and he took it and kissed it. *Okay, so she's got him literally eating out of her hand. What's so wrong with that? She's going to seal the deal.*

They walked back to their cars. The mousy little man waved to her. She said something to him, probably about an actual signing. He agreed and they parted.

So, what's next for Diane? Crystal thought as she followed two cars behind her, again feeling guilty for spying on her.

Oh, well, this makes sense. Diane had cruised around town and ended up at the Williams office. *She's going to see her boss to tell him the good news about another sale.*

Except that's not what happened.

Diane parked outside the office, down the street on the other side, where she could observe what went on but not be seen.

Crystal parked on Williams's side of the street not far away and across from Diane, realizing that she was perilously close to giving herself away, though she had no other choice if she was to find out what was going on.

A young man came out of Williams's office, closer in age to Crystal and

Diane than to the developer himself. Harry had shown her a photo of both Williamses which he had plucked from the local paper, and this one was at first a spittin' image of his father, except, as Harry had noticed, there was a nervousness about him that disturbed his natural good looks.

He approached Diane's car but barely acknowledged her, giving her a tense wave as he walked past.

He then got in his own car and both cars took off.

Crystal was now part of a caravan, a five-car outfit, which saw her, following two cars behind, tailing Williams's son Dean and Diane.

The convoy headed east out toward what Harry had described as "The Strip."

They arrived dead center in one of the seediest areas Crystal had seen— and she had seen some lowlife locales in her after-hours wanderings in her Hollywood gangster days.

They both parked and the bar they entered had a shingle outside that read "Last Ditch."

She knew she had to get at least a snatch of their conversation but she didn't know how.

She went inside and out of the corner of her eye saw Diane and Dean at a table partially obscured by the jukebox. They had chosen a spot that seemed to offer them the most privacy.

Crystal approached the bar. The bartender was friendly, and she decided to take a chance.

"What are you having?" He didn't seem particularly interested in her or, at that time of day, in anyone for that matter.

"I'd like a job," she said. "Could I have a tryout?"

There was only one other waitress in the place, which was practically deserted.

"We're not hiring, but you can have a go at it and we'll see how you do," he replied.

He pointed to the back, where she could change into the bar costume, which from what the other waitress was wearing consisted of a pink top, black skirt, black nylons and black heels.

She went into the back and changed. And when she reappeared, the bartender, who said his name was Jack Smith, smiled at how she looked in the costume and pointed to the couple by the jukebox.

She glanced at the table. Dean, out of sight of his father, was far friendlier now. She saw him put his hand on Diane's and watched Diane look down at it, smile and then gracefully remove it.

She approached to take their order, keeping her notepad in front of her face and turning to look at the bartender as if she were bored with the entire setup. Dean couldn't make out her face and Diane, for her part, was preoccupied and not interested.

Both gave their order. She turned her back to them and made to leave.

At that point she heard Diane say, "Let's get back to what we were talking about. There is something off about what happened to my father, and I think you know I'm looking into it. Will you help me?"

That was all she needed.

She put in the order, told the other waitress to deliver it when it came, and said she just realized she had an emergency at home. She went in the back, grabbed her clothes, and rushed out of the place in the waitress costume.

Wow, *that was close*, she thought. She was proud that her surveillance had succeeded and relieved that Diane had neither seen her nor that she seemed to be up to anything more nefarious than trying to trace her lineage.

Job well done, she said to herself. *We're making headway, and I hope Harry appreciates my progress on this case.*

21

I was about as low as I'd been. I was no closer to finding Sandra Chung's killer or killers. Rosa's family was about to lose their house, Esperanza was beside herself and I had really done nothing to help. I'd lost my own home and been forced to move to an even seedier location, further from my office.

To top it all off, I thought I was close to solving a murder and collecting on an oil well, and instead I had led the police to the woman who had hired me and who was now sitting in the jail of the incompetent Torrance police who wouldn't recognize a killer if he bit them in the face, or killed them.

The straw after the last straw was Sandy Muller's tale of woe about how Torrance had tortured his father to the point where he eventually did the job for them and offed himself.

I got in my car and thought I was driving blindly east and inland from the beach, though in one part of my mind I knew where I was going.

I parked my car on The Strip outside the Last Ditch, but that wasn't my destination.

The two men in the dark suits had promised a good time in Madame Thai's, and I was going to take them up on it.

A little voice inside me said this was a bad idea. There was Esperanza to think about, and the chance that maybe Crystal had come up with something useful on the Chung case. But once I was let into the place by a small but rotund Chinese doorman, those thoughts disappeared and I only wanted to forget my troubles and have a good time.

The place was dark and shadowy. But instead of the well-endowed waitresses wearing skimpy costumes who inhabited the bar across the street, the reason this place was so dim was to focus attention on a stage with a host of Chinese girls all wearing the same brightly colored one-piece pink bathing suit showing off ever more extravagant legs as they together crooned a suggestive number titled "Boys Will Be Girls and Girls Will Be Boys." As the number continued, the girls on stage were joined by a host of other girls dressed in male false tuxedos with canes and top hats. The two groups then embraced each other and kissed at the end of the number in a way that was beyond beguiling.

The packed house of white men, mostly around my age, were a little confused but nevertheless cheered the number lustily and were rewarded with both sets of girls descending into the audience, surrounding the men, who proceeded to rub their faces in the girls' chests. It was a Hollywood musical that then finished in an orgy.

I was planted at the bar, drinking my second scotch and water, and wanting to embrace oblivion as soon as it would come. One "male" and one "female" performer came up to me and started first kissing each other and then rubbing their soft, milky hands across my face. The girl in the bathing suit mussed my hair while the "gentleman," who had now unbuttoned the top buttons of "his" suit to reveal very substantial cleavage which seemed to be beckoning me, caressed my behind with one hand and started to move down toward my zipper with the other.

I was in heaven and ordered drinks for all three of us. I downed my third Scotch in one gulp, made sure they were drinking as well, and watched the same thing happening all around me.

Off to the side of the bar was a purple velour curtain, and I could see some of the men and the performers already disappearing behind it, no doubt to a series of bedrooms. I assumed that was what came next for my merry little trio.

Suddenly there was a commotion behind me, and I saw two hands with long fingernails painted with strawberry red lacquer on the shoulders of each of my companions, pushing them back and away from me.

I turned to see who was disturbing my fantasy, only to find in front of me an even more powerful one.

The woman with the long nails said two words to the other two in Chinese, and they quickly backed up and looked elsewhere for new customers in the bar.

Before me stood one of the most beautiful apparitions I had ever laid eyes on.

She was tall, taller than any of the other girls. She had gleaming black hair pulled back in a chignon and a face of the clearest glittering crystal. She was wearing a long dress clinging tightly to her thin body, featuring a slit down the side that allowed her to flash just a look at a most inviting creamy leg.

On the dress was a red embroidery pattern of a fire-breathing dragon. That should have told me all I needed to know, but in my state all I thought was, *What a nice kitty she has on her chest.*

She held out her hand, wanting me to take it and when I did, she formally introduced herself.

"I'm Madame Thai," she said.

I reached out to take her hand but instead she hoisted up her dress to reveal more of her silky flesh, and added, "But you can call me Madame Thigh."

She then grabbed my outstretched hand and ran it down her dress, leading it to caress her naked leg.

There was still enough of the detective left in me to be suspicious. Why did I rate this special treatment?

She guessed as much and answered my unspoken question.

"I run this place," she said. "And you look like some kind of cop. I pay a lot of money for protection to keep this joint open, but occasionally we get stray law enforcement in here and when that happens, I take care of them myself. We don't want any trouble."

"Oh, I won't be any trouble," I said, making sure my detective's badge was firmly planted in my pocket. If she found out I was just a private cop, the whole thing might blow up in my face and I might find myself out in the gutter.

I barely had time to gulp down a fourth scotch when she led me to the curtain, which she parted with one long fingernailed hand. She stepped behind the curtain and with the other hand invited me in.

A number of rooms stretched down a long corridor, but although many of them seemed occupied I could not hear what was going on inside.

She grabbed my hand and led me to the end of the hallway.

She threw open the door, revealing a large bedroom that, by the size of the door and the room, was probably double the width of the other rooms.

This must be the master—that is, her—bedroom.

An enormous bed inside with chiffon sheets lay smothered with what looked like hundreds of pillows. The dragon décor from her dress was taken up on the walls, with bright yellow and red creatures spewing a fiery breath.

In my state, all I could think was, *more kitties.*

I noticed the room was padded and I figured that was the case with all the rooms so that what went on in them stayed in them.

"Welcome to my home," she said, pushing me down on the bed and standing over me.

"And how do you come to run this place?" I asked, not wanting to break the spell but also overcome with curiosity.

By way of answer, she performed a striptease where, as she let loose pieces of her clothing, she also revealed parts of her story.

She unfastened what she said was her *cheongsam*, the tight-fitting dress, and as she unzipped it from the back started to speak.

"I came here as a poor peasant girl, smuggled in when there were almost no Chinese women allowed in the country," she said. She finished undoing her garment, dropped it to her knees and stood before me almost naked except for a black bra and black panties.

"That was twenty years ago when I was just a teen. I had to marry an old merchant who I met on the boat over in order to get through what they call Angel Island, but which is instead a devil's prison where they held our people."

She then reached up to take off her bra, and let that drop, revealing delicate subtle breasts with nipples standing straight up. Suddenly I was a lot less curious about her story.

"I tried to make it in the movie industry. They loved my looks, found me a perfect 'Oriental Doll,' but only offered me roles as maids and washerwomen. After a little while, I'd had enough of that, and realized it was never going to go any further."

At this, she reached delicately up to remove her black panties. What she showed off was shaven and trim, and as an added bonus she turned around to reveal an equally elegant behind which she wiggled slightly before turning around again.

"I started working on The Strip and found a wealthy patron who saw something in me and offered to bankroll me with this place. He would protect me, and my part was to find the girls and set up the show, which I also choreographed. So, you see, I did get to use my performance experience in the end."

She then approached me on the bed and climbed ever so delicately on top of me. I was beyond ready for her but she had a little more of her personal story to tell.

She rolled off to the side and continued teasing me, flitting her tongue down my body. For a brief moment my eyes started to wander. She saw I was inspecting the place and put both hands on my face and buried it in those soft breasts.

She remained quite talkative and as I was coming up for air, she told me that her most wonderful experience in life was going to the Hollywood Bowl to see Mayling Soong. I had no idea who that was and then she told me, pointing to a photo on the wall above the bed.

"She is Madame Chiang Kai-shek, who was here during the war raising funds for the war against the Japanese, the most elegant Chinese woman ever born."

She explained that the fundraiser was also a stage show that featured the Hollywood stars Ingrid Bergman, Barbara Stanwyck, Loretta Young, and, in the role of Madame Chiang's husband, the generalissimo, that sturdy Chinaman, Edward G. Robinson.

I had heard about that event. But I had also heard that the Madame my Madame admired could be ruthless, mean and savage, and that she considered herself royal-born. She didn't take kindly to those in any station below her and probably would never have allowed my companion for the evening anywhere near her. I decided not to bring that up.

She then played with the hairs on my chest, teasing me with her long nails and followed that up by climbing on me again. I was about to insert myself inside her when she again rolled off me and planted herself on all fours, motioning me to enter her from behind, almost as if she were directing a scene from one of the movies she was not allowed to star in.

She commanded me to raise my head straight up, saying she wanted all of me. She encouraged me to have my way with her as roughly as I would like and then buried her head in the pillows. I mounted her staring at the wall above the bed wondering why she was so precisely directing our scene together.

I soon stopped my wondering, and then it did not take long before I collapsed in a heap beside her.

Our business done, she quickly gathered her clothes and was about to scamper out of the room.

I asked her to stay for a moment. She sighed and pulled out a cigarette box sequestered in the drawer of a small table near the bed. She fit the cigarette into a holder, lit and smoked it, bewitchingly clasping it between those long red nails.

"Has there ever been a Mr. Thigh?" I asked as she puffed.

"Once," she said. "A Chinese boy who I saw off to the war six years ago. He finished the war against the Japanese and they sent him right back to China to fight against the Communists. He never came home."

With that she finished her cigarette, stomped it out and this time retreated from the room, telling me I could take as much time as I wanted, but that she had to be back to work.

"Thanks you," I said, as she closed the door. "It wath an enthanthing evething."

She smiled and left. I wasn't sure if she was smiling because she agreed or because, after four scotches, I was slurring my words.

I stretched out on the bed and took a look around the room. With its red velour padding, it seemed like something out of a twisted fairy tale or an opium dream. I fell asleep and was awakened, I don't know how long after, by a rapping on the door. The rotund Chinese bouncer entered and motioned for me to get dressed and be on my way.

When I stepped through the velour curtain and entered the bar, there was no sign of Madame Thai and the place was almost deserted. I must have been out for a while.

I was pretty hungover but proud that I had let off some steam in a way that didn't cost me anything and was extremely pleasurable.

In my partially dazed state, it took me a while to locate my car. When I did, I saw a pair of shadowy figures approach me. It was my old friends, the two men in black. I raised my fists, getting ready to confront them, but surprisingly they just pushed me aside into my car door.

I fell to the sidewalk and looked up at them, helpless, and getting ready for what might be the beating of my life.

It didn't come.

Instead, they threw a slew of photos at my feet.

I picked up one of them, and indeed it was me standing straight up naked in the room with Madame Thai's face concealed in the pillows but with mine on full display. I thought I might have seen the pop of a flash in the bedroom but I was too drunk on scotch and Madame Thai to take much notice of it at the time.

"Get out of Torrance and stay out," the little man said. "Or these photos are going to your girlfriend, your clients and to the local newspaper. Wise up or you'll never work again either in this town or anywhere."

They had a good laugh and walked off, leaving me in a heap surrounded by the jaded memories of what I thought was a harmless evening of fun.

22

Wow, does my heart hurt. That was my thought the next morning as I stumbled into the office. What was supposed to be a night of joy and merriment to take my mind off my troubles instead ended up making them worse.

When I got there, Crystal was in a good mood. I walked past her outer office not even nodding at her but noticing she was typing up a report which she shortly came in and put on my desk. She titled it "Dean and Diane."

"Go away," I said. "I don't want any. I already gave."

"Yeah," she said. "You didn't give at the office. I know you and you're in one of your deep dark moods which usually means that somehow you screwed up. What gives?"

"Nothing gives," I said. "The cases just aren't going well and I'm having no luck figuring them out. Just let me alone."

At that she turned, gave me a suspicious "Huh?" and went back to her desk.

A short while later she poked her head in. She was decked out today in business attire, but in Crystal style. She wore a gray top and gray pants, but she had loosened the top to let, I was guessing, prospective clients get a look at her cleavage. I assumed she was going to be back on Diane duty on the real estate beat.

"Look," she said. "It would be better if you tell me what you've done that you seem to be so down about. I might even be able to help you."

"You think you can help with these?" I said, following her back out to her office and dumping the photos on her desk.

"Oh, my god," she said, leafing through them. "You are a stallion. Or, well, you're an old stallion, maybe one almost ready to be put out to pasture."

"Very funny," I replied, though I did grunt by way of almost laughing.

I told her what had happened and what the two men had said. She was concerned but also angry.

"You're putting our business in jeopardy," she said. "I've seen you like this before and as far as I can tell there is only one way of pulling you out of it."

Uh, oh, I knew where this was going.

"It's time for you to get your head shrunk and maybe another part of your anatomy as well, though nature may already be taking care of that."

I'd had enough of her jokes. My partner rubbing salt in the wound was not helping, but I had to admit she was probably right.

I was overwhelmed and needed help and I also needed to straighten myself out.

"Alright," I said. "I'll go.

I grabbed my hat and was pushing our office door closed when she stuck her foot in the door and followed me into the corridor.

"Oh, no," she said. "You're not doing this alone. I'm coming with. This is not only your personal life. It's both our incomes and I want to hear what your advisor says."

"I don't even know if she'll see me if I drop in unannounced," I said, pushing her back toward the office. "You're probably wasting your time."

"It's our time. You gotta get right and we gotta continue the case. I'm not giving up on finding Sandra Chung's killers. We need to try to collect on the future oil well and you need to report back to Williams about his sales-woman and his son. We're going together."

I still had a headache, but my mind was clearing enough so that I could drive from our office downtown to the penthouse office on Wilshire near Western.

As we were going up the elevator, I was getting more and more nervous. I didn't want to talk about what had happened at The Strip and I especially didn't want Crystal hearing it, but some part of me knew that the only way out of this was to tell the truth and that it wouldn't hurt to have my part-ner—who from the way she was looking after me today was probably also my friend—in on it.

The door to the suite was open and we went in to find an empty waiting room. A diploma mounted on the wall read "Dr. Sarah Kellman, Doctorate in Psychoanalysis, University of Vienna."

The good doctor indeed was not just known for her credentials, having studied for a time under Dr. Freud, or so she said, but also for her practice in Tinseltown where she had a reputation as a therapist to the stars.

I had first encountered her when I was babysitting one of her biggest clients. She had helped me personally and also helped on the case. I returned the favor when she was in the process of being burgled by two FBI agents out to ransack her files. I scared them away, and for her part she offered to see me now and then when I needed her. She was, I thought, eternally grateful. But that was not the case.

After about ten minutes in the waiting room, decorated with paintings of what looked to me like garish, distorted creatures, buildings and creepy vines, the door opened, and a man I recognized from my first case with the actor came out. He looked disheveled, like he had been out of work. I knew that was the case with a good number of Hollywood writers who had been affected by the blacklist.

Dr. Kellman touched the arm of the bent-over man, and I heard her say, "This will get better and you'll get your money eventually, I'm sure."

He thanked her and exited.

She saw me, and a tired look came over her face.

"What is it, Mr. Palmer?" she said, "and who is this?"

"I'm his better half," Crystal piped up. "I'm his partner at work. I try to keep him out of trouble, but it's a full-time job and I'm exhausted."

"Come in, you two," she said, ushering us out of the waiting room and into her office which was covered with more of the garbled shapes, many of them ablaze with color.

I was staring at them, and she noticed.

"The ones in the outer office are from Berlin and Vienna before the war. The ones in here I did myself." She was quite proud as she pointed them out.

"They're beautiful," Crystal said. "I love them."

At that Dr. Kellman brightened.

"They're basically how I feel," I said, staring at one of a tall man on the street stretched to oblivion with two dancing girls lifting up their skirts on either side of him.

"It's a crooked and uneven world I'm depicting," she said.

"I do have a little time for you today, Mr. Palmer, but I would like to ask, at the request of the client who you just saw, if you would help him. He's a writer who used what they now call a front, a blind, someone whose name he could attach to his script because he cannot use his own. The front, though, is refusing to pay him."

"Have him come over," I said, dropping my card on her desk. "I'll see what I can do."

"It won't be for a while. He's trying to work through his contacts with the studio first."

I was relieved. I hardly needed more cases to screw up.

"So, what seems to be the problem?"

Unknown to me, Crystal had brought the photos, which she dumped on Kellman's desk.

"Mr. Palmer, you have gotten yourself in a mess this time. Tell me about it."

I related what had happened at Madame Thai's, my stalled progress on the Sandra Chung case, losing my home, such as it was, the bungled case with the two husbands, and my inability to halt the city in its drive to take the house of Esperanza's friend.

"Okay, Mr. Palmer," she said. "Some of these forces are bigger than you are and you may not be able to stop them."

That wasn't very encouraging.

"What we can do, though, is get a little more clarity on how you might be shooting yourself in the foot and helping these forces along."

Ouch, that hurt. To add insult to injury, Crystal, sitting beside me, was nodding in agreement.

"First, what you did yesterday could nullify your work on all of these cases as well as ending your relationship with Esperanza, who I seem to remember last time you came here you cheated on."

"He can be real scum, alright," Crystal said. "And he's put our business in jeopardy too."

Like I needed that. I was about to ask her to leave when Dr. Kellman told her that since she was directly involved and this was not an official visit she could stay.

Kellman asked about my relationship with Esperanza, and I told her about refusing her offer of sharing her home and instead moving back into a hotel.

At this point she had something to say.

"It's pretty clear," she said. "Your actions speak louder than words and, in many ways, you are what you do.

"You're terrified of any kind of commitment, not only to your girlfriend, so you go out carousing after she already took you back once, but also even to a stable place to live."

Not much I could say to that, and she wasn't finished.

"It's amazing you have any female friends at all," she said, and Crystal nodded.

"Something really interfered with your ability to form stable relationships, and since this works itself out in both using women by attacking the ones you might love and being vulnerable to ones that use you, I have to think this goes back to your mother."

We had already been through that, how she deserted me both in bringing an untold number of men into the house after my father left and then in dying from alcohol poisoning.

An image popped into my mind and I described it to her.

"I'm in a cave that is sometimes a haunted castle, and a witch appears rubbing a candy cane and then disappears to be replaced by a growling beast. It's a recurring dream."

"I do have an idea about the dream," she said. "The cave is the isolation you were in as a child which was maybe described to you by your mother as a castle. The witch rubbing the candy cane does indicate there is some kind of physical molestation going on in the cave and the castle. The beast is the actual threat of your mother's deterioration as she plunged into obscurity. I think there may be actual memories attached to this dream, underneath it."

"I still don't understand," I said.

"Was there ever a time where, unable to find a man for the night, your mother reached out to you?"

At that I felt myself growing woozy and almost blanked out.

Dr. Kellman could see I had had enough.

"I don't think we can go any further with this today, but I can say this, or rather repeat it. The combination of alcohol and sex is dangerous for you. And this is not the first time."

I remembered how I felt when I was on my way to The Strip.

"It's almost like, before I drink, I'm already drunk thinking about having sex," I said.

"Yes," she replied, "they're twin addictions, and when you combine them, you're finished."

"What do I do about it?" I said, at which point Crystal threw up her hands and yelled, "Stop drinking and stop sleeping with whoever comes down the pike."

Dr. Kellman nodded, and we continued with what was beginning to seem like marriage counseling.

"I'll give you another incentive to act on this. This will be our last free session. My debt to you is paid, and if you need further help and do not stop this behavior, I will have to charge you."

That was a shock.

"And go back to work. Once you get started again, nothing is as hopeless as it seems, and you may be able to help some of these people who need you including your partner, who is sitting next to you, seems to be a friend, and wants you to fly right so you two can figure out your business."

"What about the photos? I might be finished."

"If you just stay away from liquor and, as you would put it, 'dames,' you'll be alright and you'll figure out what to do about the photos. Trust me."

That was a lot to think about, but since we were here, I had always found Kellman helpful on whatever case I was working. I told her about Williams, the Klan, the Tong; and Crystal told her about Diane's seductiveness, which she said she was afraid might lead her into trouble either with her boss's son or with some overly aggressive client.

Dr. Kellman ran a hand through her tightly trimmed gray hair and addressed Crystal.

"I can't say for sure, but any woman who is that wild and puts herself in that much danger every day has something in their past that is driving that behavior. If you want to find out her secret, you'd best find out what that is."

Crystal seemed to have an inkling of what lay underneath Dr. Kellman's words and she blushed.

"Her secret might be a little too close to home," she said.

The good doctor nodded and may have had something more to say to Crystal, but allowed as her time was up, and her next patient was probably in the waiting room.

As we exited, she said to both of us, "Be careful, you two. You're playing with the big boys now. The people you're dealing with are powerful and violent, and you both need to keep your wits about you."

To me she said, "At least while you're on this case, no more drinking and no more 'dinking.'"

She laughed at her little joke. Crystal thought it was funny also.

I had had enough humor for one day, but I did have one more question.

"What do I do about Esperanza? Do I tell her what happened?"

"Best thing you can do right now is help her friend. Get to work and get back on the case. Eventually, though, I think you're going to have to tell her, otherwise the relationship is built on dishonesty and that's a terrible foundation."

That was a lot for both me and Crystal to take in. Once we'd left the doctor's office, I took my partner to lunch. Over two Reuben sandwiches with the corned beef piled high and topped off with melted cheese, we stared at each other, happy to be able to just pause for a bit and let the doctor's words sink in.

23

I didn't know what to do about the photos yet, but I was going to trust Kellman and believe I'd figure it out. An easy place for me to pick up was to go back to Williams and tell him what Crystal and I had discovered about his son and what Crystal had found out about Dean and Diane.

The next day, as I cruised south toward Torrance, I took the longer "scenic" route through Carson, and it proved to be educational. A development was being built there at what was called Dominguez Hills. Out in front of it was a group of what looked like angry Negro men and women with signs saying the project was nothing but a new wave of segregation. The group had buttons that read CORE, and I remembered seeing one of those in Charlotta Bass's newspaper office.

I parked and started a conversation with one of the picketers, an older man with a gray beard, dressed in a well-worn but pressed suit and holding himself in a very dignified manner. He was ready to talk my ear off and happy I stopped by.

"It's places like this in the suburbs here in Carson and next door in Torrance that are the new centers of segregation," he said. His sign read, "Black and White Together," and the protest, though mostly made up of Negroes, I now noticed had some white people as well.

One of them, an older woman in a brown flannel men's work shirt, pulled me aside.

"All we're getting here is homes for the rich or white middle class. Where are the developments for ordinary workers? That's the battle in this city right now. The mayor wants to go ahead with building affordable apartments but the city fathers led by the *L.A. Times* are so dead set against it. They're holding a recall election to get him out of office and stop the building," she explained, then frantically brandished her sign which read "Affordable Integrated Housing For All."

They were a small but hardy band, and I was glad I stopped to get their point of view.

I continued on into Torrance and parked in front of the Williams office.

I told the perky redhead in the outer office that I had some findings to report.

She said, "Good luck," and motioned for me to go back.

I found Williams in the back office, beside himself, as they say, almost literally.

This was practically a different man from the brash, confident builder I had met not so long ago, but he still seemed to be always in motion.

As I entered the office he was pacing and talking to himself.

"Come in, Palmer. What fresh hell have you for me?"

Before I could answer, he grabbed photos of his latest houses off his desk and threw them at me.

"I try to do this community a favor, building homes for everyone in what we're calling 'the only city in Southern California to have solved the smog problem' with acres of open beaches and beautiful sea breezes blowing in from the bay.

"I'm trying to turn a polluted oil town into a brand new, sparkling bedroom community, and what do I get for it, protestors claiming we're doing nothing but building segregated housing next to oil derricks and industrial waste. They got me coming and going."

"I know you're trying to clean up the town," I said, "but maybe it's too much to ask."

He then went over to two models on a table next to his desk. He pointed at the first.

"This is what I'm building in Compton. It's beautifully constructed single-family apartments for Negroes and whites in a perfectly integrated development. I'm afraid those protestors next door in Dominguez Hills will show up here in Torrance next, and I'll be accused of being a racist.

"Would I be building this if I was a racist?"

"I don't think anyone's calling you a racist. Opportunist maybe," I answered.

Oddly, he brightened at that.

"That's the business," he said. "Right now, a lot of this land is worthless, just being filled with what are increasingly abandoned oil derricks and a few companies that are probably polluting the area by dumping their waste.

"My vision is that we can turn this fallow land into acres and acres of homes at a modest price." He then pointed at the second model, the larger one, which was apparently the Torrance of the future, rows and rows of single-family homes.

"My backers and I are buying up lots here like crazy on the idea that the difference between what the land is worth now and what it can be worth once we build on it will not only shelter a good number of workers but will, let's face it, provide a big profit margin for us. As they say in this business, 'location, location, location.'"

I didn't want to tarnish his dream, but given what I had encountered in Bunker Hill, the three communities in East L.A., and what I had been told about Santa Monica by my Negro friend at The Strip, "location, location, location" might also translate to "looting, looting, looting."

I let Williams ramble. As he did, his confidence returned, and I could see the old go-getter back in the room as he swept his hair off his face and straightened up in a gesture that helped him regain his composure.

He decided to tell me about his lineage.

It turns out his grandfather was in "real estate" also, in a way.

He had come from Germany—the original family name was Wilhelm— and was proud to say he arrived in New York the same year as the Statue of Liberty. Williams puffed up at that. Apparently, he associated freedom with the ability to build homes and make a profit off of them. Not freedom to assemble or protest, but freedom to assemble prefabricated homes.

Things didn't go well for grandpa in New York, so he went West and belatedly joined the California Gold Rush, not as an honest miner, but as a buyer of saloons on land that Williams boasted was up for grabs, which I took to mean, disputed or, like Torrance's beach, "appropriated." The looser interpretation is "stolen."

The saloons, the grandson said, offered liquor and women to those who had struck paydirt or who hadn't hit anything and needed to drown their sorrows.

"He was smart enough," Williams said, "that rather than panning for gold, which had a low rate of return, he mined the miners."

He was telling me the original family fortune was made running bordellos and seemed to be boasting about it.

"What happened when the law came in and the saloons were cleaned up?" I asked.

"He would just move on to the next town and let it take care of itself," he answered.

Which meant, I guess, that the town went belly up and granddad snuck out in the middle of the night with the profits.

The originator of the family fortune died a very old man in the Spanish flu epidemic after World War I, leaving as his heir Williams's father, who 20 years ago had also "scored big" by buying up properties cheaply in the first year of the Great Depression, evicting tenants, and then raising the prices on the mortgages of the homes he bought for pennies.

"He was very enterprising," Williams said, "but not the nicest person in the world and he also died suddenly, mowed down in the street, victim of a hit and run."

"There wasn't much money left from those enterprises, but I and my backers are carrying on the family legacy here in Torrance while also trying to right the wrongs of my family. I'm a builder with integrity and I'm going to be around for a long time."

One building in his model stood taller than the rest. That was his crowning achievement, a 14-story combination office building/apartment complex with his own penthouse suite overlooking the city that he had built below.

As he said this, he strode across the room from the scale models back to his desk and seemed to gain more confidence with each purposeful step.

His old gumption had returned, and this time I thought that gumption meant his ability to carry on no matter what the challenge, or how dishonest the scheme. In his family history, gumption and sleaze were bedfellows.

I wanted to throw a monkey wrench into his plans and see how he would react.

"But who will you attract in Torrance? Isn't it just white housing," I challenged. "And doesn't that make the most money and allow you to charge the most for the houses?"

"Do you know," he said, oblivious to my charge, "that this country's first president, George Washington, was also one of its largest landowners? I'm continuing in that tradition, building, not places of privilege but places of happiness.

He was comparing himself to the father of the country, who I remembered was also a slaveholder. Hmm, maybe the comparison was apt.

"There is nothing wrong with private property if the houses are built right and offered for a decent price," he said. Suddenly, I had become an irritant.

"So, tell me," he said, now sitting at his desk and fixing me with a pointed stare, "what is going on with Diane? That is what I'm paying you for, Mr. Palmer, right?"

"Yes, and there may be a problem, not with a client but with your son."

I told him about their liaison at Last Ditch and about his son's talking to the two men in the dark suits just before they put a hurt on me.

"I never knew what to do with that boy," he said. "He drinks too much. He hangs out with the wrong people and he's liable to get into trouble. He was always his mother's favorite and I never really took to him. He's spoiled, loose, and thinks the world owes him a favor. I really don't want him near Diane. She's too sweet a girl."

I had neglected to tell him what Crystal overheard the two of them talking about. When I let that drop, he pounded his fist on the desk. First time I really saw him lose his composure. His face reddened, and for a moment the confidence was gone, replaced by stark raving anger.

"Diane's father and mother died in a car crash on Murder Mile. It's a stretch of the highway that's the automobile equivalent of The Strip, a winding, curvy road that has claimed many drivers. Her father lost control of the car on one of those curves, crashed into another vehicle and went over the guardrails.

"If my son is pushing her or helping her 'look into it,' it will only cause her more pain."

Just as suddenly, the heatwave cooled. He calmed down, became a bit more cautious, sat back in his chair and asked in a slightly more nervous way, "Is she having an affair with anyone, a client or my son?"

"Not that we know, though your son may be trying to start something."

"I'll take care of that. She's too fragile and he's too crazy. That combination would be very combustible."

Now I needed to press.

"What about his talking to the two men in black? They've shown up all over town and are very suspicious characters. He seemed to be giving orders to them in the bar on The Strip, and shortly afterwards they corralled me."

"He always wants to take the easy way out. I'm not sure, but he may not be above using 'muscle' to get what he wants. I'll talk to him, meanwhile you continue to look out for Diane."

He told me I was doing a good job, extended my contract, which was alright by me, and as I was leaving went back to the scale model on the table opposite his desk. It was the Torrance of the future alright and he was back to building it, turning a stretch of nowhere, not much more than a factory and oil well eyesore, into a prosperous town of tomorrow.

I might not agree with his vision, but he certainly had one and was proceeding with it at all costs. There wasn't much I could do about it if he didn't hurt anybody in the process.

24

I was persona non wanta in Torrance at the moment despite Williams keeping me on the case, so it was with some relief that I realized we had not picked up on a whole line of inquiry that could possibly help solve the Sandra Chung murder, for that was what I was now firmly convinced it was.

Lyn had found the acid in the car where she was imprisoned by the two Tong members. I had to know more about them and their possible motives for setting the fire.

I didn't know a whole lot of people in Chinatown, but there was one fairly knowledgeable person I could turn to who I hoped would help me.

I hadn't seen Lyn for a while and didn't know what she was up to, but the memory of our encounter with the Tong was fresh in my mind. More relevant today, though, was that the reason for the Tong's enmity was Lyn's support of her grandfather, who seemed to pose a threat to them and who might know more about why they might want to harm his daughter.

First, I had to find him. I went back again to the maze of streets located off the center of Chinatown and hoped I was on the right one. I found the building Lyn had entered as a ruse to throw off her trackers and instead approached the building next door.

There were obviously two Chinatowns. The one that Lyn had traveled on the day I tailed her was the wide open, airy city full of stores and markets. The other, where I found myself today, looked much older. Some of the buildings next door to the one I entered were left over from another time, wooden hovels, jammed close together with either shuttered windows or no windows at all.

I noticed again the old men outside the building on their way to the tiny park where they had helped shelter Lyn and me from the Tong. Begging in front of the building was a woman who, though getting on in years, still had on her face the remnants of a once beautiful appearance. She was in tattered clothes. and the old men dropped coins into her open bowl.

She tried to grab onto me as I stepped past her and started to offer herself to me. She pulled her tattered shirt down to show her naked shoulders. Her smile could not conceal the fact that she did not have all of her teeth.

I thought of Madame Thai's girls and wondered if this was how they ended up. That notion certainly cast a darker pale over what I had at first perceived as a little bit of paradise on earth.

I dropped a few coins in her bowl, strode past her and into the building next to where she had taken up residence.

The door to the room halfway down a thin, drab corridor was closed. I rapped on it, and in a moment a frail man with glasses came to the door and opened it just a crack, suspicious at who could have located him in his hiding place.

I showed him my detective's badge and explained that I was a friend of Lyn's looking into the murder of her mother and that I might have a lead on who did it. At this, instead of blanching, he brightened.

He decided to trust me and beckoned me inside.

The small studio was covered with a bookshelf that took up about a quarter of the entire place, with, as I had noticed before, newspapers piled high on a makeshift table and then spilling onto the floor. The newspapers were both Chinese and American and, apparently, he read avidly in both languages.

He went to the tiny kitchen to make tea and, when he was gone, I noticed a book on the table, whose open page was an English account of the Tong and their history in the U.S.

His name was Ahn Ti, though he said I could call him Richard, an English name he had adopted to make it easier to speak with non-Chinese.

I told him about Lyn's encounter with the Tong and her finding the acid which could have been used to trigger the fire.

She had already been there, it seemed, and related her story, so, as he pointed to the book, he explained that I had arrived at a good time because he was looking into this angle himself.

He spoke English fluently and was obviously a man both highly intelligent and also reserved in his judgments and opinions. He spoke with the kind of clarity and forthrightness that come from a lifetime of thinking, saying, and writing the truth.

I told him I had a bit of trouble finding his place because of the winding streets.

He bowed and responded demurely.

"Streets in Chinese towns are always crooked because of the old belief that evil spirits only travel in a straight line," he said.

Then he seemed apologetic about this line of reasoning.

"You may think this is primitive but the old customs are important. You came here wondering about the Tong, but to understand them you must understand something of the history of this place."

He then recounted a learned and studious chronicle of the Chinese in Los Angeles.

"The Chinese gathered and first lived as a group not because they wanted to be isolated but because they needed protection."

The original Chinatown, he explained, was founded in the last century when a street brawl between rival Tong gangs resulted in the gang's exchanging gunfire with a police officer caught in the crossfire. In response, white mobs stormed through the streets torturing, shooting, lynching, and finally burning 18 Chinese.

After that, he said, the community moved closer, bunched together in the area that is now Union Station. From that point, and following two attempts to burn down shops, when Chinese ventured outside of Chinatown, they wore police whistles to warn that danger from white mobs was near.

"The Chinese were enlisted in this country to build the railroads, dangerous work on which many died, especially the crucial stretch in the Sierra Nevada mountains. The Irish refused this perilous work, and after the Civil War Negroes, now freed slaves, could no longer be forced to participate."

He pointed to a photo on his wall of the driving of the silver spike at the meeting of the two railroad companies.

"Not a single Chinese worker allowed in that photo though it was largely they who did the work," he said.

He then talked about the history of discrimination in official acts restricting entry to only men and merchant families in the last century, and just 25 years ago an act forbidding Chinese women from entering at all.

"Americans didn't have to kill Chinese. The Exclusion Act assured none would be born."

He talked about the way that these official acts encouraged vigilante treatment of Chinese and gave rise to a litany of derogatory sayings.

"Not a Chinaman's chance in hell," which I remembered my mother used to say, came from the driving of the Chinese out of the California gold fields in the 1850s, so that their luck would never "pan out."

The famous Chinese laundry saying "No tickee, no washee" was, he explained, actually a phrase that struck fear into the heart of the Chinese owner of the business whom customers sometimes tried to cheat by claiming they had lost the ticket, which could result in violence to the laundry owner.

Even supposed reformers participated in this barbarity.

"The socialist Jack London coined the phrase 'Yellow Peril,' and Jacob Riis, who called attention to the problem of slums in America, wrote that the Chinese were not a 'desirable population,' and one which served 'no useful purpose here.'"

He collected these sayings and pointed to a sign on his wall which read "NEITHER CHINESE NOR DOGS ALLOWED."

I remembered watching a film about 15 years ago called *The Bowery,* where a white boy starts a fire in a Chinese building. While the Chinese inhabitants are burning, the Irish and Italian fire brigades, instead of putting out the fire, brawl among themselves. I recalled people in the audience around me laughing outrageously and I noticed a lone Chinese spectator cowering in his seat.

I was fascinated but not sure how this history was getting me closer to finding Sandra's killers.

Ahn was a man of infinite patience, though, and not to be hurried.

"To understand the Tong," he said, "you must understand how this Chinatown came to be."

He then launched into another history. This one struck me as oddly familiar, again a story of a people being removed from their land and homes in the name of "progress."

I knew the broad outline of it but not the specifics.

The original Chinatown was settled on land that's now Union Station. In the early '30s, just when I was coming onto the force, as Ahn explained it, the publisher of the Los Angeles Times, Harry Chandler, wanted a monumental train station to accommodate his new city and he wanted it near the *Times* building. He figured out a way of partially financing the construction based on selling the old *Times* building for over a million dollars more than it was worth, swindling the city out of the money which could then be used to help build the station which others opposed.

There were those Chandlers again at the heart of a swindle and the removal of a people from their land.

The Chinese then had to move. The first scheme was to build what was called China City, near the train station. This new movieland China, designed to look like the sets of a Hollywood version of Chinatown, was engineered by a Los Angeles socialite famous for designing Olvera Street, right opposite the train station, a kind of movieland Mexican site built in part by prison labor provided by the L.A. police chief. The sets from the film about China, *The Good Earth*, were even used to construct this Far East Tinseltown.

The shoddy construction resulted in two major fires. China City burned down, leaving the current site centered around North Broadway, a "cleaned up" Chinatown designed to look like Peking's Forbidden City. Supposedly shorn of gambling and vice, it looked something like what he said are now being designed by architects and labeled as shopping malls, though this one was to be open-air.

"However, as you can see, the bright shining exterior on Broadway is not matched by the poverty surrounding it, and the presence of forces like the Tong linger."

"How do you know all of this?" I blurted out.

At that he pointed to a framed newspaper front page hanging on his wall.

"That was my paper, before it ran out of subscribers a year ago. Actually, it was closed down by a vicious campaign against it in part by the merchants and their Tong enforcers because it was critical of Chiang Kai-shek and his Nationalist Party.

"In China I worked as a copyboy on the staff of the first paper founded by Sun Yat-Sen. I was the son of a merchant and was allowed to enter the U.S., where I started working on newspapers. Our L.A. Chinatown had, like its San Francisco counterpart, almost 35 newspapers, the most of any area in the country."

"I was a bit more critical of China's leader in the 1940s, which was okay with the government here until the 1949 Revolution and the current war of the U.S. with China in Korea. Just before that happened, the Tong came in and smashed my printing press and destroyed my ability to put out the paper. They're afraid I may be about to launch a new paper and that's why they're trying to track me down."

"And what were you critical of?"

At this he smiled. "So many things."

Generally, from what he related, his anger at the government currently sheltered on the island the Portuguese named Formosa, but which the inhabitants called Taiwan, increased as he became convinced Chiang and his people were more interested in fighting Mao Tse Tung's Revolutionary army than fighting the Japanese invader. He cited a bloody suppression of workers in Shanghai in the late 1920s in Chiang's alliance with large landowners and foreign bankers, his referring to Mao's army as "bandits," and his bombing of dikes on the Yellow River supposedly to stop the Japanese but which actually destroyed thousands of villages and towns.

Ahn claimed Chiang's ruthlessness had continued in the present with his imposition of martial law on "his" island, where amidst the suppression of all political opposition he plotted the return to his "lost domain" on the mainland.

I couldn't resist. I remembered Madame Thai speaking glowingly of Madame Chiang Kai-shek and I had to ask what he thought about her.

He was quick to reply.

"She's a power grabber, hard, shallow, and selfish, who when she was in this country was headquartered in the White House under the code name "Snow White," living like a princess and being tended to every day by hairdressers and beauticians."

"And what do you think of Mao's Revolution?" I asked.

"You better be careful there," he said. "When the Revolution succeeded, the U.S. got very scared, and the merchants here, always conservative, ran for cover and backed the Nationalist government.

"When they closed my paper, at first, I hid out and started drinking. That's why my daughter didn't want to have anything to do with me. But when Lyn, who was always interested in newspapers and politics, came around, I revived. I'm careful and sneak around but I go to the library every day and do my research, hoping it will help someone. I don't support the Revolution, as Lyn does, but I recognize that the former government was evil and corrupt."

I wasn't sure how any of this was helping me but then he came to the point.

"You want to know about the Tong. They are the enforcers for the town merchant and power structure. They still run the very profitable gambling and prostitution syndicates and they are fearful of losing their power as more and more people want to leave Chinatown.

"I can't tell you too much more but I can show you."

I didn't know what he had in mind but I was up for anything.

He got up and put on a worn and faded gray suit jacket that matched his pants.

"C'mon," he said. "Let's go."

With that he was out the door, which he didn't lock, with me trailing behind him. He seemed to be energized by our adventure, and I thought he may have been waiting a while now for an audience where he could turn over his research. The fact that I was interested in finding his daughter's killer was a big bonus, and I guess he felt it worth risk of being caught by his political enemies.

He led me down a maze of tightly interconnected streets until we came to a run-down building which nevertheless had a lot of activity outside it. Men in black shirts or more traditional long one-piece garments were coming and going from the entrance. We observed it from a distance, and he then led me to a building close by where we could peer around the corner and observe the goings-on.

"The Tong," he said, "were once guarantors of the social order, pledged to support the merchants while being allowed to control the illegal institutions. The merchants no longer have so much need for them, so the Tong have now descended into mainly just managing gang activity."

He was always the teacher and here grateful for the opportunity to take me, his pupil, out of his classroom to learn firsthand.

"This is the one of their gambling parlors."

"Could they have set fire to Sandra's house?" I asked as I took another peek around the corner of the building.

He started to answer but I put a hand on his shoulder to stop him because of what I had just seen.

The two Tong members, whom Lyn and I had encountered and who had the acid in their car, were approaching the building, greeted by two or three of those stationed in front.

That is not what caught my attention, though.

They were carrying a bundle wrapped in a black blanket. Could be some kind of Chinese vase they had lifted.

When they stopped to talk to the guardians in the front of the building, the bundle started to move. Whoever it was now was thrashing about and reaching to pull the blanket off their head.

"Let me go, get me out of here," the figure screamed.

Before they fit the blanket roughly back over the figure's head and hauled it inside, I knew who it was. It was not just seeing her face. That rambunctious teen was the only person I knew who would scream at her Chinese captors in English and expect them to obey her.

I had to figure out how to get Lyn out of there.

25

Meeting Harry's therapist had shaken Crystal up, as had this whole case. Dr. Kellman had urged Crystal to investigate Diane's past, as had Harry, who said that when he visited the developer Williams, he too wanted to know why she was so keen to find out if there was a mysterious circumstance around her parents' death.

That all meant she had free rein to pursue Diane. That was just fine with Crystal, who found Diane's lifestyle attractive. She seemed to be making lots of money and enjoying herself.

What's the harm if she uses a little seduction? That's what feminine wiles are for, she thought.

Diane said she was happy that Crystal called saying she wanted to continue to trail her and learn from her. Diane had an extra special treat today, she told Crystal. She was going to L.A. to attend a real estate convention, and the guest speaker, a famous and rich L.A. realtor, was going to talk about how to speak to clients "in the current atmosphere."

The talk was taking place downtown in the Bradbury Building. Diane wanted Crystal to meet her in the lobby.

Knowing that if she ever did want to make a transition into Diane's field, this would be an excellent place to make contacts, Crystal dressed in a tight red chiffon number that she purposely pulled down to reveal as much cleavage as possible. The dress also clung tight to her rear. She twirled in front of the mirror and liked what she saw both front and back.

This should make those realtors crumble.

When she got to the lobby, she was stunned to see that Diane had outdone her. Her "mentor" had a less dressed-up but sexier look. She sported a tight red sweater with what looked like a push-up bra underneath, allowing the men in the room to contemplate what lay beneath. She let her long blonde hair fall loosely on her shoulders, cascading down her back and almost touching the black pants clinging to her hips for dear life.

Diane preferred to walk up the stairs to the atrium at the top of the building where the conference was taking place. The two women passed a number of men, happy to see that their outfits were working, because they got a host of "Hello's" and "Nice to see you's."

They created quite a stir walking into the room and sat near the front so that again everyone could get a look at them.

"This is going to be good," Diane said. "This guy sells about a house a week and he's building a home in Beverly Hills. He's at the top of his profession. You're going to learn a lot."

The lights in the hall dimmed, and a giant spotlight came up on the stage.

The speaker entered over a song that had been a hit that year, though it was around for a long time, "I Can Dream, Can't I?"

Probably in his late 30s, in white suit and carefully slicked-back black hair, the speaker bounded on stage seemingly wanting to impress the audience with his energy.

Introducing himself as Teddy Regal, he launched first into what Crystal believed was a standard speech that she'd already heard from Diane about the "missionary" duties of a real estate agent.

Then he got down to brass tacks, his real reason for coming. Crystal noticed several of the men—in an audience with only a few women—perking up.

He wanted to talk about how to sell homes in the "current climate," which to him meant increased pressure to integrate neighborhoods.

"The problem," he said, "is not that Negroes want to live in a better neighborhood."

At this Crystal sighed with relief, since she had already viewed Torrance prejudice firsthand at the home of the first wife Harry had sent her to investigate.

But then her hopes were dashed.

"The problem," Regal said, "is selfish neighbors who want to sell for a high price."

He went on to argue that it's these "traitorous" neighbors who are placing their own short-term material gain over the good of the neighborhood.

"You've got to convince your clients to look out for their neighbors and not to sell to a non-Caucasian. Otherwise, the entire property value of the area will go down and you will lose money in the end."

He talked about a "community action," where in L.A., in South Compton, to maintain the neighborhood, a group was formed called Friendly Neighbors, which bought a property that was about to be sold to a Negro and would have "brought down the value of the entire block."

Especially among the men in the audience, he stirred a good deal of interest, and several of them cheered him on.

He saved the best for last.

"It's only by loving our neighbors that all of us, realtors and clients alike, can protect our community."

His big finish was hailed with huge cheers.

Diane grabbed Crystal's arm and wanted to go backstage to introduce herself, but after realizing where this was going, Crystal was not so eager. Regal's speech attributed no ill intent to real estate agents who, from her look around a room full of well-dressed men, seemed to be doing quite nicely. There was no talk of greed on the part of his well-off audience Instead, he blamed "greedy neighbors."

But her job was to trail Diane, so Crystal feigned interest. They walked to the side of the stage, where Diane ran her long nails with their silky, soft pink polish along the security man's arm, and he quickly let them back.

Teddy Regal was holding court in a tightly crammed dressing room, but he immediately noticed Diane and Crystal and approached them.

"Did you find what I had to say helpful?" he asked.

Diane immediately went into fawning mode, blushing and giggling before him.

"Yes," she said, "very inspiring. I work in Torrance and we are often accused of being in collusion with the banks to sell only to white customers. It's ridiculous."

"It sure is," he said, laying a hand on Diane's shoulder, and before she turned to leave, being sure to slip her his card.

"Come back any time," he said. "And give me a call next time either of you are in town."

The girls curtsied coquettishly and left. Crystal was surprised to be included in his invitation and thought, *Wow, he'll take advantage of anybody.*

"What did you think?" Diane asked as they walked down the Bradbury Building's five-story exposed staircase.

Crystal decided to level with Diane, at least a bit, thinking she ought to if they were really going to work together.

"I don't like the exclusion. It just doesn't sit well with me," she said.

"That's not usually what happens. There is no real collusion, and where we sell is much more open than you would think. In fact, honey, sometimes it works the opposite of the way Teddy laid it out."

She was already on a first name basis with this slippery character.

"When a Negro or a Mexican or a Chinese buyer moves in, what they call it in the trade is 'busting a block.' But what we can do, if we see somebody wants to sell and doesn't care who they're selling to, we offer to buy the house ourselves. We take it off their hands, since they're eager to leave, and we sell it for a profit. Sometimes we can make $10,000 on their selling too hastily."

"But who do you sell it to?"

"Well, we don't allow the block to be busted," Diane said.

Diane had a client that day and wanted Crystal to come along. She offered to drive Crystal out to Torrance.

Crystal accepted and, on the drive, decided to ask about Diane's parents and upbringing.

"Sounds like you can make a lot of money in this field," Crystal said, though from what she had just seen, what she meant to say was "in this racket."

"Did you have much money growing up?"

"We always had enough. My father made a decent living as a carpenter, but for a while, after my parents died, I floundered, until finally I was taken in by a friend of my father's and his family. They gave me a home and he doted on me."

"And who's this friend?"

"Not important," she said. "But he did save me and I am eternally grateful."

Diane then asked Crystal to look for a map in the glove compartment, saying she wanted to try a new route out from L.A.

Crystal at first pulled out a green booklet, thinking it might be a map.

"Put that away," Diane said. "The map must be underneath."

Crystal found the map, and they took the alternate route.

When they got to Torrance, Diane parked on Oak Street in front of one of Williams's new homes with a huge FOR SALE sign outside.

"Now you can see how I make a sale," she promised.

The man in front of the house was not of the shy, retiring, timid kind as Diane's former clients had been. He was over six feet, big and brawny, and when Diane got out of the car and approached him, he immediately patted her on her rear. She didn't recoil. Instead, she smiled.

"On second thought," Diane said, turning to Crystal, "wait for me here. There's a coffee shop around the corner. I'll be out in a little while and I'll come get you."

At that, the man smiled broadly. Diane lifted his hand delicately off her behind, put it on her arm and led him into the building.

Crystal knew what she needed to do.

Diane had locked the car, but in their off hours Harry had been teaching her how to use a coat hanger to reach inside the driver's side window and jerk the lock. She just needed to find a coat hanger.

She walked around the corner to locate the café and as luck would have it, next to it was a drycleaning shop.

She went inside, and the middle-aged man behind the counter, who was all business with the elderly female customer just leaving the shop, smiled, and leaned over the counter when she entered.

For a moment she had forgotten how she was dressed, but now realized that could be useful.

"I wonder if you can help me," she said, leaning over and into the bugged-out eyes of the graying man behind the counter.

"Stupid ole me just locked my car and then when I bent over dropped the keys down a manhole. I have a spare set of keys in the car."

"You want me to see if I can get the car door open for you?" the overeager man asked.

"That's so nice of you, honeychile, but I can do that myself. I just need one of your hangers," she said, leaning a little further over the counter.

She came by the poor dumb Southern girl routine honestly. It was part of her rural Georgia upbringing and worked well in the big city.

He ran to get a very thin hanger which he said he'd had to use himself sometimes when he did the same thing.

She beat it out of there, but he ran after her to give her his card. She took it and made sure he saw her inserting it into her pink bra, which she allowed him to take a peek at.

He'll remember me but he won't think twice about the fact that I'm breaking into someone else's car.

She returned to Diane's Oldsmobile, a car with a slightly sporty exterior that Diane said she was hoping soon to upgrade to an even sportier Jaguar, a sign that she was definitely on her way up the real estate ladder.

She was glad Diane had not yet made the trade because the Oldsmobile lock was easier to pick. She inserted the hanger and quickly jimmied the lock. *At least Harry taught me something in all those hours hanging around the office when we had no work.*

She slid inside and made right for the glove compartment. She had to be quick because there was no telling when Diane would return.

She led out a whoop when she opened the book.

Inside, indeed, was a series of maps as she'd originally thought when she'd pulled it out of the glove compartment. But these were no ordinary maps. The town of Torrance, as well as Carson and parts of Southern Compton, were shaded in either green or red. She ripped a page out of the book which had both shadings, to show Harry.

She put the book back, locked the car again, and was about to go to the café when she looked at her watch.

It had been almost 45 minutes, and Diane had not returned. She was getting worried because the buyer had been so aggressive. She decided to wait a few more minutes and then go in.

At almost an hour, she entered the house and heard no sound.

She walked through the place and finally heard a commotion from the back master bedroom.

The door was just opening, and the man came out buttoning his shirt and putting his suit jacket on.

He was surprised to see Crystal, but as he left simply waved in the direction of the bedroom and said, without a trace of embarrassment. "She'll be out in a minute."

Diane then exited the room, hastily pulling her sweater down and refitting it over her pants. Diane started rubbing a spot on her back, and Crystal wondered if whatever had happened had gotten rougher than anticipated.

"I told you to wait for me," she said.

"I was worried," Crystal said. "What were you doing?"

"Making the sale. I do what it takes," Diane countered, now fully dressed and once again the capable and successful broker. Except that as they left the house, she crouched over a little, still favoring whatever was bothering her about her back.

Geez, Crystal thought, *this business isn't very different from the movie industry. Diane just got off the casting couch. Except, the part paid a lot less than a movie star's salary and given who she was mixing it up with could be a lot more dangerous.*

26

Lyn's grandfather, frail old newspaper editor that he was, rolled his fingers into two fists when he saw the Tong had captured his granddaughter and wanted to make a direct assault on their gambling den. I had a better idea.

"I think they grabbed Lyn to make her tell them where you are," I said. "How well do you know these streets?"

At that he smiled.

"I've lived here longer than any of the Tong. I can run them ragged."

He may be frail but at that moment, flexing not his arms but his legs, he also looked spry.

"I hope this works for both of your sakes," I said. And I told him what to do.

Shortly after, the three men stationed outside the hall were greeted with a strange sight.

Ahn leaped out from around the corner building we had stationed ourselves behind and started flailing his arms and yelling, "Wǒ zài zhèlǐ. Lái zhuā wǒ," which he had told me meant, "Here I am. Come get me."

He then took off crossing the street and disappearing into one of the blind alleys just across the way. It worked much better than I thought. Not only did the three men outside take off after him, but apparently the commotion outside caused the two Tong who had kidnapped Lyn to see what the disturbance was. They joined the posse and all five of them took off after Ahn, who I hoped knew what he was doing.

I sprang from my perch around the corner of the building and made for the entrance.

I had no idea what I would find inside, but luckily the front door was unlocked, likely because that was not needed due to the guards in front.

Just inside, in a corridor leading to the entrance of what must have been a mammoth gambling hall, lay a bundle, thrashing about on the floor. The two Tong had tied Lyn up again and rebound her in the blanket.

I quickly lowered the blanket, threw it off her, and untied her hands.

"Thank you, Mr. Palmer," she said. "But I am quite capable of taking care of myself. Another few minutes and I would have gotten loose."

"No doubt," I said. And at that she smiled.

"But right now, we have to get out of here."

We made pell-mell for the door, and she led me around the corner of the building her grandfather and I had used to conceal ourselves.

I told her what had happened to Ahn.

She was not concerned.

"Granddad is in good shape," she said. "He can take care of himself just like I can."

"So, I was right," I said. "They were after you to find out where Ahn is hiding."

"That's only one of the reasons," she replied. "They'd been looking for him for a while. They think he's about to restart his paper and they've been ordered to find him.

"And that's not all. They know I found the acid in their car and they suspect I will go to the police and accuse them of setting the fire that killed my mother."

"And did they do it?"

"Don't know. Like you, I'm still investigating," she said.

With that she beamed. She was now a private detective.

"You're your own little Carrol Chan," I said.

"Charlie Chan is a white invention," she corrected, "but I like the nickname. Carrol in Chinese means 'champion.' And that's what I would like to be.

"But Mr. Detective, there's one additional thing you don't know about what they wanted."

I bowed to her.

"I am all yours, esteemed daughter," I said.

She smiled again, but her answer was all business.

"I was on my way to a rally to support Chairman Mao and the Chinese Communists. The Tong has been trying desperately to find out where these rallies are being held. They think I know and they're right."

I could see her grandfather in her, this young woman before me who was so firm in her beliefs and willing to go to any lengths to defend them.

"There might be trouble," she said. "I might need you and you're coming with me."

I begged to differ—I needed to get back to the case—but she wasn't taking no for an answer.

"As far as I know, we're still paying you. The Tong are suspects, and this is what my mother and I need from you today."

There wasn't much I could say to that, so I followed her as she led me on a circuitous path through the maze that was the real Chinatown, rather than the shopping plaza designed to attract both Chinese regulars and Anglo visitors. If the idea was to ward off evil spirits, I didn't see how any of them could have followed us through the twists and turns she led me around.

On our way, as we veered momentarily across North Broadway, we saw two men in business suits strolling the streets, and we realized the sight of a middle-aged man who looked like a cop and a Chinese teen-age girl caught their eye.

"Let's get out of here," Lyn said.

"They look like Feds," I said, as she led me around the corner with the men in pursuit.

Just around the corner, we ducked into what looked like an apartment building but was not. Instead, it was another huge meeting hall, probably a former gambling arena.

"I hope they didn't see us," she said as we entered the main hall, decked out with red flags, some with hammers and sickles and some with a red star.

She pulled me aside before we went to grab a chair facing a lectern with an array of speakers seated behind the podium.

"You're right," she said. "They're FBI and Chinatown is full of them, along with the Immigration Service, all of them looking to deport any supporters of the Revolution."

I wanted to ask more questions, especially about the role of the Tong in all this, but Lyn silenced me by putting her index finger to her mouth. She wanted to hear the speaker.

At the podium was a woman who was talking—in English—about equal rights for women.

She said it was time to end the old feudal idea that "the boy is everything, the girl is nothing."

She talked about women working with men under the Revolution and said the old hierarchy was ending, where girls didn't need to know anything since their duty was to get married and have children and respect the old order of father, husband, son.

The speaker, a woman not in Chinese dress but in a Western business suit, then talked about the wages of Chinese women in the city's garment shops where they sewed everything from women's blouses to overcoats to men's shirts. She said they worked three split shifts that began at 7 and ended at 10 in a 10-hour day. She was getting more excited, as were the women in the audience, about thirty percent of the group, who were now cheering her on.

Her fellow workers, she said, were cheated of even their meager wages by being forced to fill out timecards claiming falsely that they were being paid the legally mandated rate of $1.65 an hour when they were actually getting below one dollar. She was reaching a crescendo now and the cheers were getting louder from the women in front of her.

"The answer," she said, "is to unionize both against the Anglo bosses downtown and against the Chinese bosses."

Lyn leaned into me and whispered, "It's amazing how the Chinese exploit themselves."

The woman at the podium bowed demurely but went back to her seat on the podium smiling.

The next speaker had a very learned air. He told the audience he was a doctor and wanted to strike a blow against Chinese humiliation and the blind following of the old ways.

He began by plucking a red flag in a holder at the side of the stage and waving it.

"This is the first anniversary of the Revolution and we're celebrating it," he said, to lusty cheers from everyone. Lyn stood on her feet and whistled. I didn't know what to do. It was too late to crouch down in my chair and look invisible.

What the hell, I finally thought as I gave a little yell, *when in Shanghai, do like the Shanghainese.* I wondered if I got that right.

The doctor, though slight of build, was a firebrand.

"We've gotten rid of our colonial masters," he shouted. "The Kuomintang, the old power, barely fought against the Japanese. It was the Communists who liberated China along with the Russian Red Army in the North. Now Mao is building bridges across the Yangtze, creating highways and machines for the people, and engineering huge rice paddies, so that the white man can't look down on us anymore.

"The People's Army is now distributing land so that everyone has a home, giving ordinary people a chance to go to school, and making sure there is a job for everyone, including women."

He raised his fist and then launched into a description of how China was being transformed, so that it was no longer a "semi-colonial" or "feudal" country where the old power passed through inheritance. He said "lineage" claims were being destroyed, as peasant cooperatives were replacing the control of "clan elders." This was all new to me but I did notice the audience was at rapt attention.

He then started a fiery harangue against the Tong as the symbol of this old power.

"All they do," he said, "is prey on the poor."

As if right on cue, the doors of the hall suddenly burst open and a crew of men mostly dressed in black burst through, one of them carrying a puppet effigy of Mao that he then lit on fire.

A general panic broke out in the room. The Tong were armed with fierce sticks with handles, that they held in either hand and whirled about to clear the room.

"They have *tonfas,*" Lyn said. "I wish I had one."

They were led by the two men who had kidnapped Lyn, and though she wanted to fight back, I knew I had to get her out of there before they caught her.

Several of their members ran up on the stage and starting tearing down the flags.

In the middle of all this commotion, I noticed the two white men in dark suits at the back of the hall that Lyn and I had seen on the street. They were nodding in approval at the scene before them. They must have recognized Lyn, tailed us, and alerted the Tong.

Two of them hauled the doctor and the ladies garment worker organizer off the stage and were about to deliver a series of blows to them when I had had it with them and couldn't take it anymore.

Lyn joined me. I grabbed one of them from behind as he was wielding his stick and threw him on the ground. Lyn did better than that. She raised her leg in a kick and knocked the other one onto the floor of the hall.

Then I saw the two Tong from the funeral who were leading the charge making for us.

"We got to get out of here," I said.

The doctor and the woman fled stage right with some Tong in pursuit, and we fled toward the exit stage left.

As we left the hall, the two men spied us and started chasing us.

Lyn led me down a series of streets with the men on our heels.

"I have a friend," she said. "He will help us."

Just ahead of the two, she pulled me into a somewhat ramshackle one-floor shop. The owner came to meet us.

Lyn explained the situation to him in Chinese.

"Get in the back," he said, pointing to a wool curtain behind his counter.

Lyn led me to the back. Once again, I was surprised that a narrow front led into a wide-open space. Inside, mats lay on the floor and cushions and blankets against the walls.

"He looks like a humble shop owner but he's actually my teacher and trainer," Lyn said. "Mr. Mung is also one of us."

I think that meant a partisan of Mao's Revolution.

We listened to see what was going on outside and I was pretty sure I heard the door of the shop open and close.

There was then a long conversation in Chinese, and I expected we would need to defend ourselves. I had had enough of fisticuffs. I pulled out my gun. There was plenty of evidence against the two Tong, having possibly committed arson, murder and kidnapping, to not fool around any longer.

But they never came through the door.

I heard the front door open and close again. Mr. Mung poked his head through the door to the training room and said it was safe to come out.

"I hope you learned your lesson about not getting involved in politics," I said to Lyn as we stepped into the store.

She pulled me aside and jerked me back into the training room.

"The only thing I learned," she said, now assuming a fighting stance aimed at me, "is that they desperately fear the Revolution and will do anything to destroy it. They claim now with the Chinese crossing the Yalu River and entering the war that 'You Chinese are killing our boys in Korea.' But what are they doing there? MacArthur wants to use Korea as an excuse to invade China and crush the Revolution. The Chinese are fighting for their lives and their ability to free themselves from the Western yoke."

Now she was really adamant and started flexing her arms. She had to restrain herself from kicking with her legs. A lot of teenage energy was in that training room.

"Mark my words," she said, "MacArthur will be defeated and the Revolution will endure. They have nuclear weapons and may even threaten to use them but our side has a Revolutionary army fighting for its life and its existence. Our army is massing for a battle now in Korea at Lake Changjin. We have nothing but ordinary weapons and our own human ingenuity against the might of the most powerful army on earth, but we will hand MacArthur and the United States the greatest military defeat it has ever suffered and establish the right to have our own system of government."

She was winding up and I was getting the point.

She grabbed my arm and now was pleading her case.

"So, Mr. Palmer, I hope you learned *your* lesson."

But there was still the matter of the Tong, who might be waiting for us when we exited the building.

That worked out better than I could ever have expected.

"They must have known we came in here," I said to Mr. Mung. "Why didn't they check the back room?"

He was surprised also, and still a bit in shock, as he relayed what happened.

"They wanted to talk. What they were after today was breaking up the rally, but they kidnapped Lyn because they had something to say to her and they claimed they sometimes just get a bit too rough."

"What did they want to say?" Lyn asked.

"Believe it or not, they wanted to tell you that they had nothing to do with your mother's death and they want you and the white detective to stop bothering them."

"Do you believe them?" Lyn asked me.

"I don't know," I said. "We'll have to file that claim under 'Subjects for Further research."

"I'm on it," she replied, and I realized that not only was I again at the center of solving the murder of her mother, I was now also needing to keep tabs on and keep a wild teenager safe. The second task was the bigger challenge.

27

After our adventure with the Tong, I was confused. Part of me had pegged them as the killers, especially when Lyn found the acid in their car, but if they were, since they probably knew Lyn and I were hiding in the back of Mr. Mung's shop, why didn't they come in and take us?

Was it possible they could be telling the truth or were they just trying to throw us off the trail? If they were to be believed, the finger was pointing again at either the Klan or my two friends from The Strip who had roughed me up, Mick and Tony.

There were so many strands I didn't know which one to pursue first, and somewhere out there, if I got too curious, were the photos of me at Madame Thai's which could still be used to get me off the case and get me out of my job.

I was almost relieved to get a call from Esperanza, though she sounded anxious, not relieved. The city official Beame had been out to Palo Verde to see Rosa and her family, claiming that the city was at that moment drawing up papers to claim Rosa's house as part of its public housing project.

She wanted to know what I could do to help. I had an idea. I asked her to come to my office so I could give her a camera. I told her that next time Beame came to Palo Verde, especially if he was with my two friends Mick and Tony, she should hide herself in Rosa's house and take pictures of all three of them. I wasn't sure where that was going to lead but I thought those photos might be useful.

When Esperanza arrived, she was very friendly, and since Crystal was in Torrance with Diane and the office was empty except for us two, she spread herself out on the sofa I used to nap on next to my desk.

"Have you got time for a roll in the hay, Meester Palmer?" she said, as she undid her kerchief and reached for the buttons on her yellow shirt.

That would usually be a moment of ecstasy, but instead guilt kicked in.

Dr. Kellman had told me that eventually, if the relationship was to succeed, I would have to tell her about my, to put it politely, "dalliance" on The Strip.

I was not in a truth-telling mood. Dr. Kellman did say "eventually," and I took that to mean when the case was over.

I felt too terrible, though, to take advantage of Esperanza's offer, so I claimed I needed to be somewhere and begged off. How much longer was what my mind told me at the time was "just a little harmless fun" going to torture me?

Esperanza was taken aback. She buttoned up and almost ran out of the office, feeling, I guess, the sting of my rejection, when I realized I needed something from her that might be helpful for both Rosa's and Sandra's cases.

I asked her about the professor who had testified at the hearing we attended. I thought I might pop in and pay him a visit, since he had such a clear idea about how the real estate market was developing in the city and the county.

She stopped as she was about to slam my office door, paused, and gave me his address in San Jose. She realized there was a wider issue at stake here and decided to be helpful.

"He's up this week for appointment to the city Planning Commission. He's Edward's candidate and it's likely he'll be accepted, though many of the other Council members don't like him at all."

"Goodbye, Harry Palmer," she said, this time gently closing the door. "If you want me, you know where to find me."

I felt a strange mixture of attraction and repulsion, attraction at her intriguing offer and repulsion at my not being able to accept it with a clear conscience.

I would have lots of time to think about why I had done what I had done on the drive to San Jose, which was almost eight hours, a full workday. I hoped this trip was worth it.

I decided to make the trip even longer, following the road along the coast though the scenic seaside towns of Santa Barbara, San Luis Obispo and Monterey, and then turning inland to San Jose.

It was a beautiful clear morning with the sun gleaming off the ocean. I didn't resolve anything about the case or cases but did figure that I could not move forward with Esperanza without telling her what I had done, regardless of the consequences. I felt better about that resolution and hoped I could keep to it.

Professor Gonzalez lived on a sleepy, tiny street in the center of the town, not far from the college he taught at, which I drove by on my way.

I parked near his house and as I approached a well-kept lawn, I heard voices and shouting from inside. "For your health, it's not a good idea if you accept this post," one of those voices said. I recognized that voice. It was my friend Mick, the bigger, burlier of the two men in black.

I'd had enough of them. I circled around the back of the house in what was an equally well-manicured backyard and tried the back door. It was not locked and I stole in through the kitchen.

I peered around the corner into the front living room. Mick, standing over the professor seated in an armchair, was holding a blackjack in a way that indicated he was quite comfortable with how to use it. He was just about to lower the boom on the frail, aging man in the chair. Tony had grabbed Mick's arm, trying to restrain his companion.

I brandished my gun and stepped into the room.

Tony didn't like that and reached into his pocket about to pull out his own weapon. It looked like we were going to shoot it out in the living room.

At that point, the little man in the chair leaped up.

"Get out of here, both of you," he said to the two men. "I will not be threatened and I will take any office I want."

They decided that they had lost this round and started to head for the door.

Mick turned to me before leaving.

"Next time, you won't get a bead on us and you won't come out of it in one piece," he said.

His partner was a bit more subtle.

"We've got some photos that are going to start popping up all over town," he said.

And they both left.

The professor collapsed in his chair. He was terrified after his brief moment of defiance.

"Thanks, Mr. Palmer," he said. "This is the second time you've gotten rid of those two thugs."

I was glad he remembered the incident at City Hall since it might make him trust me more and have more to say.

He motioned for me to sit and offered me some tea, which I declined. I wanted to get to the point.

He wanted to tell me what my two friends were doing there.

"Their bosses are trying to intimidate me and keep me off the Planning Commission. It's mostly made up of real estate salesmen, luxury apartment developers, and corporate lawyers. None of whom have the best interests of the majority of the city's residents in mind.

"I head a small part of the sociology department here called Urban Studies, and if I say so myself, I am well qualified to serve on the commission. Edward is going to nominate me."

He explained that he grew up in Boyle Heights in a family that was second generation from Mexico, knew Roybal for a long time, and had done research for his campaign.

"And what does the Planning Commission do? Why is so important to them to keep you off it?"

At that he beamed. He sat up in his easy chair and addressed me as if I was a student in one of his classes.

"What the Planning Commission mostly does," he said, "is ratify the decisions of the developers who often hold the real power. But it has to look like it's an open process, one where the public has input. The Commission is all about making it seem like the people have their say while ultimately making sure the developers keep control. Edward and I want to change that, give ordinary people and minorities in L.A. more power and the 'city fathers' view that as a threat.

"But you didn't drive all the way up here to talk about the planning commission. What is it you wanted to ask me?"

"Two things," I said. "The first is general. The second is very specific."

"Okay," he replied, "let's use deduction. We'll go from the general to the specific."

I could respect that logic. On the LAPD we did the opposite, going from the very specific and making sure that that whatever crime we were investigating never got to the general question of what was causing it and who was actually behind it.

"What is going on in the town, right now?" I said. "I've come across three incidents and they all involve Chinese, Mexican and Negroes losing their land in Torrance, Palo Verde and Santa Monica, not to mention me being run out of Bunker Hill."

Now Professor Gonzalez was sitting straight up at attention. This was a serious lesson he was about to deliver.

"It's an old story," he said, "and there's a name for it. We sometimes call it 'accumulation by dispossession.' City enhancement projects to attract wealthier renters are often built on centrally located land where poor people live."

That described everywhere I was talking about to a T.

"But do these forces have a name? Who is behind this?"

"In L.A., their name is the Chandler family," he said. "Not just owners of the *Los Angeles Times* but landowners and developers as well."

He described Harry Chandler and General Otis, whom Charlotta Bass had talked about, and their original scheme where they claimed to bring water from Owens Valley to L.A. They then largely diverted the water to the San Fernando Valley, where they had just bought what was thought of as worthless property, because there was no irrigation, for $3 million, but which, with the water, was then worth $120 million.

The Chandlers, he said, were also the motivating force behind Union Station, which I knew from Lyn's grandfather had "dispossessed" the Chinese.

They owned huge parcels of land outside the city and were in the process of engineering highways to develop them, all of which resulting, the Planning Commissioner nominee said, in "planning" that was mainly meant to enhance the wealth of Chandler holdings. He said that those holdings also included companies that profited from the building of the new highways. I thought about following the men in black to the Chandler-owned gravel pit and got a glimpse of how all this might fit together.

He summed up.

"A great deal of Los Angeles as it is taking shape today is based on the drive to improve Chandler wealth."

And he had something else to add.

"You may think the *Los Angeles Times* is a public institution in the service of the people, but actually it is a private institution in the service of the Chandlers' crooked deals."

He smiled.

"I didn't say that. That's a quote from William Randolph Hearst, who said the paper 'prostituted' itself for the 'private unworthy ends of its owner.'"

Hearst, their competitor, was a rabid "yellow journalist," but in this case, since they both attacked each other, it was two equally dirty pots calling the same kettle black.

"That's helpful," I said. "And now there is something I want to show you. It's a page from a book of maps that my partner found in a Torrance real estate saleswoman's glove compartment that she didn't want anyone to see."

I pulled from my pocket the page that Crystal had given me with its green and red shadings.

He studied it carefully and before answering specifically he had some more generalities.

"Yes," he said, "in these land development schemes there are winners and losers, and these maps are about keeping the two apart."

He explained that maps like these dated back to the early 1930s, when they were used by banks to refuse loans to those in the red areas, mostly made up of minorities, and approve loans to those in the green areas of white residents.

"The maps were originally put together by the federal government's Home Owners' Loan Corporation," he explained. He added that they then became the basis for racially restrictive covenants, and that created a housing market that channeled and then maintained real estate wealth that was almost exclusively white.

"This is a part of a map of Torrance and its surrounding cities and it's even worse in L.A.," he said. "The city has been refusing federal money to help its poorest residents by claiming there are no slums. One 'surveyor' said that there are 'only Negroes, Mexicans, Chinks and Japs in those neighborhoods' and they should be forced to get along on their own.

"The term the banks use for this is 'redlining.' They work in conjunction with the Klan to keep unwanted populations out. One method of discrimination is institutional and the other is personal and individual."

I wondered if the personal in the form of the Klan was what had murdered Sandra Chung.

"The green areas on your map, all in Torrance, are called 'hot spots,' and thought of as 'well-planned sections of the city,' as 'good' parts, whereas the red areas, which on your map are parts of Compton, are thought of as 'undesirable' and 'bad.' Maps like these allow inequality to spread and create areas wider than just those in extreme poverty. What they show is a hostile attitude toward all non-whites and people of color."

At this he got heated.

"White communities in places like South Compton and Torrance are fighting like hell to keep everyone where they are, and if that doesn't work to flee to newly built green areas.

"It's a war going on out there and it goes on every day."

He was disgusted at his conclusion and this sedate professor seemed to even surprise himself that he was angry enough to swear, sounding more, for a moment, like a Marine than a scholar.

He then looked more closely at the page and turned to me surprised.

I had not really studied it, just figured I would bring it to someone who knew what it was.

"There are pencil marks on this page. They're light and may have been actually made on a previous page that will show through if we etch them.

He asked if it was okay that he shade them. I agreed, kicking myself that I had not discovered this.

When he ran his pencil over the marks, they revealed a name and a phone number.

"It looks like 'Dean,'" he said, "and this must be his number."

Crystal had told me that the two met, but that Diane did not seem interested in Dean other than for information. Could this be a sign of a deeper collusion between the two?

I put that in my own "Subjects for Further Research" file and thought it would be a good idea if, along with Crystal, I took another look at Torrance's sexiest real estate agent.

28

Diane had not contacted Crystal for a day or two, and Crystal was beginning to worry about her. The lifestyle that had once seemed so glamorous now had more than a trace of unwanted danger about it.

I'm going to have to take this bull by the horns, Crystal thought as she made the drive out to Torrance, maybe for the last time. *I'm not sure if she'll even talk to me after I caught her out*, but she decided it was worth the effort to warn Diane about what lay ahead. She had been on a similar path before Harry had pulled her out of the bars: She had watched her roommate and friend Jade do herself in with drugs and then be done in by those who feasted on innocent girls like her.

Diane had a separate office a few blocks from Williams's, but when Crystal went to check, she wasn't there, and the place looked like no one had been in for a day or two.

She then walked to Williams's office, and coming out of it was Dean, his son, who looked to be in a hurry.

Crystal stopped him and introduced herself as a trainee and friend of Diane. Dean said he had no idea where she was, that he hadn't seen her in the last few days, which Crystal knew to be a lie since she had seen them together in the Last Ditch.

He said he had a client to meet and rushed off, but on the way down the sidewalk he turned back and shouted, "I don't think she was doing any selling today, but you might try the bar where she makes her sales. Sometimes she just hangs out there."

Crystal then remembered Dealmakers, got back in her car, and drove further downtown, but no luck. The lunchtime crowd was just starting to gather, and the hostess, dressed in a business suit with a carnation in her lapel and all business for the occasion, told her Diane had not come in today.

"She's here quite a lot, but I'll tell you the last time she was in, she didn't look to be in good shape. I shouldn't say this, but since I saw you two in here together I will. When things get a little out of hand, she doesn't come here. She goes to the Last Ditch and drowns her sorrows.

"You didn't hear that from me," the hostess concluded as she abruptly turned away and ushered a patron to his seat. The man in an elegant gray suit requested a booth in the back. On her way out, Crystal saw a woman in an equally elegant pink business suit pass her. She watched as the woman then made discretely for the back booth, where she and the man embraced. *There's a lot of kinds of business that go on here*, she thought. She watched from outside as the man in the back booth got up and crowded into the same side as the woman, throwing his arms around her and kissing her passionately. *He's certainly giving her the business*, she thought, a little envious of their clandestine rendezvous.

Crystal made her way out to The Strip and found herself in luck. There, parked in front of the Last Ditch was Diane's Oldsmobile.

She went inside the place, with a few scattered souls at the bar and almost no one at the tables. From the jukebox came the mournful sounds of the current hit "My Foolish Heart."

Behind the bar, pouring drinks, was the leather-clad man that Crystal had tricked into giving her a tryout to spy on Diane and Dean. He was none too friendly when he recognized her.

"Here for another quickie?" he said.

"I'm sorry about that. I just had to get some information. I did come with a peace offering." She had retrieved the waitress outfit from her car and handed it over to him. She ordered a mai tai and dropped a huge tip, which came from the daily expenses Harry was now allotting her.

"I was angry and jealous about my girlfriend Diane's new boyfriend," she said. "But I'm over that now. I accept him and I wanted to make up with her."

Jack Smith, as he introduced himself, was not too busy and he pulled Crystal aside.

"She's not in a good way today. I don't know what it is, but something happened recently that has shaken her. She could use some cheering up."

She thought Jack was a good bartender and a good friend.

"But where is she?"

"She had something to drink already, and I'm letting her sleep it off in the back room. You can go wake her up if you want."

Behind the bar was the side room which Crystal knew was used for the bartenders and waiters to dress.

Inside she found Diane sleeping peacefully. She was wearing much more casual clothes on a day when she wasn't working, a tight pink sweater and even tighter jeans.

Even asleep she looks great, Crystal thought as she tapped her shoulder and rolled her gently to wake her up.

"Huh? What's going on," Diane groaned as she was coming to.

"I think you are still recovering from what happened the other day," Crystal said. "I came to rescue you."

"Thanks, I can use some rescuing."

Crystal was relieved that Diane was no longer angry at Crystal having intruded on her sale.

Diane sat up.

"That's a cute outfit," she said, looking at Crystal's more business-like orange dress with orange heels.

"Let's get out of here, I know a place we can go."

Crystal helped Diane to her feet. She staggered a little at first and then walked off what she said was "just a little morning refresher."

They walked out to the bar, and Jack waved to them. As they were going out the door, two men in black suits were just coming in and both seemed to pay a lot of attention to Diane.

She seemed to never mind flirting and when she saw them eyeing her, she pulled down her sweater to make it cling to her even tighter.

Crystal was a bit concerned at Diane's flashiness, and as they were leaving the bar, she noticed the two men walked outside and continued to stare at them.

"Where are we going?" Crystal asked, as they were about to clamber into their two cars.

"Just follow me," Diane said. "It's my secret place."

Diane led her on a merry chase through the streets of Torrance to near the outskirts, though in the end actually not far from The Strip, on Abalone Avenue.

She stopped and parked in front of what looked like a Williams house but this time without a FOR SALE sign on the lawn.

When they both got out, Diane led Crystal by the arm up the lawn and through the front entrance.

"They use this place as a demo house to show customers what the other houses look like. The nice thing about it is that it includes all the features of every home."

Once inside the door, Crystal was impressed with how huge the place was. Diane gave Crystal a tour. The front room and each of the four huge bedrooms had a custom fireplace as well as, as advertised, the cedar roof and the oak floors.

"I've got to use the bathroom, but, when I get back, we can get something to eat from the kitchen. The fridge is fully stocked."

When Diane was gone, Crystal went to the kitchen and checked to see if the wall phone was working. It was, and she called Harry to tell him where she was. He had wanted to question Diane about some new information he had about the map Crystal had found. He was in the office and said he would come right over.

Crystal heard Diane exit the bathroom and was unable to get back to the living room where Diane had left her.

Diane came into the kitchen, and Crystal walked away from the phone and threw open the refrigerator. There were layers of steaks and piles of chicken.

"Wow, this stuff looks good," she said. "When do we eat?"

Diane didn't reply. Instead, she closed the refrigerator door, took Crystal by the arm, and led her to the huge master bedroom.

"We eat right now," Diane said, throwing Crystal down on the bed.

Before Crystal even knew what was going on, Diane rolled her over, undid her dress and pulled down her matching orange panties.

"Those are cute," she said. "I love them."

But she quickly tossed them aside and rolled her warm tongue against Crystal's mouth and then all the way down her body, pausing at her breasts to swallow each of them, and finally arriving at her trimmed vagina.

"I hope this is okay," Diane said, already beginning to lap Crystal and warm her with her tongue.

"It would be hard to stop now," Crystal said. "And who wants to?"

She'd had other experiences like this in her club days, but they were different.

Usually with another girl and essentially at the service of one of the gangsters. This was just about the two of them.

Diane eagerly devoured Crystal in a way that led her to believe this was not her first time with another woman. She seemed poised and experienced.

When it came, the feeling of release was one of the most exciting Crystal had ever felt.

She had been with men who "went both ways," but most of them were simply in it for their own pleasure. This was more mutual.

Diane, when she had finished, caressed Crystal's breasts, and Crystal returned the favor.

"And I thought mine were big," Diane joked, and they both laughed.

Diane then poked in one of the drawers of a chest by the side of the bed and came up with a pack of cigarettes.

"Would you like one?" she said, lighting up. "I don't usually indulge but this is a special occasion."

Crystal nodded approval, and Diane took out another cigarette, lit it, and passed it to her. Crystal had to admit that she agreed because smoking might loosen Diane up, and there was still a lot she didn't know about her.

"Is this really a special occasion, or just a regular occasion?" Crystal asked.

Diane deposited both cigarettes in an ashtray and held Crystal to her.

"It's special," she said. "I usually come here alone. I wanted you from the moment I saw you."

"But," Crystal said, "you are so forward around men and have so many of them coming onto you. Why me?"

"The truth is," Diane said, picking her cigarette back up and exhaling a luxurious puff, "that I hate men. I can't stand their grubby paws on me. They're dirty and I always want to shoo them off."

"So, this whole show is just for work?"

"Yep, just for work."

Crystal couldn't help but recall what Dr. Kellman had said about a secret buried in Diane's past. She decided to probe, while also feeling guilty about still being on the job after Diane had opened up to her.

"It must have been difficult for you after your parents died."

"Yes, one moment they're there and the next they're not. At first, I went into an orphanage but I was rescued from that by someone who took an interest in me and then things got better."

She seemed reluctant to say more, so Crystal tried another tack.

"And what was your past life with men like?" Crystal asked, deciding to be direct.

"I learned growing up that they just take what they want, and I had little say in the matter. So, I decided that I could play the same game and get what I needed from them."

"Sounds a lot like my life," Crystal said. "But what happened the other day? Did that guy hit you?"

"He liked to play rough, and it turns out he may not even buy the house. What a louse."

Crystal wanted to find out more about how Diane thought about the job, since after she had discovered Diane being accosted and with all that Harry had told her, she was souring on the real estate business. She told Diane she found it shady.

"Yes, you're right," Diane said. "Do you know that even here in Torrance, to build these new homes, the company had to foreclose on mortgages and make a lot of poor people homeless?"

"I've heard about it happening elsewhere," Crystal said, "and it's disturbing."

"A part of me wishes I could get out of the business, but it's all I've ever known."

Crystal was glad Diane at least had second thoughts.

"And what about your boss's son Dean? I saw him the other day and he's quite handsome. Should I be worried?"

Diane scoffed as she started to dress.

"Him, no way. I've known him for a long time. He's interested, but not me. Sometimes he gets jealous and he also hangs around with shady characters. I think he might be able to help me with something I'm working on, though."

Crystal knew what the something was but had to be careful.

"And what's that?"

Diane continued to get dressed and threw Crystal's clothes on the bed for her to do the same.

"I miss my father and I still think there is something fishy about how he died. I really don't know who to go to about this and I was hoping Dean could help me."

"What makes you think it wasn't an accident?" Crystal asked, dying to tell Diane that she and Harry could help her but afraid to reveal who she was and why she was pursuing her. Crystal felt dirty herself.

"Let's see what I can find out on my own," she said.

They were now fully dressed and as they stepped out onto the porch, Crystal spied Harry outside.

He had a scared look on his face as he raced up the lawn. He had seen something on the other side of the lawn.

It was at that moment that she heard a *whoosh* and then a *ping* as something cascaded off the wood on the porch.

Harry grabbed Diane and started to throw her to the ground, but before he could push her Crystal heard a second ping—this one not so loud.

She looked down and realized the second shot had struck flesh.

"I saved her," Harry said, bending over Diane and not noticing the red splatter on her sweater. "They were aiming at her head."

Crystal cradled an inert Diane in her arms and looked up furiously at Harry.

"You pushed her into the line of fire. The bullet hit her heart. You killed my girlfriend."

Act 4

Home (Bitter) Sweet Home

29

"I'm sorry, Harry, I know you were trying to help."

It had been a frantic 24 hours. Diane had passed out from the shock of being shot. Crystal, practically in shock herself, thought she was dead, but I wasn't sure. I used the phone inside to call an ambulance and they arrived quickly.

After he gave her oxygen, I asked the medic how she was. He shrugged and said, "Could be worse."

They operated immediately at the hospital nearby in Carson. The doctor removed the bullet. He showed it to us and told Crystal and me in the waiting room that it had come within an inch of penetrating her heart. They had saved her, but there was more than a bit of luck that she was still breathing.

Crystal wanted to rush in to her immediately, but the doctor said we needed to wait a little for her to recover before she could receive guests.

My partner was still confused about what had happened and now, with a little time on her hands, she wanted to know what I had seen and why anyone would want to kill Diane.

"The second question, I can't answer," I said.

"But the first, when I pulled up to the house I saw the red Chevrolet Bel Air, a hard car to miss with the two men in black, Mick and Tony, in it, and I figured something was up. I was keeping one eye on them and one on the house at the address you gave me when I suddenly saw a high-powered rifle poking out the window of the Bel Air. I ran up the walkway and pushed Diane down on the porch, in time to save her life but not in time to keep her from getting hit."

"Actually, Harry, you did save her life," Crystal said, patting my arm in gratitude. "But who would want to kill her?"

I showed her the photo I had snapped in front of what was once my hotel. Dumb of me not having shown it to her before. She nodded.

"Those two were at the Last Ditch. They were coming in when we were going out. Diane flirted with them and they followed us out of the bar."

"We know the who, but we don't know who's behind the who," I said. "I do know this though, at their hangout, the last time I was there I saw them talking to Dean Williams and then they put a hurt on me. They could be working for him."

"It's possible," Crystal said. "Diane says he's jealous of her. She's not interested in him and he could've been getting his revenge."

I told her what I had discovered about the page from Diane's book with Dean's name and phone number. This seemed to confirm that the two of them were working together, and perhaps that one of them had tried to dissolve the partnership in a serious way.

"And are you and Diane wife and wife?" I asked.

At this she blanched.

"Wouldn't you like to know," she said. "Are you jealous?"

"A little," I said, "but I don't go around expressing it with a gun."

Which reminded me to do something I'd been meaning to do since the case began. I'd had Crystal out on the shooting range in our down time prior to the case, so she at least knew how to hold a gun and fire it without shooting herself in the foot. We then got her a license.

When I retrieved my own gun, I brought along my second gun for her, and now in the waiting room I slipped it to her and told her to be careful with it. She was glad to get it.

At that point, luckily, a nurse came out into the waiting room and said we could go in and see Diane.

She was already sitting up and despite the operation still looked stunning.

She was in hospital bedclothes without makeup, but her blonde hair was flowing and she even had a mischievous look on her face.

She grabbed Crystal's hand and held it close, not noticing me.

When she looked up, she did recognize me as someone who had been a prospective client.

"What is he doing here?" she asked.

I think this made it all a little easier for Crystal, who had apparently decided to come clean.

"I'm not who you think I am," Crystal said, holding Diane's hand even tighter.

"I just think you're spicy," Diane said, but as she did, she pushed Crystal's hand away.

"So, what's going on?"

Crystal told her about Sandra Chung's death, which was not news to her, about finding the map with the red and green territories, and about the Klan activity in Torrance.

"But who are you people?" she asked, grimacing in an effort to sit straight up in her bed.

I let Crystal answer.

"We're private detectives hired by Sandra Chung and we're trying to find out who murdered her."

Crystal did not tell her we were also hired by Williams to keep tabs on her, but I guess she figured that was only for her own good.

At the word "murder" a shocked look crossed Diane's face.

"Harry is an ex-cop and maybe he can help you find out if there was anything suspicious in the death of your parents," she said.

At this Diane brightened and took Crystal's hand again.

"Will you, Mister—?"

"Palmer," I said, maintaining my distance. "Okay," I answered, not sure I needed another case.

Crystal stepped aside and pushed me forward toward Diane. "Of course, he will help."

Now Diane sat straight up in bed.

"My parents died on what is called 'Murder Mile.' It's on the opposite side of The Strip, and many cars have crashed there."

"So, it's likely this was just one more," I said, reluctant to commit myself.

Crystal poked me in the back. "Listen to her," she ordered.

"But my father didn't drink. He set a good example—which I haven't followed. And he was an excellent driver. When I was a teen, well before I could get my license, he used to take me driving to teach me. He never exceeded the speed limit and never took risky curves like the one the police claimed knocked him into the other car and then off the road.

"I'm assuming you two have been spying on me. If you have you can at least help me."

Crystal stepped forward and took Diane's hand. "You bet we will," she said.

"Agreed," I said, "but we also need some help from you."

"I'll do what I can," she said.

"What do you know about the Klan in Torrance and in particular a rather seedy character named Frank Chase? Is he in league with your boss or his son?"

Diane looked at a photo I had taken, studied it, but then shook her head.

"I've seen him around town. But Dan wouldn't have anything to do with him. He doesn't like the Klan, thinks they're primitive and stopping the town from developing and him from selling houses."

"Does Dean have anything to do with Frank Chase?"

At this she thought a long time.

"It's possible. He's the one who introduced me to the Last Ditch and there is no telling who he meets there. Except for my friend the bartender, Jack Smith, it's a very dangerous place.

"I grew up near Dean. He always had a hankering for me and he was always nervous and slightly annoying, but until now I assumed he was harmless.

"One other thing. Dean's the one who gave me that booklet with the red and green shadings telling me where I can and can't sell. He slipped his number in it when he gave it to me. Personally, I think it's ridiculous. Anybody should be able to buy wherever they want."

Crystal heaved a huge sigh of relief, and I felt relieved also. Diane could turn out to be very helpful.

And now the million-dollar question.

I showed her the photos.

"These are the men who shot you. Do you recognize either of them? Dean seems to know them rather well."

"No, never seen either of them before that day at The Strip."

She appeared to be telling the truth.

And now there was one more piece to the puzzle she might be able to help with.

"What happened in the orphanage?"

Crystal told me that was where she'd been sent for a brief period after her parents died.

At this she crouched down in her bed, and a look of terror and pain came over her.

The nurse walked in when she saw me leaning over Diane.

"That's enough for today," she said. She was an older woman, matronly and supremely protective of her patients.

She ushered me out of the room.

Crystal begged her to let her stay, and Diane nodded that she was in favor of that also. The nurse agreed.

As I walked out, I saw Crystal gently kissing Diane, which luckily the nurse did not see.

There wasn't much I could say to Crystal. The last thing she needed after a harrowing experience was me telling her it was dangerous to get involved with a client. Besides, I wasn't good at that part of the profession myself. My last three girlfriends all were involved in cases I was working on.

There was one thing I could do to help.

I figured that my friends Mick and Tony might come back to finish the job when they found out it wasn't done. For now, Diane was safe with Crystal with her, but she couldn't be there 24 hours.

I didn't want to, but I had to pay a visit to my friendly neighborhood police station, a place of quiet and peace there to serve the community in whatever way they could.

"Get out of here," McGinty said, rolling his fist into a ball the moment I entered the station. "Or I'll throw you out."

I would say he was in a bad mood, but I think bad was his only mood.

Once again, Lance, most likely having heard his desk sergeant bellow, intervened.

He came to the outer office and waved me to accompany him. I tiptoed past McGinty, who was still eager to clobber me and again looked deeply disturbed not to be able to accomplish that task.

"Sit down," the investigator said, motioning me to a seat. I wondered why he was being so polite.

"We know about the shooting. We got a call from Dan Williams, who was very concerned about his saleswoman being shot. You did good saving her, Palmer."

I thanked him and now had a further favor to ask.

"The two men who shot her are fairly dangerous and we don't know if they might try again. Would it be possible to station someone at the hospital with Diane for the next few days?"

"Yes," he said. "I guess we can accomplish that."

He rang a buzzer on his desk, and almost immediately a young man ran into the room from the back, still buttoning his shirt and adjusting his cap. He was rawer than raw and looked to have just been hired.

"This is Padewski, our newest recruit. I'll assign him to hospital duty."

Lance dismissed him. Padewski saluted and left the room. I noticed that in his haste to report to his chief he had forgotten to cinch his belt, which was still flying loose around his pants.

"Thanks," I said, "for taking this seriously."

What I wanted to say was, "Do you think he can even find the hospital?"

I guess I was back in the good graces of the Torrance police, but there was one thing more Lance and I needed to talk over.

"Are you still holding Fran McCordle?" I asked.

"That's pretty solid evidence *you* provided us with," he answered. "Until there's something to counter it, we're keeping her and we're probably going to charge her."

I knew she was innocent and I had to get back on her case.

With my somewhat but not entirely botched attempt to save Diane, at least I was able to operate in Torrance again and that was a major gain.

I thought about what had happened on the drive back to my new digs in L.A. I was relieved that Crystal could tell Diane the truth and that Diane accepted her. She didn't kick her out of the room and the two of them seemed to be getting along fine. I wondered if this might carry over with Esperanza, but I also realized that while Crystal had fooled Diane, in sleeping with another woman, I had betrayed Esperanza's trust at a far deeper level. I had no idea once I told her the truth whether she would accept me again or if she even should.

Maybe I just wasn't to be trusted.

30

The most logical lead to pursue at the moment was that of Williams's son Dean. He knew the men in black and had a motive for the attack, wanting his revenge on Diane who had rejected him.

He also seemed to be adamant about closing off the town, keeping non-whites out, since he gave Diane the maps marking off various territories.

I decided to pick him up at his father's office and see what a day in the life of Dean Williams was like.

I was parked outside at 11 a.m. when he came out, walking briskly to his car, apparently a man on a mission. He was dressed in a sparkling white suit with a pink tie. He deftly maneuvered into a sporty red T-bird convertible with the top down. He looked spry and jaunty at the wheel. I don't like spry and I hate jaunty. It would be a pleasure taking him down.

His first stop was at a local gathering of Torrance homeowners. They were parked in front of a house with a FOR SALE sign out in front. They were a mixed crowd, men and women, carrying placards that read "Save Our Community" and "Keep the Rabble Out."

The guy carrying the "Rabble" sign was middle-aged with a day or two's stubble and a checkered shirt that looked a little ragged. What was he doing here at noon on a workday? It looked like the "Rabble" sign could equally apply to him.

When the group—there were about ten of them—saw Dean, they cheered. He got out of his car waving his hands, and they crowded around. He said a few words to them and then got back in his car. They patted him on the shoulder and back as he left.

I decided to go talk to them. I would lose track of Dean but it might be worth it.

When I approached them, they were curious to know who I was and why I was interested.

"I'm a prospective homeowner," I said, showing them a brochure I had picked up from the Williams office. "I want to make sure this place is safe."

"That's what we're here for," Mr. Rabble Rouser piped up.

"And who was that man I saw talking to you? Is he part of your group?"

"That's Williams's son," said the man, who introduced himself as Morgan. It turns out Morgan was on disability, didn't work. and so had plenty of time to spend keeping the neighborhood "clean."

The woman next to him, holding the other sign, punctured that fairy tale.

"Morgan, you're not really hobbled," she said and then turned to me. "He supposedly had an accident at the oil derrick but we all think he might have faked it."

At that Morgan stormed off.

The woman said her name was Mamie and also seemed eager to talk.

"Dean's a friend of ours. He doesn't always agree with his father but he's in the forefront of keeping our town safe for all the residents."

"And what is he up to today?"

"He's trying to organize something for the City Council and he wants us to be there this afternoon at 2. He said right now he's off to the city government office."

"I hate to say this, but I've heard there is a seedy part of town and some less than reliable characters who frequent that place hang out there. I saw two of them recently and I snapped them. Have you seen either of them?"

"No," she said. "Not them," and now she was starting to get suspicious.

"Who are you anyway?"

"Honestly, I'm just a cautious prospective buyer. One more question. Do you know this man?"

I showed them a photo Crystal had snapped of Frank Chase.

"And why do you want to know?" she said. "Morgan, get back over here. Somethin' off about this guy."

Oops. It was time to be heading for the wide-open spaces, heeding the words of Horace Greeley to "Go West, young man." Only in my case, that meant getting in my car and driving the few blocks west toward the City Hall offices.

The demonstrators, though, started running after me and I tore out of there.

They didn't have pitchforks and pikes, but with the angry looks on their faces they might as well have, and this Frankenstein was making tracks.

But they had steered me in the right direction.

When I got to the town hall the red convertible was parked out in front. The top was still down. It was as though Dean owned the place and had nothing and no one to fear.

I got in past the town secretary, a pretty little number with fiery red hair and a winning smile, by telling her I was a friend of Dean's hired to help him on his project. She pointed me in the direction of a slew of offices. I walked past them until I came to the "Land Claims" office, where I spied Dean inside.

"I'm going to take some definitive action to keep this town safe and to preserve property values," he was saying.

I stationed myself outside. Again, whatever their unwholesome business, they didn't feel any need to conceal it and had left the door wide open.

The spectacled man behind the desk in a gray striped suit was listening attentively.

"I want the backing of the city offices, your office, Planning, and the town clerk."

"We're with you, Mr. Williams," the man said. "I think I can safely guarantee you that the city bureaucracy will back you."

Dean thanked him and practically rushed out of his office, on to his next stop.

He took me by surprise. As he shuffled past, I pulled my hat down over my brow and sauntered past him in the opposite direction. He was in such a hurry and, as his father had said, in such an agitated state, that he didn't notice me.

I was surprised where our little entourage showed up next.

He pulled into the Torrance PD station.

There was no way I could be a fly on the wall there, so I just waited the half hour or so it took him to come out.

I knew where he was going to show up later, so I let him drive past me.

I was pressing my luck, but I was going to try one more time to get past McGinty.

He was absorbed in reading another trashy police pulp, holding the magazine up in front of his face. The cover had a half-naked blond screaming in the grip of a ratty mobster on a run-down street while a handsome cop was pulling up to the curb and about to jump out to save her.

This was apparently McGinty's fantasy, but given his rotund shape and abrasive manner I was sure that fantasy it would remain.

I stole past and entered Lance's office.

"What are you doing here?" he barked, forgetting that we had kissed and made up. I didn't care. If we were going to break up, so be it.

"I'm trailing the primary suspect in the shooting of Diane Chestnut and I'm wondering why you were just meeting with him."

Rather than responding immediately, Lance cleared his desk and began filing papers strewn across it so that it was again tidy.

"We don't think he had anything to do with the shooting," he said. "I told him to come in anyway, questioned him, and he said he didn't. He's as surprised as you are about what happened."

"And you believe him?"

"What are you doing here Palmer? He's one of our leading citizens and we've cleared him. I was just typing up the report. That should be good enough for you."

Was he now going to try to sell me a piece of the Brooklyn Bridge?

"And what else did he want?"

"Not that I need to tell you, but he's rounding up local support about neighborhood safety. We're backing him. That will certainly make our job a lot easier."

I had nothing to say to that.

I just retreated from the office and left.

It was well past noon, time for lunch, and I had an inkling of where Dean was likely to be.

Dealmakers was full when I entered. The hostess, a 20-something brunette in a shapely dress with a blue floral pattern, asked me who I was meeting and said there were only a few booths open.

I looked around and saw Dean in a booth facing someone with his back to me whom I couldn't make out.

"I'm with them," I said, pointing in Dean's direction. She let me file past.

I couldn't believe my luck. Practically the only booth open in the place was just in front of Dean and his lunchtime companion.

I plopped down in a seat facing Dean, keeping my head down low and buried in the menu the hostess had given me.

Dean and the man with his back to me had ordered and were eating. Dean had a salad and the other man was munching on a hamburger.

"I need you and your group to back me," he said. "We have a similar agenda."

The other man continued eating, didn't look up or pay much attention to what Dean was saying.

"This hamburger is good," he said. "It tastes even better since you're paying."

I recognized the voice, both nasal and gravelly at the same time. It was the pock-marked man, Frank Chase.

Frank seemed to be enjoying his moment of power. He continued chewing and did not answer until he finished his burger.

"I think I'd like some dessert," he said.

Dean motioned for the waitress and Frank ordered apple pie with vanilla ice cream. Dean just had coffee.

"Yes," Frank Chase finally said, "we'll back you. What do you need done?"

"Nothing right now, and no burning crosses or whatever you guys did with the Chinese family, but if my resolution isn't approved, we may need to be out in the street in force."

Frank Chase didn't reply to that. He just nodded.

Dean Williams at least thought Chase was the one who set the fire in the Chungs' house.

Williams then leaned in toward Chase. "I hear that sometimes in your 'missions' you're clumsy with matches and that's why you've got those marks on your face."

"Don't you worry about it. I'm plenty good with them now," Chase replied.

I wanted to hear more, but at that moment the hostess came to me and asked if anyone was joining me. I said no, and she then told me they were very busy and I would have to sit at the bar.

That was okay with me because the last thing I needed was to be seen by either of the two in the booth behind me.

When I got to the bar, I looked at my watch, said to the hostess, "I guess she's not coming," and took off.

I waited for the two men to come out. They shook hands and made for their respective cars. Williams's convertible and Chase's more than slightly used Chevy made for a sharp contrast as they exited the parking lot one after the other.

Chase was likely going back to work. There was nothing further to be gotten from him today, so I kept a safe distance behind the younger Williams because I knew where he was going.

It was nearly 2 when, one after the other, we pulled onto the grounds of the municipal parking lot.

I waited a spell and then entered Torrance City Hall and asked what was now a male receptionist where the City Council was meeting.

This was the City Council, I remembered, that had once both elected and then summarily dismissed William Muller when he tried to reform the town.

The council, all six members, sat on the raised dais, and when I walked in Dean Williams was addressing them.

"And that is why," he said, "I am in favor of the motion Councilman Talbot has proposed that we close the town to strangers, no more settlements. It's too dangerous."

I had heard of towns doing this to keep the population white since "strangers" usually meant Negroes, Mexicans, Chinese and other Asians.

There, on cue, was the Land Claims officer, Lance from the PD, and Morgan and Mamie and their band, all cheering him on.

A general roar went up from the audience and it looked like the motion would pass when suddenly the door to the chamber was flung open and in strode a tall, tousled man in a white suit of his own. He commanded attention from the moment he entered the room.

Dan Williams put his hand on his son's shoulder as he approached the dais and then quickly withdrew it.

"This is a foolhardy motion," he said. "My son is well-intentioned, but it will be impossible to grow the town if we close it off to strangers. We will be truly cutting off our nose to spite our face.

"This is a boom town and it's going to leap ahead in the next five years, but we've got to let that growth occur."

That took the wind out of everyone's sails, especially Junior who just slumped down in his seat in the front row before the podium.

The motion was then quickly defeated by a vote of five to one, the lone vote coming from the councilman who introduced it.

Williams Senior abruptly left, and on the way out he grabbed Junior and pushed him out the door. They both saw me, but neither said anything to me.

"Just stay out of my business," Senior said to Junior, as I followed them out into the hallway.

"And don't let me hear you trying any rough stuff."

With that, he let go of his son's arm, which he had been pinching, and walked briskly out of the building, presumably to get back to his work of making the town safe for the future.

I was more concerned with how Junior was going to take this, and whether he would be contacting Frank Chase.

That didn't happen. Rather, he retreated to the Last Ditch to lick his wounds. The waitress I had seen him with the other night came over to his table with what was, I guess, his standard drink. He held her hand, and she leaned over and kissed him.

He was drowning his sorrows, and I decided to let him be, still feeling like I might like to join him and drown my own, but instead I heeded Dr. Kellman's words, got out of there and returned to work.

When I got back to my office, Crystal had opened a package that had been delivered that afternoon.

It was the photos of my escapade at Madame Thai's with a note attached. "Boss," she said, "you're still quite the drunken stallion."

She then showed me the note. It read, "Last warning. Get out of Torrance and stay out or these start getting delivered all over town."

I was making progress on the case, but all that would have to wait, because first I needed to deal with this threat to my livelihood and my career.

31

Lyn was puzzled. Why had the Tong who seemingly had trapped them in her mentor's shop not burst through Mr. Mung's curtain and taken her and Harry?

She decided she was "on the case" and would be pursuing them. She would take a lesson from Harry Palmer and follow them.

She stationed herself outside the gambling den that they had taken her to when they kidnapped her.

She had been watching it for a few days and had observed the activity decreasing there.

In China, the Tong's power was based on maintaining lineage claims, that is, by grafting onto the power of local landlords and warlords who had fractured the country. Mao and the Revolution had laid waste to that power by distributing the land in a national reform program that her grandfather had described to her. They had seized the clan associations and ancestral halls the Tong defended, and turned them into schools and meeting places for peasant groups claiming control of their villages.

This undermining of their traditional power carried over into the Chinese diaspora, where Chinese men who had fought in the war were now attending college on the GI Bill. Women also were becoming more assertive, wanting jobs as secretaries and office workers, not just as sewers where they were almost slave laborers in the garment district, as the speaker at the rally had described.

What was left to the Tong was gambling and prostitution in the place of their traditional role of enforcing the power of Chinatown merchants.

On the second day of her stakeout, Lyn struck, as Palmer might say, "paydirt."

She saw the two Tong members who had grabbed her approaching the gambling hall and talking to three other Tong members outside.

From her perch on the corner of a neighboring building, she watched them, this time with an improvement over the day before.

She had bought binoculars and she noticed, though the two were roughly the same size, a tattoo on the index finger of the slightly smaller man, which looked like a coiled serpent with a Chinese word underneath it. She had to pull the focus on the glasses to its smallest measure and was able to make out the word "*mingyun*," which translated in English to "destiny."

The two men did not go into the hall. But they received some instructions from one of the other men outside and were now departing.

Lyn was going to follow them when an arm snaked out, grabbed her, and pulled her back around the corner.

She coiled into fighting mode, raising both arms to counter this thrust and started to ready one foot for a kick when she saw who it was.

"What are you doing here?" she said.

"Getting you to safety. You shouldn't be hanging around here," Harry Palmer said.

He took her arm and led her down the street and into a nearby tea shop where they could be seated.

"I told you I was going to find out what they were up to," she replied when they had ordered two jasmine teas.

"And I will help you, but first I need a favor."

Harry told her about his "adventure" at Madame Thai's and his subsequent blackmailing.

"Detective Palmer put wee-wee where it does not belong?" she said, clamoring to see the photos.

"Number one daughter too young for photos," Harry said.

He told her that he figured the negatives were still with Madame Thai, who he thought would want to hold onto them for whatever power they would grant her.

Lyn began to get the idea where this was going and she wasn't sure she liked it.

"I know it's dangerous, but I want you to go in there and get them for me."

"You're right, number one daughter risking her hide getting photos for white detective. What in it for number one daughter?"

"While you're there you can see if the Tong and Madame Thai are con-nected. It might also lead us closer to who killed your mother."

That was enough. She accepted.

"You'll be inside, but I'm giving you a device that will help you. If you get in any trouble, Crystal and I will be outside listening and we'll come get you."

Harry took her to his car and showed her the device, which he said was on loan from a friendly sound man he had met on his first case.

It was clumsy, and not small, but it would fit inside her shirt.

"Okay, I'll do it," she said. "But after this, I want to be at least on call for your detective agency and, if you use me, I want to get paid."

"That's a deal," Harry said. "Now let's talk about how you're going to get in there."

Harry was right. He had sussed out that there was always a need for a cleaner in Madame Thai's place, and they put together a story that Lyn could tell.

They had bought her a plain, second-hand black shirt and black pants and dressed her as what Harry described as a "scullery maid." He also had her practice her demeanor, so that she behaved humbly and didn't flex her martial arts muscles. He had her bend over and walk slightly crooked.

When she entered the place early afternoon the next day, it was prac-tically deserted. Madame Thai herself was resplendent even in what for her was probably casual wear, a loose-fitting pink dress that had the signature slit revealing her right leg.

She was smoking a cigarette and talking to a few of the girls gathered around her. They were discussing a new number for the show that evening.

Her girls were even more casual, most without makeup at this time of day, and some with their black hair falling loosely on their shoulders.

"And who might you be?" Madame Thai said, when Lyn entered, making sure she looked lost and out of place.

"I need job," she said. "Will clean entire place, almost for free."

She hoped she wasn't overdoing it.

"And where have you stumbled in from?" Madame Thai asked. The girls around her were making fun of Lyn and pulling at her frayed shirt.

"In Chinatown, live in small apartment divided into two bedroom with mother, father, and us four daughter. Mother, father, and youngest daughter in one room, me and other two in other room. Need work for family."

"And what brought you here?" she asked suspiciously.

"Man I met told me might be work here. He wanted me for something else but I only want to work as cleaner. I clean very well. Make floor and window spotless."

With that she bowed.

"We can use a really good cleaner, but I can't pay you much."

"Mai Ling not need much," Lyn said. "An honor to serve."

"You can start today."

Madame Thai had one of the girls show "Mai Ling" around the place and get her a cleaning cart and a white apron.

The girl who stepped forward was probably not much older than Lyn. Without her severe makeup, she looked like an ordinary young woman. Actually, Lyn thought, slightly plain looking. She showed her the rooms where the girls took their men for the night and poked open the door of the large room at the back of the hall, Madame Thai's bedroom, which she said Mai Ling should be extra careful in cleaning.

"You must have good job, make lots of money," Lyn said.

"It's not that easy," the girl, who called herself Blossom, replied.

"The place I worked before got raided all the time. The police would haul the girls off to jail and then try to send them away to some Christian mission, but they would never touch the owners.

"The owner paid the police for protection but still got raided, though he didn't get arrested, just us. The cops would then raise the price for protection and the owner would pay it.

"That doesn't happen here. We don't know who is behind this place, but whoever it is, they've got the cops in their pocket and we don't get raided."

"Is American Dream," Lyn said, bowing to Blossom.

"Hardly. My American Dream is I want what Americans have, a two-car garage, two bathrooms, and steak every night. I was raised in poverty like you, and someday I'm getting out."

But Lyn noticed that she said this not in an upbeat hopeful way but with a kind of resignation. She felt sorry for the girl, realizing that she may never be able to leave what was still a kind of slavery.

Blossom left her to start cleaning the rooms in the back, where the girls both lived and did their business.

Luckily, she was a good cleaner. She and Sandra had a small house and growing up, since Sandra was at work all day, after school Lyn was responsible for keeping the place, as her mother said, "ship shape." She had probably learned that phrase from one of her clients at the dentist's office.

The rooms were generally a mess. She sprayed them down before beginning the hard task of cleaning, but when she had done a few, she decided, since no one was stirring in the hallway with the girls either out for the day or gathered with Madame Thai in front working on tonight's show, that she would move to the main stage herself.

Madame Thai's room was huge and already spotless. Nevertheless, in dusting and cleaning every corner she had a perfect chance to inspect the room to see where the photos were hidden. She could find nothing. No secret drawers or panels in her dressing closet.

But she knew that poised above the bed was the camera set-up from which someone had photographed Harry. She tapped the wall at the point where the camera would be placed from the way Harry had described the photos.

There was a hollow sound behind the spot she tapped, indicating a room behind this one. How to get to it?

Thinking there might be a secret panel in the hallway, she finished dusting and moved her cleaning tray out of the room.

Just in time, too, because Madame Thai came down the hallway past her and entered her bedroom. She was not alone. With her were the two Tong members Lyn had been keeping an eye on who may have killed her mother.

The three entered the room, and Lyn parked her cleaning cart outside the room next to it and tiptoed to Madame Thai's bedroom door to hear what she could make out of their conversation. Since the room was padded, she had to press her ear tightly against the door to make anything out.

"I have little to say to you gentlemen," Madame Thai began in an irritated tone.

The Tong spoke in Cantonese, the language of Guangdong province, where many Chinese in Los Angeles came from. Luckily for Lyn, her ancestors had come from there too.

They were indeed trying to muscle in on Madame Thai's club, wanting a piece of it.

She boldly told them in a mixture of Cantonese and English that that was not going to happen. She ended her speech in English with a threat.

"Try and make a move on this place and you will find yourself in an American jail very quickly," she said.

With that the two Tong stormed out of the room. Lyn was startled and just managed to leap back from the door, but not before the man with the serpent tattoo got a good look at her.

He recognized her for sure, but said nothing to Madame Thai, who followed them out of the room.

Lyn made as if she was going to ask her boss a question about what to clean next but Madame Thai waved her away and said, "First, I must see these gentlemen to the door."

The trio then paraded down the corridor and out to the main room of the club.

Lyn decided she would gamble that the two Tong would not betray her since they were at cross purposes with the club owner. They may have recognized her as a spy and might even think she could be helpful.

Still, she didn't know how much longer this cover would last and figured she had to move fast.

She went back into the bedroom and made right for the strip of wall above the bed, but still there was no visible opening. She was about to give up, when out of frustration, she moved the bed, thinking to stand on a chair to look at the place on the wall where the camera was concealed. To her surprise, that movement unlocked a hinge behind the bed, and a panel in the wall opened revealing a room behind the bedroom.

Mounted on the wall in that room was the camera, but behind that was a smaller room that as she entered turned out to be a darkroom which, she figured, must be where they developed the photos that were then used for blackmail. Harry had called what Madame Thai was doing a "honey trap," but Lyn thought, *Maybe it should be called a lychee trap or, given what was on the walls of the bedroom, a dragon fruit trap.*

She knew she had to work fast. It would be all over if Madame Thai came back in the room. She could signal Harry and Crystal, but it would be too late, and the burly security guard at the door would probably dispose of her.

There were a whole series of plates in the darkroom. She didn't recognize any of them, but all the men were in the same position. They were all white men, probably prominent in L.A., she figured.

There were two piles, and on top of the second pile were the negatives of the photos with Harry.

She grabbed them, got out of there, and stepped through the trick room back out into the bedroom. She put the bed back in place and that move-ment this time snapped the panel shut.

She had thought to bring her cleaning cart back into the room, and as she was depositing the plates under a pile of towels, Madame Thai entered the room.

"I thought you were finished with this room," she said, seizing Lyn's arm and holding it tight.

"Remembered some dust on the wall and came back to clean again," Lyn said, hoping this would work.

"Wow, you are thorough, and the room does look good," she said, releas-ing her arm.

Lyn was starting to sweat as she hauled the cart out of the room and down the corridor.

She grabbed the plates and hid them under her apron as she entered the outer room.

The bouncer looked at her suspiciously as she moved toward the exit.

"Worked hard, time for cigarette break," she said, and he let her leave.

As she walked out, she saw Harry and Crystal making for her. She gave

Harry the plates with the negatives, but, outside the club, she also spied the two Tong members. She told Harry to watch out for her because she had an idea. He said okay since she was still wearing the listening device.

They were standing around the corner from the club. She approached them, and they did not retreat or try to grab her.

"I think we might be on the same side," she said, "but first I have to know, what was the acid doing in your car?"

The smaller of the two, after a pause, answered.

"We were going to use it on the rally for Mao," he said. "But we decided just breaking up the meeting was enough."

"Did you set the fire that killed my mother?" she asked, and then assumed her fighting stance with her hands flat but pointed at them.

"No, why would we do that?" the smaller one, with the serpent tattoo asked.

"Because she's leaving Chinatown and its old power structure of which you're a big part."

"We've been attacked and accused by the Americans as well," the shorter one said.

The taller one piped up. "After Pearl Harbor we had to wear buttons with a Chinese and American flag so they wouldn't think we were Japanese and beat us up."

"Gentlemen," Lyn said, instead of threatening with her hand now holding it out to them, "I think we might be able to help each other catch my mother's killer if we can put our political differences aside."

She knew that on that front they were closer to Madame Thai, who Harry had told her adored Madame Chiang Kai-shek. The conservative Chinese elements in the U.S. wanted her husband returned to power and even favored an invasion of China to destroy the Revolution. More enlightened voices, however, favored peace between the two countries and were trying to halt the drive toward war.

At the moment, though they were on different sides of that important battle, she knew she might need them.

They shrugged at her offer, said they would think about it, and moved away.

Harry ran up to her. Crystal fell right behind and hugged her.

"Number one daughter is number one detective."

Lyn smiled and then collapsed in Crystal's arms, suddenly overwhelmed with the realization of how close she had been to a much more dangerous outcome.

32

The two men in black had returned to Palo Verde, threatening a home nearby Rosa's. Esperanza, as I had suggested, snapped their photos, and had them developed. Now we had photos of them both in front of my former hotel in Bunker Hill and in East L.A. at two scenes of the crime.

I was still avoiding Esperanza, preoccupied with the case and not ready yet to come clean to her. So I felt relieved when she suggested that instead of me coming to her house, we go out together to a gala to which her boss Edward Roybal had invited her.

It was a black-tie, formal dress affair at the Hollywood Bowl, which had recently been saved from oblivion. Massive charity events had raised money to keep the outdoor concert hall alive and pay off an enormous debt. To celebrate this resurrection, last month there was a big show on the Hollywood Bowl stage titled *The California Story*, which to me sounded like a lot of rich people celebrating themselves and, from what I had been experiencing, not much about the other California of Mexican, Negro, Chinese and American workers trying to hold onto their land in this state.

The show was an extravaganza with two hundred chorus girls and hundreds of Hollywood actors, stretching out beyond the stage and into the Hollywood hills. It was helmed by a famous Russian director I'd never heard of, and the story was told on stage by Lionel Barrymore. If Edward G. Robinson could play Chiang Kai-shek, why couldn't the fading celebrity Lionel Barrymore star as California? In Hollywood anything was possible.

Why on earth would I want to dress up and go to this gaudy display of wealth? is what I thought when Esperanza asked me to be her date. I think she knew what my response would be because she explained that there was something in this gathering she wanted me to see, something that would help the case. She asked that I bring the photos along and told me she was bringing hers also. That was intriguing, and I also decided to go because accompanying her might put credits on my side of the ledger when I came clean about my recent exploit.

I had to rent a tuxedo, which I guess would come out of my expenses for the case, though I wasn't at all sure that any of this was relevant.

For the evening, they had disassembled a portion of the stage and instead mounted a simple central podium where the full stage would have been. There were about 400 guests, a small crowd for the Hollywood Bowl but a very large gathering of L.A.'s elite. The lights were dimmed, and everyone in the audience below was facing the raised podium.

On the dais was the power of the *Los Angeles Times*. Striding forward to address the crowd was the *Times* publisher's wife, Dorothy Chandler. Norman, the husband, was seated quietly and obediently behind her. They were a strange couple. Norman parted his neatly trimmed steel-gray hair in the middle in an antique style made fashionable by actors like Ronald Reagan and the singer Rudy Vallee. His wife had the female equivalent, the same neatly trimmed and suavely stacked graying hair. She was much more animated than him. She mounted the podium in a way that suggested she had total command of the evening. He suppressed a yawn and looked bored behind her.

She was there apparently to outline her vision of a new Los Angeles.

"The city," she said, "has to be a hub which the suburbs circulate around. We must revive downtown and we're going to do it by creating a world-renowned culture center.

"This city has too long been a runner-up to New York and Chicago. We're going to create a city that is recognized around the world and where here we promote 'civic respect.'"

She asked everyone to applaud themselves for having participated in her campaign to "Save The Bowl" and preserve open-air classical concerts in Los Angeles.

She then described her plans for, first and foremost, a classical music center which would feature a Los Angeles orchestra to compete with other cities and, particularly in California, with the San Francisco Symphony. Her complex, as she outlined it, also included two theaters, one large, which would inject L.A. with a Broadway flourish, and the other smaller and more experimental, a kind of off-Broadway.

I was starting to yawn myself when she explained that these cultural forums would be built just above downtown on what was still Bunker Hill. Suddenly, what had happened to me became clearer. Esperanza already knew this and touched my hand when Dorothy Chandler got to this part of the speech.

Dorothy was now moving into her pitch, starting to rev up her campaign.

"And where will the money come from for all of this? It will come from all of you concerned citizens who want to make this town the equal of any other.

"So, enjoy the evening and when it comes time to donate, please open your wallets and give generously."

With that, cheers rang out from the audience, along with chants of "Go, Buff."

She was resplendent at the podium, smiling and basking in the glow of her stardom. Esperanza told me she was planning on naming the concert hall after herself, already rejecting an idea that it instead be named "The Peace Pavilion." I noticed Norman barely clapping on the stage as people around us applauded wildly.

"He's the businessman of the two," Esperanza said.

"He looks kind of henpecked," I replied.

"Yes, he's rumored to have said that he wonders 'if anyone will ever name even a closet after me.'"

Next up on the podium were the combo of the song-and-dance man Danny Kaye and the singer-actress Dinah Shore who performed a duet. I was a fan of neither, but Esperanza told me they had been in a war film together called *Up in Arms* and were doing a number from that.

Their real reason for being on stage was revealed when through the Hollywood Bowl front gate a fresh-faced, blond-haired young man drove a Cadillac El Dorado.

The duo then explained that to get the charity ball rolling they were holding a raffle for the car where tickets could then be purchased.

They left the podium. The lights came back on and we were met with an onslaught of Chandler reps accosting us. First came the food, lots of hors d'oeuvres, several kinds of cheese with broccoli and celery and meats, beef, ham, and chicken, with assortments of crackers. These were followed by a second legion, this time of girls in skimpy costumes right out of a nightclub selling the raffle tickets.

Esperanza guided me past this charity phalanx to Edward, who was shaking his head at the whole scene and standing next to a companion.

At this point he recognized me.

"Esperanza has told me about your helping her and losing your home," he said. "Now you see this alternate version of Los Angeles. Bunker Hill becomes a corporate playground with its 'cultural' temples to the rich, and most likely the three villages in East L.A. are just laid waste to become, who knows, maybe a sports palace. They've been trying to get a baseball team here since the 1930s. Maybe they'll accomplish it.

"But it's all instead of building public housing, which is a much greater priority for the city. It's about serving the expensive taste of the well-to-do."

He then shook my hand, patted Esperanza on the shoulder and walked off.

Roybal's companion, a small man with a thick mustache, looked out of place in this gathering and lingered with us since he seemed to know Esperanza.

"This is Emilio Diaz, our accounting consultant," she said.

The man smiled and lowered his head, a bit overwhelmed at the formality of the occasion. In front of the podium, the Benny Goodman Quintet was performing and a scattered few of the crowd were even dancing, awkwardly it looked to me, but dancing, nonetheless.

"Dorothy is quite a dynamo," I shouted to the accountant, trying to be heard above the music.

He had a different take.

"It's a lot about her own power," he said. "They call her 'the greatest fundraiser since Al Capone.' They both know how to strong-arm an audience. She controls the society pages of the *Times* and that's her bully pulpit. If you want to be in those pages, you need to contribute to her charities.

"She's trying to create this group called the Blue Ribbon 400, who are going to be asked to each contribute $1000 every year to the music center. That's $400,000 a year. The idea, my sources tell me, is that if you want to do business in this town you have to be one of the 400—and no Mexicans or Negroes need apply."

I thought about the contrast between *The California Eagle's* Charlotta Bass, who used the society pages of her publication to rally Negro ladies to defend the hard-won housing gains of her readers trying to secure a better place in Dorothy's society, and Dorothy's organizing of the rich in a way that excluded everyone else and furthered their own power.

Diaz found me a willing audience and wanted to keep going.

"They'll get the money however they can," he said. "The voters have already rejected an appropriation for her plans for an opera house, so now they're in the process of lifting almost $14 million from the county pension fund administered by the county supervisor. The whole idea of 'civic respect' is to lay the groundwork for the supervisor approving the funds, so they don't have to put it before the people. Every public bond they've floated so far for this project has been rejected by the voters. Despite what you see here"—and with that he pointed to the crowd reaching for their wallets—"the majority of money isn't coming from donations. The plan is to 'appropriate' it from working people's pensions."

I couldn't help thinking about the jazz and particularly rhythm and blues clubs on Central Avenue where new kinds of music were being discovered every day, and new, more lively song stylings like those practiced by my ex, Dinitia. Nobody was "appropriating" money to support them.

The accountant then shuffled off pursuing not the chorus girls with the raffle tickets but the waitresses with the food.

I thought it would be a good idea to join him, when who should come striding through the crowd but Dorothy herself.

As she approached us, Esperanza let me have a bit of her history. Her father owned a chain of expensive department stores, with the family name of Buffums, a kind of California version of the high-end Gimbels in New York, only Buffums started in Long Beach.

With this merchant background, when she married Norman, whom she met in college, she was not accepted into the idle rich of Pasadena—which initially led her to see a psychiatrist who counseled her to go her own way and not pay any attention to the old wealth surrounding her.

So Dorothy, called Buffy—and by her close friends, Buff—moved to Los Angeles and began her control of L.A. society using the power of the newspaper.

As Esperanza was finishing her summary, Dorothy and her entourage, which included Norman looking uncomfortable and trailing behind her, approached us.

"Who have we here?" she said, addressing Esperanza and myself.

"We're big fans," I said.

Esperanza added, laying it on a little too thick I thought, "And you're such a strong woman."

Dorothy blushed. "I'm not, really," she said. "I owe it all to my husband."

At that she took Norman's hand, and he cringed and backed up, embarrassed at the attention.

"I'm just a loyal wife," she said, pulling him back to her and corralling him around the neck with her arm.

I'd had about enough of this.

"We do have a question," I said.

"Go ahead," the great lady responded, "we're all friends here."

Esperanza and I then showed her the photos of the men in black and I told her where they were taken.

She let out a little gasp and managed to stammer out a reply.

"We're trying to turn idlers and unproductive space into a modern city," she said, and quickly pivoted away.

I saw her talking to one of the discreet security members circulating in the crowd who quickly approached us.

"Are you two buying a raffle ticket?" he asked.

"Not planning on it," I said. "We're just here for the finger food."

I knew the gig was up and didn't see any reason to prolong the agony.

"I'm afraid you two will have to come with me," he said.

At that point, another two security members emerged from the crowd, and the three of them escorted us out the front gate, watching as we made our way down the hill toward our car.

Esperanza invited me back to her home in Boyle Heights, and this time I couldn't refuse. I was still not comfortable doing anything more than cuddling until I had told her the truth. I imagined that might be a bit uncomfortable but I was sticking to my resolution.

When we got back to Boyle Heights, we noticed that across the street from the apartment building, a crowd had gathered around a local electronics shop watching television through the show window. Most people on Esperanza's block probably could not yet afford a set of their own.

What they were watching was glowing coverage of the event we had just witnessed.

"That's KTTV, a station partly owned by the *Times*," Esperanza said. "They give Edward hardly any coverage at all."

The *Times* had apparently decided the future was in these huge green sets which they thought would soon be in everyone's living room. And according to who I hoped was still my girlfriend, they had even bought what was an independent movie studio this year to use to launch the station.

The paper was everywhere. Buff's "civilizing mission" was part of remaking a town that, when it resisted that mission, might be compelled by whatever means necessary to accept it.

33

I was starting to feel like I was back on track. Lyn had probably erased the danger of the photos since it was likely that Madame Thai kept the negatives and made copies in her darkroom. That didn't tell us who was bankrolling her, nor who was using them to try to get me off the case. But the immediate threat was past.

Lyn believed that her new friends the Tong did not have a hand in killing her mother, and I tended to accept that—and also to think that this new unholy alliance might be useful.

The most promising lead might still be Williams's son Dean and his own linking up with the pock-marked Klan man Frank Chase.

There was the messy affair of Dean's relation with Diane, but beyond that lay the question of who wanted Diane dead. I had a strong intuition that might have to do with her own quest to find out what happened to her parents in their fatal crash.

The logical first stop for me in investigating their deaths would be the police station, but that wasn't the friendliest place lately and I wanted to see if I could steer clear of it.

I went instead to the Town Clerk's office. It turns out that in Torrance police arrest records and reports were public.

I asked if this was because everyone had a right to the information.

He replied "No," and explained.

The reason was that the police didn't want to be bothered with keeping the records, so they foisted them off on his department, where they sat on some dusty shelves since hardly anyone ever looked at them.

He let me in the back to search through the documents, and in about an hour I found a series of reports under the twin headings "Coroner's Corner" and "Murder Mile." This section of the road, all angular curves, had no traffic lights, signs, or any attempts to slow traffic. There was one particular section more dangerous than the rest—the corner of Newton Street and Pacific Coast Highway—and it was known as "The Dark Corner."

The file contained a history of accidents on this stretch which had, in the last three years, amounted to almost 60 injuries.

The town was petitioning the state offices in Sacramento to install safety devices, but as yet there was no response.

In that pile was only one twin death, and I figured this was Diane's parents. The name, of course, was not Chestnut, Diane's phony real estate moniker, but rather Burnett, Mr. and Mrs. Bob Burnett, killed in a crash 11 years ago. The file contained photos of the aftermath of the crash which the report said had indeed occurred at The Dark Corner. It was a grisly sight. The police had photographed the car at the location and next to it both bodies, mangled and covered in blood.

The report also said the other driver, whom they had crashed into, Blaine Henry, escaped with only minor injuries.

I had to have those photographs and I didn't figure it would be too difficult to get them out past a clerk who regarded the records as a burden he shouldn't have to bear.

But when I stepped out of the records room in the back and entered the front office, he struck an official pose.

"I'm going to have to search you," he said. "I'm charged with making sure these records remain intact."

He then patted me down, feeling inside my coat, searching my shirt front and back and with that, let me go.

It wasn't the most elegant solution, but it worked. I had fitted the photos against my ankles and pulled my socks up over them.

My next action was to drive Murder Mile and see for myself how dangerous it was.

The stretch was well named. I had to swerve a couple of times myself to avoid oncoming cars. The Dark Corner was especially treacherous. The curve was practically 90 degrees and it was almost impossible to see who might be coming around the corner. I had to slow to almost a crawl.

Once around the corner, I parked on the thin curb that was just wide enough for my car. I took out the photos and went back to the corner.

Lo and behold, the photos of the accident did not match the corner where I was standing. The police report was incorrect. The death had not occurred where they described it, so I started walking the stretch of highway to see what matched the photos.

I found a stretch of terrain that was an exact match, except there was again a problem with the report. It had stated that the Burnetts lost control of the vehicle as they rounded the curve, but the area where the photos were taken was a completely straight part of the highway, probably the safest short stretch of Murder Mile.

As usual with the Torrance police, something was fishy.

I had to find Blaine Henry, the other driver.

That was not difficult. He was listed in the Torrance white pages. He lived not far from the scene of the accident on Madrona.

I approached his house, smaller than the others on the block and a little more unkempt. Inside, I found a man who looked to be in his late 50s, a bit unkempt and run-down himself, but eager to have any visitor.

"What can I do you for, mister?" he said.

"I'm a reporter doing a story on Murder Mile to get the state to clean up the place. I wanted to get your version of one of the most notorious accidents to happen there."

He seemed a bit confused and reluctant.

"My paper offers a reward for sources who contribute to our stories, who step forward because of 'civic respect.'"

Who would have thought Buffy Chandler's phrase would actually come in handy?

I pulled out a fifty-dollar bill. That came in handier.

He grabbed it and motioned me to a seat.

"Well, of course I remember," he said.

"That was tragic but I didn't have anything to do with it."

I told him I knew he didn't and he relaxed.

I wanted to know about the other car.

"First of all, where on the road were you? The police said it was the Dark Corner."

"Well, that's not quite right," he said. He got up and went to a battered desk and pulled out a map.

"No, it happened right here." He pointed to the spot on the map that I had identified, a short distance from the deadly curve.

"Their car started swerving left and right and coming straight at me. I ducked to avoid them and they went over the embankment and crashed into the side of the road. I'll never forget it. The car jumped the pavement and overturned. I called the police and then I left. I was too shocked to follow the story in the papers at the time. I wasn't aware until you just told me that the police report claimed the accident took place at the Dark Corner."

"I looked at the police report and it suggested he had been drinking. Did you get that impression?"

Blaine put his hand to his jaw and, as he might say in his careful manner, "ruminated" about it.

After a while, he was ready to speak.

"I can't be sure, but I don't think so. He didn't seem drunk."

That matched what Diane had said about her father.

Blaine continued. I was certainly getting my money's worth.

"The swerving seemed to me, in the moments just before I got out of the way, as if he was trying to control the car. I will never forget the look on his face. It was a look of terror, trying to bring the car to a halt before he got to the Dark Corner. He also, I think, chose to go off the road rather than hit me, and he may have saved my life."

I had heard enough.

It was time to seek out my old friend the County Coroner to get his view of the death.

He had signed the death certificate, verifying the police report, and I needed to know, given what I had found out that morning, if there were additional irregularities in his report.

I had to drive back to L.A. and visit my old stomping grounds in Boyle Heights, but it was worth it.

Phineas Poole, last time I'd seen him, was about to retire. He had never met a police report he didn't go along with, and I had needed to strong-arm him in the past to get anything out of him.

This time that wasn't necessary.

He was holding a freshly lit cigar and spraying the ashes all around the morgue, just missing covering the body he was examining with soot from his smelly stogie.

"What are you doing here, Palmer?" he asked, looking up from his work, cigar in one hand and what looked like a hacksaw in the other.

"I could ask you the same question. I thought you were retiring."

He had a minute for me.

"I was. Had the testimonial and everything."

He put down the hacksaw and reached inside his pocket to show me his retirement gift, a gold watch.

"But I got in a little financial trouble, a money arrangement I've had to work off."

"You're telling me you have gambling debts with the Mob and that's why you're still here?"

Phineas was as corrupt as the day was long.

"I didn't say that, but if that's what you think I can't stop you."

"Your secret's safe with me. I just want your opinion on a car crash that happened in Torrance eleven years ago.

He knew immediately what I was talking about.

"That was a funny one," he said.

I didn't think he would say anything more but instead he even put his cigar down in an ashtray next to his latest corpse.

I told him what I had discovered and he was not surprised.

"I'm no fan of Torrance or the Torrance police," he said, and I realized he may have lost his money in one of the gambling houses on The Strip.

"Had some bad experiences in that place."

"Well, okay. Here's your chance to get revenge. They claim Burnett was drinking. Did you find any trace of alcohol when you did the autopsy?"

"Well, first of all. The local police didn't request an autopsy. But I took a look on my own and no, there was no trace of alcohol in either of them."

"Then what was making him swerve like the driver of the other car described?"

Phineas thought about that. Thinking for him necessitated picking up the cigar again, and this time, lost in thought, he absentmindedly flicked some ashes on the corpse.

"There is one thing I've seen that could cause that," he said.

"If someone had drained the brake fluid, he would be frantically pumping the brake trying to stop and might have chosen to go off the road before he hit the deadly curve. I've seen the Mob 'fix' accidents like that."

"Thanks, Phineas," I said. "You've done your good deed for the year, and I hope you work off your debt before they drain your brake fluid."

He motioned for me to leave, took a long toke of his cigar, picked up the hacksaw, and resumed work.

I was always relieved to get out of there.

My next, and I figured last stop was to track down the Torrance officer who had signed the report.

His name was O'Reilly, and he too was listed in the directory.

He was on the other side of town from Blaine at the end of Maricopa Street. His house was in even worse repair. The lawn looked like it hadn't been mowed in ages, with thick underbrush crawling up and strangling the porch.

I rang the front door, and a man in his mid-60s came out in dirty white t-shirt and black pants that had a lot of last night's hamburger and ketchup on them.

This was not going to be pleasant.

"Yeah," he growled, as he opened the door. "What do you want?"

"I want to make sure you keep getting your pension," I said. "I've got enough information about a crash you investigated to know there was a coverup."

He looked in both directions to make sure none of the neighbors had heard me, then motioned for me to come in.

"What you buttin' into?" he said.

"I'm a private detective, working for Diane Chestnut. I know about falsifying the report to claim the accident took place at the curve and I also know that Diane's father probably wasn't drinking."

A look came over his face that I had seen before, mostly on crooked cops. It was as if he had been waiting his whole life, or at least his whole retirement, for someone like me to show up and reveal what he had done.

"Nothin' you can do about it," he said, pouring himself a hearty portion of the bottle of scotch that lay open on the table in front of our two chairs.

"There's something *you* can do about it," I said. "You can tell the truth. I'm not after you, and it would probably be a great relief."

He confirmed what I had told him, and now we were facing his moment of reckoning.

"When you examined the car, was the brake fluid drained?"

He didn't answer at first, just took another big gulp of the scotch, draining the glass.

Finally, he nodded, in answer to my question.

"Yes," he said. "It was just before I was to retire. You're right, the brake fluid was drained."

"So, what seemed to be an accident was a murder?"

"That's what it looked like," he said. "I've been waiting all these years for it to catch up to me."

"Who bought you off?" I asked, realizing this was the hardest question of all.

I took a look around the place. "You couldn't have made much money off of the deal."

He rubbed his belly. "Cirrhosis of the liver," he said. "It all went to the doctors, and in the end hasn't done any good.

"I will tell you this, and it might help you. What I found out in the course of the investigation was that Burnett was not their real name."

"Thanks," I said, "but who do you think did this?"

In answer, he got up, walked to a chest of drawers which looked like it should have been in the bedroom, and pulled out something.

I thought he was going to show me some new evidence. But what he took out was a Smith and Wesson .38, probably one he had kept from his time on the force.

I was going to rush him, but before I could, he turned his back on me and headed into the bedroom.

I was heading there myself when I heard a blast, and then the thud of a body as it hit the floor.

Whoever was behind this killing was someone more powerful than O'Reilly could deal with. Given what he probably thought could happen to him, I suppose he had taken the easy way out. Or maybe he was just consumed with guilt, eating away at him in this house at the end of the world until it finally ate him up.

34

Though the sound came from the back bedroom, the gun made a loud noise. A few minutes later a nosy neighbor came poking at the front door.

I went out onto the porch to meet her, an elderly biddy wearing a bathrobe and hair curlers she hadn't bothered to remove. Her curiosity had gotten the best of her, outweighing whatever sense of decorum she might still be clinging to.

I told her that her neighbor had committed suicide. She shrugged, hardly surprised, she said, since he had seemed to be in a constant state of drunkenness. She went to call the police.

I had to work fast. O'Reilly was one of their own and they would probably be here quickly.

I didn't particularly want to face the body in the back. I was just going to assume the bullet had done its job. I had heard of enough police suicides in my time, and they were most likely to occur in retirement, when the men on the force had time to think back about what damage they had done and who they had done it to.

On a hunch, I went to the drawer from where he had pulled the gun and rummaged through it. I didn't have to search long. Near where the gun had lain was a piece of paper.

I unfolded and read it. It was typed out, very neat and tidy, like a standard police report, only instead of transcribing someone else's confession, O'Reilly had written his own.

He had indeed been paid to make out a phony report, misidentifying where the accident had occurred and implying that there may have been alcohol involved, all to discount the eyewitness account of the other driver, and most important, to suppress the fact that upon examination of the car, he had observed that the brake fluid was drained.

He definitely covered up a murder and I had the proof. What I didn't know was who had drained the brake fluid and why.

Time was getting short, and I thought I heard off in the distance the sound of a police siren.

O'Reilly, it turned out, had one more thing to tell me from beyond the grave. It was as if dead he was admitting what he could not bring himself to confess alive.

I found a check in the same drawer. I assumed there had been a series of payments and this was the last one, which I guess he never cashed, again perhaps wanting his secret to be found out.

The check was for $500 and it was issued from AA Milne Ltd. I had never heard of the company but I assumed whoever was behind it was part of the coverup and the murder.

The bathrobe lady returned. I told her I was a friend of the cop and that he had two papers he wanted passed onto his family. I asked, as a favor to the deceased, if she would mind holding onto them until the family came to pick them up.

She agreed and left. Shortly after, McGinty burst through the door, followed by Lance.

McGinty had his revolver drawn. Brave cop, knowing he was here to investigate a suicide.

He couldn't help pointing it at me.

"On your knees," he said, but Lance halted him.

I addressed Lance and hoped once again cooler heads prevailed.

"Let's check the scene of the crime," he said.

They went into the back room and a few moments later McGinty came staggering out.

"What a brave man," he stammered, by way of an epitaph. "They don't make them like that anymore."

There was something almost touching about one corrupt cop eulogizing another.

Almost touching, but not quite.

I had some business with both of them.

I had a hunch and wanted to act on it.

"I know you've just had a shock," I said to McGinty, while Lance was still in the bedroom with the body. "But I was wondering if you could look at these photos and tell me if you recognize either of them?"

I pulled out my handy dandy snapshots of the two men in black.

McGinty's reaction was confounding, even given his possible state of shock.

At first, he smiled, as if they were old friends, then, when he remembered who he was in front of, he frowned and reached for the photos to try and tear them up.

"These aren't relevant to any of the cases here," he said.

I snatched the photos away from him.

"Anyway, thanks," I said. He had told me what I wanted to know.

Lance then returned from the bedroom, telling McGinty to get on the horn and call the County Coroner. The brawn went into the kitchen to make the call and I was left with the brain.

That was good for me because I had business with him too.

"O'Reilly was a shady character and involved in a coverup more than a decade ago."

I told him about the case. It was before Lance had transferred to Torrance, but he had heard of it.

"He left a confession linking himself and the Torrance PD to the crime. I've also got a check that was probably part of his payoff."

"And where is this confession?" Lance asked, realizing that McGinty would return soon and the two of them could probably lift it off of me.

"It's safely stored away," I said, "where it will stay. There is no reason to involve the department in this."

He liked that.

"That is, on one condition."

He looked puzzled. What was I up to?

"I have a strong hunch about who killed Stan Cardiff, and it wasn't his second wife. I want you to let her go and drop the charges."

"Why would we do that?"

"It will be a lot less grief for the department. We won't dredge up the past. And I will bring you the killers all tied up in a neat little bow and you can take the credit. If I fail, you can always arrest Fran again and charge her."

Surprisingly, he agreed. On my way out, I knocked at the neighbor's door. She came out onto the porch, excited that all of this was happening on her street.

I showed her my PI license, said I would also be investigating, and asked if I could come in for a cup of coffee.

When she went to the kitchen to get it, I noticed that she had set the two papers down on a table beside her couch.

I grabbed them and got out of there quickly. None too soon, it appeared, because on my way out McGinty and Lance arrived to question the neighbor who had phoned in the shooting.

I tipped my hat to them and got out of there pell-mell.

I burned rubber, smiling as I took off. It was always rewarding to come out ahead of L.A. County's finest, even if that wasn't much of an accomplishment. When you're being dragged down into a sea of corruption, sometimes it helps just to briefly come up for air.

<hr>

The nature of Diane duty certainly had changed. Crystal had been at her bedside almost from the moment she arrived at the hospital, worried that, after they removed the bullet, she might not heal properly.

Diane thanked her and was a little embarrassed at all the attention. She didn't say much, just held Crystal's hand and sometimes pulled her to her bed and kissed her.

That was enough.

Padewski, the rookie officer, had arrived and stationed himself outside in the hall. He was having such a good old time reading magazines and ordering food that he barely had a minute to keep an eye on Diane. He was such a raw recruit that if the men in black returned, Crystal wasn't at all sure he could handle them, and that was another reason she was staying.

That was not to last, however. Harry told her he had work for her. He wanted her to trail Frank Chase, the pock-marked man, who Williams's son Dean at least thought had set the fire that killed Sandra Chung. After Harry had snuffed out his and his fellow Klan members' burning cross, he had headed in the direction of The Strip, but then Harry had lost him and that was just before the fire broke out.

It was late afternoon when Crystal parked herself outside the plant where Frank worked. He came out of the plant with two of his buddies. They sat for a moment together in front of what was probably Frank's car. Frank took out some cups and poured each what looked like a slug. They downed the grog and then took off, all three cars in a line.

They didn't go far. The caravan pulled into the parking lot of a tavern only a few blocks away, and all three got out and entered. She wondered if the other two were also Chase's recruits for the Klan.

Crystal wasn't sure it was even necessary to follow them inside. It just looked like all that was going on was more drinking.

About an hour went by, and no movement from any of the trio in the bar. Crystal had bought a series of magazines with names like *Home Beautiful* and *Building Your Castle*. That was before she had caught Diane in the act of what was sometimes really necessary to "make the sale," and before she had found the green book saying where you could and couldn't sell.

The truth of what lay beneath the profession had pretty much soured her on the work, so she threw the magazines in the back seat and instead read an article she'd found in the *L.A. Daily News* about the real estate industry. The reporter had talked to a number of agents who were up in arms about the policy of the National Association of Realtors, which apparently held the patent on the word "Realtor." That is, no agent could call themselves a realtor unless they paid membership dues to the organization, which consequently had over 500,000 members as well as owning millions in assets. *What a profession*, she thought. *They're so greedy, they're eating each other.*

There were also rumors: The reporter wrote about the male leaders of the association having improper relations with female brokers. Crystal flashed back on the speaker who had invited both her and Diane to meet him in what he may have imagined would be a tasty threesome, and about Diane's having to sell herself to her male clients to make the sale.

It's a corrupt organization and a corrupt business through and through. She decided that if she and Diane were going to continue—and she hoped they would—things were going to have to change.

She had just reached this conclusion when all three of the men exited the tavern. They had apparently downed a number of drinks because none of them were walking straight. Chase especially was slipping and sliding and slapping one of his pals on the back. He tried to slap the other one, missed and fell forward. The first guy caught him and the two hauled Chase to his car.

They're not going to let him drive, Crystal thought, but, apparently, they had no such qualms. The other two, one of whom Crystal recognized when she was waiting with the girls in the parking lot, probably were then on their way home to those wives.

Oh boy, the wives are going to be in for a fun evening.

Chase, though, didn't have anyone to go home to.

Now's the time to follow him, but not too closely. Crystal remembered that he had seen her at the plant the other day.

He headed west and she had a pretty good idea where he was going, so she could relax and not be on his tail.

He was heading in the direction of The Strip and she was pretty sure that he would end up at the Last Ditch.

She was so sure that's where he would end up, she gave him a twenty-minute head start.

But when she arrived at The Strip, she couldn't find Frank Chase's car. It had disappeared.

This was exactly what Harry had described the night of the fire.

She had an idea, though, of what might have happened and decided to go see her favorite bartender, Jack Smith.

She ordered a mai tai, not because she particularly wanted a drink, but just because she liked the red and yellow umbrellas that came with it.

Jack was in a good mood when she entered and prepared her drink with a grand flourish. He was also delighted with her tip, courtesy of her daily expenses from Harry.

He lingered after bringing her the drink.

"How's my favorite would-be but not really waitress?" he asked.

"A little miffed," she said. "I was supposed to meet a date here but looks like he hasn't shown up. He's a guy from the Dow plant, Frank Chase."

At this Jack grunted.

"I think you can kiss your date goodbye for tonight," he said.

"Well, that's no good. Where is he?"

"He's in the back, sleeping it off."

This was the same room where she had found Diane. That was a mission of mercy; looking in on Frank Chase would be a mission from hell.

"He told me to meet him here but I almost didn't come in because I didn't see his car outside."

"Yeah, he's a 'special customer,' per Dean Williams, who always gets his way. When he comes in like that, and it happens every few weeks, he often passes out at the bar. The waitresses let him sleep it off in the back, and the other barkeep drives his car out behind so nothing happens to it."

"He's a peach of a guy."

Crystal proceeded with her inquiry.

"This is the second time he stood me up. I should have learned my lesson. The first time was two weeks ago."

She gave him the date of the Chungs' fire.

"I seem to remember that as the last time we had to do this. Yeah, it was. I was on that night and not supposed to work. I was substituting for someone. Yep, he's stood you up twice, alright. Are you planning to make it a lucky three?"

"No," Crystal said, "I've had enough."

She left the bar and drove back to the hospital in Carson. She was quite proud of herself, and when she got there, she found Harry outside Diane's room. She told him that Frank Chase was not involved in Sandra's murder and he told her he had discovered that Diane's parents were murdered.

"Now we need to find out what she's been keeping from us," Harry said.

Crystal didn't like the sound of that.

Harry assured her it was most likely that rather than being guilty, Diane was the victim.

Diane lit up when she saw the pair enter the room.

Harry told her what he had discovered about the death of her parents and showed her Officer O'Reilly's confession.

Diane was no longer relieved. Now she was angry. She sat straight up in bed and made two fists.

"I think you know who killed your parents. I think you may have always known," Harry said.

"Before, I asked the wrong question. I thought there was a problem in the orphanage. But that's not correct. The problem was with who adopted you."

At this a look of sheer terror came over Diane's face. Crystal held her hand. She had a suspicion of where Harry was going with this, and it was not going to be easy for her new lover.

"So, what was your parents' real name, who took you in from the orphanage, and what happened in that home?"

At this, Diane burst into tears. She did not want to answer, but finally, alternating between crying and raising her fists, she told her story.

35

Harry had an elaborate scheme for both trapping the men in black, getting them to confess, and then corralling their boss. Crystal was to be in charge of the initial part of the plan.

He first made a couple of calls. One was to the soundman Kelly, who was expert at fixing up recording devices. Harry needed two of them. The other call was to Lyn. He spent some time on the phone questioning her about Chinese herbal remedies and then asked her to come to the hospital with her "new friends."

Kelly showed up first with two fairly bulky recording devices, one for Crystal and one for Harry. He showed them how to use them, but wasn't at all sure how they would function, if they could be concealed and, if the recording was successful, if either of them could be used in court as evidence.

The two men in black had been difficult to find. It was always hard to determine their whereabouts. Harry figured, and Crystal agreed, that since they had not finished the job with Diane, they might likely be back to get it done and get paid.

There was the matter of Padewski, the ineffectual rookie cop on guard outside Diane's room who, rather than watching Diane, seemed to be peeking in now and then to watch Crystal.

Right on cue, Lyn arrived with her new friends, the two Tong members she had formed an uneasy alliance with to solve and possibly avenge her mother's murder.

They all crowded into Diane's hospital room, and Lyn pulled out what she said was valerian root, a pungent Chinese herb that she left with the nurses to brew and then insert into a cup of tea which the nurses placed on the stand next to Diane's bed.

Crystal put on red lipstick and tightened the belt on her jeans so they hugged her hips. She then took the tea to Padewski.

"You must be awfully bored out here by your lonesome," she said, puffing out her red lips and making sure he was gazing at them. I brought you this tea. It's very refreshing."

Padewski thanked her and asked what she was doing after she left Diane.

"Well, why don't we just find out later?" she said.

That old Southern charm never failed.

She returned to the room, and shortly heard Padewski snoring peacefully. Lyn told them the herb was used to treat insomnia and never failed to put its user to sleep, or in this case knock him out cold.

Harry then had Crystal call McGinty at the Torrance PD and tell him she was very afraid because Padewski was asleep and they needed reinforcements.

After assuring Crystal that she could handle this, Harry told her he was off.

"Where are you going?" she asked.

"I'm going to see a man about his son," and with that he left.

It was not too long afterwards, with Padewski still enjoying the rest of the weary or, Crystal thought, *the rest of the rookie*, that two men stole past the recruit and entered Diane's room. There they saw a female body in the bed with the covers pulled up over her head.

They pulled back the covers to reveal the female figure, sleeping face down.

Mick, the tall one, grabbed a pillow and was about to smother the figure when she suddenly turned over and pointed a gun at both of them.

"Don't move," Crystal said, and the two men froze. She'd seen this scene in movies many times and it was a thrill to enact it in real life.

From the closet, the two Tong emerged, and Lyn rolled out from under the bed. The intruders were completely surrounded.

Harry had noticed last time they had talked that the sergeant seemed to recognize the men in black and he figured he would alert them. Meanwhile, the hospital had cooperated by moving the drowsy Diane to a nearby room past the "unconscious" rookie who Crystal told them was faking being out cold to catch Diane's killers.

The rookie was still sleeping—Crystal wondered if he would ever wake up—when she, Lyn, the two Tong and their captives paraded out of the hospital. Crystal informed the desk they had caught the killers and were taking them to the station while Padewski waited upstairs to make a full report when the other officers showed up.

Crystal removed a trunk from her car, and they made their way to the Tong's van, the same one where they stowed Lyn at her mother's funeral. They all crowded inside with one Tong in the driver's seat. Crystal trained her gun on the men in black while Lyn, in black fighting outfit herself, faced off, ready to confront them if they made a wrong move.

The other Tong had gone to search the red sportster, which they had seen parked near the hospital. He returned carrying something, and they were on their way.

They drove north lickety-split for about twenty minutes, pulling onto the far edge of Chinatown, then a short way up the hill just beyond it to a cottage which was more camping lean-to than abode. Nevertheless, it had a plainly furnished first floor but, more important for their purposes, a narrow stairway leading to a basement that was padded on all sides.

This was apparently where the Tong took those who resisted.

Crystal gave Lyn the gun to train on them and dragged her suitcase down the stairs.

"What's that for?" Tony, the short one asked.

"It's some extra clothes. I'm not sure how long we're going to be here."

"If you're waiting for us to talk, you'll be here a long time," Mick, the big one said.

At that point Lyn addressed the Tong in Chinese.

They went into a corner of the basement and disappeared for a moment.

"What did you say to them?" Crystal asked.

"I said, 'Show them the instruments,'" Lyn replied.

When the Tong returned, the two men looked at each other, and for the first time since she had been watching them, Crystal saw fear in their eyes.

I called Williams and told him I had some sensational news about Diane and her would-be killers. Eager to hear what I had to say, he told me to meet him at his newest construction project. As I had seen in the scale model in his office, he was building a 14-story tower in Torrance, the largest structure by far in the town.

He was in his office off the lobby, the only floor in the building that was finished. Girders were everywhere, and an elevator that I presumed went to the top floor.

This was a different Williams from the last time. He was brimming with confidence and bubbling over with enthusiasm.

"What do you think of my triumph?" he asked.

"It's big," I said, "and like you, full of vision and energy."

I thought I would pamper him.

He wanted to talk about the place.

"I have to admit I get a little dizzy with heights, but in this home, I'll just be dizzy with success. Just to make sure not to jinx myself and end up like my grandfather and father, there is no 13th floor, so the 14th is the 13th."

That to me sounded like the same thing.

"It's the future," he said. "Offices on the ground floor, apartments on the middle floors, and on top, so I can look out over the city I built, my penthouse."

"And how is the future looking?" I asked.

"Rosier than ever," he said. He explained that he had kept the protesters I had seen from Dominguez Hills at bay by having the town form a home-owners' association, or what he called a Common Interest Development. In it, he said, individuals not only own their own homes but also control the streets, public areas, and local city functions. The community association with no government interference or control is free to enforce whatever housing restrictions on whoever they want, since they are the ones managing street paving, lighting, local security, and garbage removal.

"We don't have to worry about the riff-raff," he said, sitting bolt upright at his desk and getting more excited by the minute. "We just keep the rents or the purchase price high enough to manage who comes in by making it too expensive to live here for those who are unwanted."

This was his plan for an all-white town.

"The wonder of it is, if we do let a few of those others move in"—he deigned to say the words Negro, Mexican or Chinese—"since their choice is so limited, they will have to pay more for what they buy."

As he was speaking, I opened a briefcase I had brought with me hoping he would think it was full of incriminating papers I wanted to show him.

"We can continue building out middle-class paradise without even saying the word segregation. Instead, we talk about freedom, property rights and individual responsibility. We'll have model communities with high tax bases and residents who won't have to witness poverty and desperation, completely cut off from those communities. All they will experience is an abundance of jobs, beautiful individual homes, plenty of goods to buy and loads of entertainment. In my All-American city there will be growth without strain."

I had flipped the "on" device on the recorder because it was time to talk turkey.

He saw what I was doing, got up from his desk and dumped the recorder on the floor, causing it to break into pieces.

"We don't need that," he said. "And now let's talk about my son."

The Tong opened a leather satchel and spread out on the floor in front of the men in black an assortment of knives of all shapes and sizes, along with two medium-length swords, a longer sharp blade, and what looked like an axe.

The man with the serpent tattoo grabbed Mick's arm and planted it on a table in front of the two men who were sitting in small, tight chairs.

Carefully, after some thought, he selected one of the shorter blades and sharpened it on a stone which he pulled from the satchel.

He raised the blade and was about to lower it severing Mick's finger when Mick cried out.

"Stop, I'll tell you want you want to know."

Tony just sat there with his eyes bulging.

It's amazing, Crystal thought, *how two bullies, so brave when they were beating up on those they had the drop on or outnumbered, become cowards when the tables were turned.*

Harry had briefed her on how to get started.

First, she had to reach inside the suitcase.

She told the men in black she was going to change into something more comfortable.

She hovered over the suitcase for a moment and pulled out a pink sweater.

"This ought to do," she said.

Harry had helped her with the interrogation in advance.

"When did you kill Stan Cardiff and why did you leave his body in his car?"

Harry had remembered the blackjack that had knocked him for a loop and he remembered that his landlord Johnson also had been hit on the head and he had seen Mick threaten Professor Gonzalez by holding it in the same way.

The answer wasn't long in coming.

Mick, whose finger was still being held to the fire—or rather to the knife—got the ball rolling.

"We broke into the garage and I hit him in the right spot and he died instantly. Not many people know how to work a blackjack that way."

"You're immensely talented," Crystal said. "Keep going."

"The wife heard a commotion in the garage and opened the door. We didn't know what to do so we stuck him in the trunk of the car. We had figured out the combination of the outside lock so we snuck out for the night.

"We didn't think she used the car and we were surprised to see Palmer when we returned a few days later to retrieve the body.

"We knocked him out and were told to see if we could frame the second wife which we eventually did after our plan to dispose of the body in the swamp didn't work. We buried the body in her backyard."

Lyn was up next.

"I saw you two at my house the day the fire was set," she said. "And my partners found this in your car."

She pulled out the vial of acid, similar to the one she had found in the Tong's car and told them she knew this was a device used to trigger a fire.

Mick pulled his finger back and shut up at that.

Both Tong then grabbed Tony and instead of his finger put his head on the table. The one with the serpent tattoo then grabbed the axe and held it over Tony's outstretched neck.

Tony at first chirped, Crystal thought, and then began, as her Mob dates used to say, "*singing like a canary.*"

"We did it," he said. "And it was good work too. Made to look like an accident. We poured gasoline on the stairs and once the fire started it whooshed up them and surrounded the bedrooms. We snuck out through an outside entranceway that led to the cellar."

Lyn was furious, and Crystal had to hold her back.

"There's more to come," Crystal said. "And they're going to pay."

"I can imagine you think my son must be really evil and heinous and that you are about to accuse him of a number of crimes," Williams said.

I was out of options. He had spoiled my plan to tape his confession, and I just had to sit there and listen.

"But the truth is, he's just an amateur, trying to break into the business as best he can, he's a kind of ne'er-do-well always mucking about. His association with the Klan is repugnant. I never wanted to have anything to do with them. As I explained, we have other, more civilized, ways of accomplishing the same thing. We don't use their primitive, racist terms and call it segregation. We call what we're doing 'home-owner independence.'"

Suddenly, he was back on topic.

"I hope Dean hasn't got himself into too much trouble."

May as well try a frontal assault. Can't do any harm.

"I don't think your son had anything to do with this series of murders," I said, "though I appreciate you trying to pawn them off on him.

"Since this is just a conversation between friends, and now not being recorded, how about telling me why you ordered Stan Cardiff killed."

"I'm not saying I did and I'm not saying I didn't but you probably know the reason."

"You wanted to keep the oil in the ground. There's probably oil under a lot of these houses and if people start digging and turning them into oil wells, there goes your plan for an ideal city. That oil needs to stay where it is and you got wind of it when Cardiff bragged about it at his job."

At this he smiled. I had hit the hammer on his head.

"I also bet that somewhere in this office is the will leaving the house to the second wife."

His eyes went to a cabinet to the side of his desk, and I filed that look away.

"I'm gonna guess you ordered Sandra Chung burned out of her house to keep your middle-class white paradise safe from outsiders."

"I'm not admitting to anything but I will say that we couldn't afford to have that block 'broken.' The death was an accident, but it had been done before with some Negroes in Fontana and it worked."

I remembered that incident and "it worked" in Fontana, a town where I had visited a Klan meeting, because a family of four died. Williams was undaunted.

"First Chinese, then more Chinese, then Negroes, then who knows who? The town isn't ready for that yet, and my company isn't ready for the rapid fall in property values that would entail."

He made murder seem very logical.

"I'm also guessing you have a stake in Madame Thai's and that you use the club to ward off city officials or anyone who opposes you in the local administration."

"That's my little honey pot, and you fell into it, Mr. Palmer. But I'm not the only one who owns a piece of that place. There are other more powerful backers as well."

He was not going to go any further on that, and for a moment we had reached a stalemate.

At this point Mick and Tony were about ready to admit to anything. Lyn was buzzing around them and the Tong looked like they too might want to enact a bit of revenge for Sandra's death.

"She was my dentist," the one without the tattoo said.

Crystal stepped forward.

"If you two want to get out of here alive, you better answer my next questions quickly."

They both looked confused. There was more?

"Who drained the brake fluid in the Burnetts' car?"

Mick reminisced fondly, forgetting for a minute where he was.

"That was our first job for one of our steady employers. After we drained the fluid, we chased their car out onto the highway near Murder Mile. When Burnett swerved to avoid the oncoming car, the driver was both trying to stop, knowing he was approaching the curb and couldn't brake, and also trying to get away from us. We saw the car go over the embankment and drove off."

Tony put his head in his hands, knowing that they had probably sealed their fate.

"And who ordered Diane to be shot?" Crystal asked.

That put them in more fear than even the Tong induced.

"We can't tell you that," Tony said, glancing at his companion and nodding for him to go no further.

"You just admitted to the shooting," Crystal said, going over to her suitcase. "And when I took out the sweater, I put on this recorder and we have the whole confession on tape."

The Tong then tied them up.

"Leave them here," Crystal said. "We're going to deal with their boss."

⌗▨▨▨◻◻◻◻⌗

"Mr. Palmer, you have a call," the perky redhead, who had transferred from his other location, said, poking her head into Williams's office.

"I'll take it at your desk," I said, leaving Williams, who had gotten up from behind his desk, pacing.

I returned to his office quickly. Now I was excited and effusive. That was a good word from Crystal's and my novel reading.

"We've got a confession from your henchmen," I said, neglecting to tell him that they hadn't given him up.

At this point he stopped pacing and just sat in a heap at his desk.

"Why did you kill Diane's parents, your brother and sister-in-law?"

"Yes, it's true," he said. "They changed their names because they didn't want to be associated with me and what Bob called my 'corrupt business practices.' They refused to sell to me and I needed their lumber for my building. When they died, I bought the shop."

"But that's not the only reason," I said.

At this, a look of terror came over his face.

On the wall was a photo of a company named AA Milne.

"What's that?" I said.

"It was my old company that I've since abandoned," he replied, thinking he wasn't revealing anything.

"It's the company that issued the check used to pay off the cop who set up the cover-up," I said.

I had him on that one.

"He was a business rival," he said, "nothing more."

I guess in his mind he had forgotten he was also his brother.

"And why did you put out a hit on Diane?"

"What makes you say that?"

"We have a confession from your thugs but beyond that you called the police station and reported her shot before anyone else knew about it."

"And why would I do that?"

"You wanted Diane," I said. "You were fixated on her probably from the time she was young. She told us you read to her from *Winnie the Pooh* and so you named your former company after the author of that children's story."

It was lucky Crystal was an avid reader and helped me figure that out.

"It wasn't the orphanage that messed with her head. It was what happened afterwards. You took her out of the orphanage. At fourteen she was the big prize in your eliminating her parents. You brought her home and you molested her."

He had his hands over his eyes and was peeking out from behind them, not wanting to face this accusation.

"You groomed her to be your ace saleswoman. She was as important a part of your business as your brother's lumber. She didn't get very far away from you, but though she worked for you, because of what you did to her, she refused to have her office with yours."

"You also probably gave her that phony name 'Chestnut,' a little memory of your poking her."

"All part of the sale and the come on," he said, now not in the least bit ashamed.

"What's the point of dredging this up, Palmer? Yes, I was in love with her. Even at 14 she was the most beautiful girl I'd ever seen. So what?"

"The point is that everything was okay until first you thought your son, her cousin, was after her, which he was, in a case of the apple not falling far from the tree, though you didn't regard him as competition. You couldn't stand it, though, when your men reported that she had taken my partner Crystal to her love nest. She had had other lovers before but you were worried this one might be serious. You got insanely jealous. I saw a flash of it in your office last time I was here. And you ordered her shot."

"Okay, Palmer, is there more?"

"One more thing. Who's backing you? Where did the money initially come from for all this building?"

He was, oddly, regaining his composure. For him, the worst was over.

"This is all between us," he said. "You have no proof and your recording scheme didn't work. My men will never betray me, like I will never betray my backers.

"I'll give you a check for your so-called 'work,' and then I never want to see or hear from you again."

With that, he sat calmly, wrote out a check, handed me the hush money, and ushered me out to the lobby.

He approached the elevator which ran up the side of the partially built structure.

"You and those like you will always be trapped on the ground, Palmer. But me, I'm a man of vision. I'm going up and up and up and up."

He strode majestically into the elevator, but before the door closed, a hand snaked around the corner and waved. Imprinted on the hand was the tattoo of a serpent.

I watched the elevator crawl up the side of the building as Crystal and Lyn appeared next to me.

Suddenly a figure plummeted off the side.

"And now," I said, "you're going down and down and down and down," as Williams fell in a heap almost at our feet.

Epilogue

There Is No Place Like (Someone Else's) Home

I had two stops today, a few weeks after Williams's death, to finally close out the case. The first seemed like the greater challenge, but for me that was manageable, while the second was terrifying.

The Tong had cleared out quickly after Williams's fall. His death was blamed on what he had said was his dizziness and his challenging the gods by halting his building on the 13th floor, even if he called it the 14th.

I used the confusion after the "accident" to go back into Williams's office and rifle it. In a concealed bottom in one of his desk drawers I found Stan Cardiff's will. I later tore it up, deciding that indeed it was best to keep the oil in the ground and not deprive one of his "wives" of their home.

I also found a gold-plated card, which I took to be some kind of exclusive admittance, and which I was now on my way to use.

With the help of my old pal Nader on L.A. homicide, Crystal and Lyn turned over Mick and Tony's confession to Lance and the Torrance police, who had no recourse but to investigate, using the confession as a way to locate leads. They found enough in their respective homes to put the men in black away for a long time.

Williams's payment—or payoff—was substantial, and I split it three ways, myself, Crystal, and Lyn, who, if she also wanted to pay the Tong, was fine with me. The street criminals had proved in the end to have more integrity than the criminal in the suites.

Lyn liked her time as an investigator and planned to use part of her share to go to college and study law. Following Professor Gonzalez, whom I introduced her to, she said she was particularly interested in real estate law, helping Chinese secure homes throughout Los Angeles County.

She will be a formidable and tenacious lawyer, I thought. *I wouldn't want to tangle with her.* She also reminded me that she was going to work her way through college as a new member of my team. I was okay with that. She had earned it.

Diane recovered from the shooting, and she and Crystal were going great guns. Diane got out of real estate and was using the money she'd stowed away to fully recuperate and figure out what she wanted to do next.

Dean, of course, took over his father's business and seemed to pick up right where his father had left off, another rotten apple not falling far from an orchard full of them.

I was driving downtown from my hotel on Sunset, and I heard on the radio that my "old friend"—L.A. Police Chief William H. Parker—was testifying in a hearing as an expert, urging the City Council to cancel any plans the city might have for building public housing. In his testimony, he called those that favored affordable housing "communists." Since when was the police chief a public policy advisor? The current political climate was getting stranger and stranger.

The second piece of news, which went along with the first, was that Richard Nixon had won the election as the new U.S. Senator from California. He was victorious not only by attacking his female opponent as too "emotional," but also by smearing her as a "communist sympathizer."

I was on my way to the *Times* building. I had business with the Chandlers. The guard tried to stop me in the lobby but I showed him the gold card with Norman and Buff's name on it, and I was allowed to go up to the top. The view was spectacular with windows stretching around the entire floor. There was the magnificence of downtown, but also on one side I could see the now more hollowed-out space of my old home in Bunker Hill and on the other side the now disappearing homes in the three villages in East L.A. On the wall hung a huge drawing of what Bunker Hill would one day look like, all gleaming skyscrapers next to Dorothy's cultural center. It was almost as if the drawing was a decal to be smeared over the terrain to cover what the *Times* viewed as unsightly, but which was in fact the way real people lived.

I was told to wait in the outer lobby, which I did, and I was then told it was okay to enter the inner office. Who should I meet coming out but Richard Nixon? He should have been in a good mood, but he wasn't. He was muttering to himself. I heard him say something like, "Chandlers think they can control me. I'll show them."

He had a droopy-eared cocker spaniel on a leash who apparently was not in a hurry to leave. He had to drag the dog out into the lobby. Finally, to get the dog going, he kicked it. "Let's go, Checkers, you piss ant puppy," he said. He seemed to really love that dog.

When I was let inside, only one Chandler greeted me.

"Where did you get that card?"

I told Buffy it was "passed on" from Williams. She said, as I assumed, that it granted access to the bearer, and the fact that she honored it was a tangible link to the now deceased builder.

She sat straight up at her desk with copies of the society pages on the wall behind her. Her hair was slightly graying, and she presented herself as prim and proper, without a shred of her business suit out of place and her hair meticulously manicured.

I think she knew who I was, and had apparently decided to take me into her confidence, figuring that I was inconsequential.

"Congratulations on the election," I said.

"Him?" she replied, pointing toward where Nixon had exited.

"He's a vicious attack dog who we use to clear away our enemies. He's as corrupt as the day is long and we hope his political dealings and shady campaign spending don't come back to bite us.

"He's still young, but they say he's got 'an old head on his shoulders.' Maybe, but that old head is petty and tawdry."

She then told a story of Nixon at an elegant dinner with his extended family, where she saw him pour bourbon in his milk to hide it from his mother.

"He's 'Tricky' alright and sometimes not in good ways. We keep him around because he knows how to redbait anyone and that is really quite useful."

"Speaking of shady characters," I interjected, "I've got you and Norman linked to two shady characters who are right now being charged with several murders and an attempted assassination, not to mention the card that got me access today which I found in the possession of a homicidal developer."

"Please, Mr. Palmer," she said with a wave of her hand, "don't you go being tawdry yourself."

"The fellow you're referring to died a tragic and unnatural death. Meanwhile, I understand you've been quite an irritant to the city projects of redeveloping Bunker Hill and reviving Chavez Ravine, but that has nothing to do with us."

"I can't prove it, but I think the two of you bankrolled Williams and have been using the two felons to intimidate landlords and tenants in the areas you want cleared."

"I wouldn't know. That's really Norman's province. He loves riding and he's out at the Tejon Ranch getting ready for our annual fox hunt. They don't use foxes. They use mangy gray coyotes, but they've got the dogs, the pink coats and the ascots and they romp through the arroyos in the San Gabriel Mountains. I suppose it's a lot of fun for them."

"That's not what I was told. I hear you're the brains of the outfit."

I had been to visit Professor Gonzalez again and he described Dorothy as "a power-hungry matron who never took 'No' for an answer" and who kept the Chandler dynasty alive, chiding Norman for not being enough like his swindler father.

At this she smiled.

"I'm always saying to him, 'Posture, Norman, posture,' reminding him of his duty and responsibility to the Chandler tradition."

"And to Chandler real estate?"

Gonzalez had told me that the father, Harry Chandler, had moved from real-estate speculator to industrialist-developer, and Norman and Buffy were the inheritors of that.

"It's true," she said, with another wave of her imperious hand. "When Norman took over the newspaper in '41, Harry told him the key to its coverage lay in 'what is good for real estate.'"

"I followed the two goons to a gravel pit which I found out the Chandlers secretly owned. The whole push of the paper into the suburbs is all part of a Chandler profit machine as far as I can tell."

"Right again," she said proudly, explaining the family had a stake in every aspect of the highway and automobile suburban expansion except actually making the cars. She listed them: gravel for the highways, rubber plants for tires, knowing where the roads are going and buying land along the route, as well as a controlling interest in an oil company to fuel the vehicles and, of course, owning a real estate company.

"But that's the suburbs, why are you trying to clear out the city and opposing public housing?"

"We're going to turn Bunker Hill into a cultural center, with corporate skyscrapers and a series of quality high-rise apartments.

"As Norman would say, Harry would turn over in his grave if he knew there was public housing with all its crime and transients next to our expensive real estate. As for East L.A., those are just small shacks that we're demolishing."

"And for what?" I asked, throwing up my hands.

She decided to take me into her confidence.

"We're building a new residence right here in the city to enhance the town. It will have Doric pillars and a classical front. Inside, an extravagant library, a curved marble staircase and the crowning touch, a music room with, if I can get it, the wallpaper in Mozart's composing room at the Viennese Court and a harpsichord once played by the great Amadeus himself."

"That will be a great benefit to you but how will it help anyone else?"

She was surprised by the question.

"It will raise the standards of everyone," she said.

"But what about the rest of the population of the city who will no longer be able to afford to live here?"

Now she was getting exasperated.

"Norman says this about the paper, but it's equally true of the city: 'Our future is not in trying to be a paper for the Negro and Mexican population or the low-income white population.' I don't want to read, and none of my friends want to read, about Negro foster parents and Spanish women or about a woman with ten children who has never been married and who survives on city handouts."

I had had enough. I think she had just let me on the real meaning of "civic respect."

"I can't tie you directly to any crime, but I've got enough to go to the *News* and they would print a hell of a story about two goons the family seems to have a relation with and about a developer connected to a string of murders."

"And what do you want to not tell them that story?"

"Two things. One, I had to move, and I want my rent paid for a year and, two, I want the home of Rosa Morales in Palo Verde not to be touched."

"Done and done," she said, getting on the intercom and ordering a check to be written. She then made a call to the city official Beame and told him to leave Rosa's home alone for the time being.

"And now," she said, "goodbye, little pest."

With that she once again waved her hand and expected me to disappear in a puff of smoke.

I followed her wish, exited, and picked up my check.

There wasn't much more I could do, but I planned to turn over everything I had to Gonzalez and see what he and Roybal could do with it.

My last stop had me shaking and my stomach fluttering.

Esperanza was overjoyed to see me, and when I told her I had saved Rosa's home she kissed me and wanted to take things further.

I backed off from her on the couch.

I told her what had happened at Madame Thai's.

She listened silently to my tale. When I finished, she looked down at the floor for a moment, then looked me straight in the eye.

After a few minutes, she spoke.

"Get out. I can't do this anymore."

I had cleaned up the case. But I was not so lucky in my personal life. Not everything can be fixed or repaired, and this was one of those things.

As I left, I felt dazed. I didn't know where I was going, but I knew that wherever I went, it had to be different than it was now.

Bibliography

California Eagle Archives (1949-52). https://archive.org/details/caleagle

Daily Breeze Archives, courtesy of Torrance Historical Association.

Gibbons, Andrea (2018). *City of Segregation:100 Years of Struggle for Housing in Los Angeles.* Verso Books. Kindle Edition.

Gottlieb, Robert and Irene Wolt (1977). *Thinking Big*: *The Story of the Los Angeles Times, Its Publishers, and Their Influence on Southern California.* G.P. Putnam's Sons.

Huang, Yunte (2023). *Daughter of the Dragon: Anna May Wong's Rendezvous with American History*. Liveright. Kindle Edition.

Ibsen, Henrik (2019). *The Master Builder*. Herstellung und Verlag. Kindle Edition.

McDonald, Patrick Range (2023). "Is a LA Times Reporter Shilling for Big Real Estate?" *L.A. Progressive.* https://www.laprogressive.com/the-media-in-the-united-states/shilling-for-big-real-estate

McDougal, Dennis (2001). *Privileged Son: Otis Chandler and the Rise and Fall of The L.A. Times Dynasty*. Perseus Publishing. Kindle Edition.

Nee, Victor G. and Brett de Bary (1972). *Longtime Californ': A Documentary Study of an American Chinatown*. Pantheon Books.

Shatkin, Elina (2018). "The Ugly, Violent Clearing Of Chavez Ravine Before It Was Home To The Dodgers," *L.A.ist.*

https://laist.com/news/la-history/dodger-stadium-chavez-ravine-battle.

Stein, Samuel. *Capital City* (2019). Verso Books. Kindle Edition.

Vidor, King, director (1949). *Fountainhead*. Warner Brothers.

GRATITUDE

So many people contributed to the writing of this book that I hardly know where to begin. I must say, though, that while the historical accuracy and insight are theirs, any distortions and errors are all mine.

I will start by thanking Leroy Jackson of the Torrance Historical Society, who researched Torrance development and sent me a number of useful articles from the local newspaper in the 1950s that were absolutely essential to the making of this book.

I must also thank Los Angeles's Chinese American Museum for an excellent exhibition on the history of the Chinese in California and Los Angeles.

Dick Price, editor, and publisher with Sharon Kyle of *L.A. Progressive*, took time from his busy day to give me a wonderful background interview on the current state of L.A. segregation. Since this book has an eye on the present and is in part a recounting of how the city got to where it is today by its actions in the 1950s, that interview was extremely helpful.

On the subject of city planning and planning offices I was greatly enlightened by a generous conversation granted me by former San Francisco City Planner and now superb full-time writer and critic Michael Berkowitz.

A great storyteller and fountain of information on L.A., as usual, was Ryan Erlich, whose recounting of past cases with the city helped me create one of the crucial through lines of the novel.

Teresa Gonzalez, a writer and organizer, arranged a wonderful reading of my last book on Boyle Heights and continued to be a fountain of information on the forced disappearance of city neighborhoods in the rush, in the past, to Urban Renewal, and, today, to Gentrification.

Ying Ying Wu's recounting of her family history in San Francisco was extremely useful in creating the character of Lyn's grandfather, the journalist and historian.

I have to thank Melissa Mandracchia and her husband Gil for another great stay (and a timely rescue from a less than desirable apartment). Their studio was once again a comfortable and affordable place from which to write and do research.

I would like to acknowledge two new friends here in France where I live whose support for the project and both my first and current trilogy was refreshing and helpful. First, Roger Martin, whose own French translation of Ed Lacy's *Room to Swing*, featuring the first Black private eye, is stunning. His book on Lacy's career is a marvel in the French tradition of discovering American authors too long neglected. Second, Benoît Tadié, whose extensive work on American hard-boiled authors was revelatory and who is also a good friend and warm companion.

As usual, I must thank, for all his support and encouragement, Barry Forshaw and *Crime Time* for his and its continued embracing of my work.

Kudos also to Olivia Castillon, the publicist of Quais du Polar in Lyon, a place to share the excitement of writing crime fiction with many of its top global participants, as well as Cécile Dumas, the festival's media assistant, for all her help and personal warmth.

As usual, I would like to thank the Cinémathèque Française's Elodie Dufour for her wonderful aid, and programmer and film scholar extraordinaire Jean-François Rauger for in this case a wonderful recounting of the films of Douglas Sirk, which introduced me to Sirk's version of *The Master Builder* as well as many other films that have furnished visual images on which this book draws.

Also encouraging and helpful on my path toward becoming a full-time crime writer was Gunnar Staalsen, called the Nordic Raymond Chandler and rightfully so.

For a number of thoughtful comments on the series, I would like to thank my fellow detective novelist Michael Paul.

For a careful read and wonderful encouragement, thanks to USC's David James, an extraordinary film critic who proved equally prescient about the history of L.A.

Helpful as always and with always an encouraging word was my editor at *Culture Matters* Mike Quille, as well as a superb editor and wonderful critic at *People's World*, Eric A. Gordon, who did double duty as copy editor of this book.

I would like to thank Prairie Miller and Jack Shalom of Pacifica Radio's *Arts Express* for their acute political awareness in the area of cultural politics, and, increasingly, politics in general, and their trumpeting of my work and helping to spread the word about the fractured adventures of Harry Palmer.

For constant tech support above and beyond the call of duty I must thank Long Island University's Stuart Alleyne.

Now we come to the more personal acknowledgments.

For once again, and as always, helping with all aspects of marketing and with making my stay in L.A. a pleasant one that included a number of spirited and enlightening conversations, I would like to thank my nephew, Jordan Broe.

Avid readers of my novels, with always a pleasant word to say about them, are my sister Margaret Fitzpatrick and brother Pat Broe. Your support is important.

Crucially welcoming in my visit to Los Angeles and a great lunch and dinner companion was my longtime friend Linda Provenza.

Many thanks are owed to James McLaughlin for his wise counsel and constant encouragement, and to Charles Ellison for enlightening me on contemporary redlining and for always being there.

I have to thank also the many members of a series of L.A. meetings which made my stay a healthy and enjoyable one.

A hearty tip of the hat to the economist extraordinaire Alexis Crow, whose travels often coincide with mine, providing many pleasurable hours talking about and looking at art.

Thanks in Paris to James Anderson and Annemiek Determann for their warm support and, as well, to Sean Dwyer for his enthusiasm and for his technical knowledge and aid.

I could never have done the book without the constant support of my writing group which has endured now for more than a decade and seen me through at least seven books. To the novelist Mathilde Merlot, the playwright Dan Kavulish, and the psychologist and self-help author Judith Chusid, my warmest appreciation.

A wonderful librettist and faithful friend Ed Levy was always there with an encouraging word. He has been over the years a crucial anchor in my world.

I love my every Saturday conversations with the philosopher, educator, and editor Michael Pelias, not only a superbly informed interlocutor but also a kindhearted companion.

Especially helpful on this book, but always and perpetually a source of validation and enduring friendship, is Bob Spiegelman. His comments on the book and his careful listening not only proved valuable but also were a highlight of each week that I was writing it.

I hardly know where to begin with this final acknowledgement. My wife and chef extraordinaire Sri saw me through this project with infinite patience. It absolutely could not have been done without her. She tended me when I was sick, cooked extraordinary meals, and restored me to health with an array of her own medicines that were a better remedy than any doctor could offer, all done with an abundance of love which astonishes me every day both by its consistency and its magnitude.

Dennis Broe's First Harry Palmer L.A. Trilogy consists of: *Left of Eden*, about the Hollywood Blacklist; *A Hello to Arms*, about the postwar buildup of the weapons industry; and *The Precinct With The Golden Arm*, about the LAPD and the Hispanic Community of Boyle Heights. He is an expert on 1940s Hollywood cinema, the crime film, and art and culture of the Cold War. His contemporary writing on film, television, art and aesthetics is available at *Cultural Politics For Those Who Care*. He haunts the *petite salles de cinquième*, the little cinemas of the Latin Quarter watching crime films, melodramas and westerns.

Printed in Great Britain
by Amazon

38911025R00169